ISLAND CHRISTMAS

An Isle of Man Romance

DIANA XARISSA

ISBN: 1548253537
ISBN-13: 978-1548253530

❀ Created with Vellum

For everyone who loves romance and believes in happily ever after.

AUTHOR'S NOTE

Welcome to the fourth book in my romance series set in the wonderful Isle of Man. While the romances can be read in any order, this one does open where *Island Heritage* left off, so I suggest you do read that title before this one.

Many of the characters appear in more than one of the romance novels. Additionally, some characters in the romances make appearances in my Isle of Man Cozy Mystery Series as well. The cozy mysteries are set about fifteen years before the romances (they start circa 1998), so the characters from the romances that appear in those books do so as younger versions of themselves.

This is a work of fiction. The historical sites and landmarks on the island are all real, however all of the events that take place within them in this story are fictional. Manx National Heritage is real and their efforts to preserve and promote the historical sites and the history of the island are incredible. All of the Manx National Heritage staff members in this story, however, are fictional creations. Castle Rushen is a beautiful medieval castle, but they do not hold an annual "Christmas at the Castle" event there (at least not yet).

All of the modern characters are a product of the author's imagination. Any resemblance to actual persons, living or dead, is entirely coincidental. Similarly, the names of the restaurants and shops and other businesses on the island are fictional, but may coincidentally resemble actual shops or businesses on the island.

This book is also missing the American protagonist that the first two romances had, so once again I've put a glossary in the back of the book. Please check there for words or terms that are unfamiliar. As ever, a few Americanisms have probably snuck in as well, for which I am sorry.

Those who have read my other romances will remember the ghost of Charlotte de la Tremouille, who appears to women in the throne room at Castle Rushen. If she smiles at you, the man who brought you to the castle is your soul mate, but if she is crying, he isn't the right man for you. The story is, unfortunately, entirely fictional. To the best of my knowledge, Charlotte does not haunt Castle Rushen providing such assistance to the island's dating population.

I really hope you enjoy the story, and I would love to hear from you. My contact details are also in the back of the book.

"I now pronounce you man and wife," the minster said solemnly.

Darcy Robinson brushed away the tear that threatened to smudge her eye makeup. She couldn't have been any happier for her dearest friend, Lisa. Now she followed the happy couple back down the aisle to the back of the church, smiling brightly at the young groomsman who offered his arm as she went.

A seemingly endless half hour of hugs and handshakes followed as everyone congratulated the newlyweds and had a quick word with their attendants. Darcy kept a smile firmly fixed on her face, no matter what anyone said.

"So nice to see that Lisa's found someone special," one of Lisa's aunts told her. "I always worried about your influence on her."

Gee, thanks, Darcy thought.

"Never thought Lisa would beat you down the aisle," one of their old school friends laughed. "Of course, I figured you'd have had about five husbands by now. Each one a little bit older and a lot richer than his predecessor."

Darcy bit her tongue.

"Darling, this is deadly dull. Let's get out of here and fly to Rome," Finlo Quayle whispered in her ear when it was his turn to speak to her.

Darcy shook her head. "You promised to behave," she reminded the man.

Finlo sighed and then gave Darcy what looked like a forced smile. "I will," he said in a grumpy voice. Finlo was tall, with dark hair and gorgeous blue eyes. Even his fake smile made women swoon.

Darcy laughed lightly and then turned to greet the next person in line. "Andy, wasn't it a lovely ceremony?"

She was determined to keep the smile on her face as she spoke to the man she'd with whom she'd only just recently broken up. His continued refusal to make any real commitment to her had finally driven her to end the relationship.

"I don't really believe in marriage," Andy replied with a shrug. "But they seem happy enough."

Darcy nodded and then quickly moved on again. Seeing them together, Darcy was surprised how much Andy and Finlo resembled one another, but she didn't want to think about that right now. For now she was conscious that Andy was watching her closely, but then so was Finlo. It was going to be a long day.

The reception was being held at Castle Rushen, and Darcy knew the food would be delicious, as the island's premier caterers had been hired for the occasion. Her smile was only a little bit forced as she joined the rest of the wedding party in the limousine.

"Are you okay?" Lisa hissed to her as someone popped open a bottle of champagne from the car's bar.

"I'm fine," Darcy said insistently. "Don't you worry about me. You just have a wonderful day."

Darcy had only just told Lisa about the breakup with Andy and she knew her friend was concerned, but she really didn't want Lisa worrying about her, especially today.

"Are you going to be okay with Finlo?" Lisa asked.

Darcy flushed under Lisa's hard stare. "It'll be fine," she muttered. There was no doubt that Lisa understood why Darcy hadn't wanted to come to the wedding alone, but Darcy suspected Lisa would have preferred that she'd invited just about anyone other than Finlo to come with her.

Darcy and Finlo had dated off and on for many months. Finlo was another man with commitment issues, and Darcy had finally dumped him for good just before she'd started dating Andy. This occasion was not about getting back together with Finlo, though, it was just about having a man by her side so that she didn't feel all alone on Lisa's special day.

Lisa was still staring at her. "Really, it's all good," Darcy told her firmly. "I'm over the moon happy for you and I'm going to have a wonderful time today. But no matter how much of a couple Finlo and I look at the reception, we are definitely not getting back together, I promise."

Lisa looked as if she wanted to say something, but was interrupted by her new husband. "Champagne?" he offered.

Lisa took the glass and then handed it to Darcy. "You probably need this more than I do," Lisa suggested.

"Indeed," Darcy replied with a wry smile. Glasses were quickly passed throughout the car and everyone toasted the newlyweds. Darcy drained her glass in a single swallow, hoping that she'd told Lisa the truth. Finlo was very attractive and he could be incredibly persuasive when he wanted to be.

When they arrived at the castle, Finlo was already there, ready to help Darcy from the car. The medieval castle looked beautiful in the bright June sunshine. Finlo's expensive black sports car was parked at the kerb near the castle gates. It was just one of the many luxuries that owning his own charter air service allowed him to indulge in.

"I missed you," he said as he pulled her close.

"Oh, please," Darcy whispered. "I told you to pretend we're a couple, but don't get carried away."

Finlo chuckled, a sexy sound that made Darcy shiver. "But I really did miss you," he told her softly. "You were dating Andy Kenyon for six long months and I missed you."

Darcy shook her head. "You didn't have time to miss me, not with all the women you went through over the last six months," she said sharply. "I appreciate your willingness to be my date today, but we aren't getting back together. You're just here so that no one thinks I can't find a man."

Finlo laughed. "Someone would have to be blind to think that," he told her.

Darcy sighed. She knew she was attractive, with her long red hair, bright green eyes, and naturally generous curves. Men had been telling her how beautiful she was since she was a teenager. What she wanted was for a man to tell her she was smart and interesting and that he wanted to spend the rest of his life with her.

She took Finlo's arm with a resolute smile. He'd agreed to pretend to be her boyfriend for the day, which meant she had to play along.

The food was, as expected, excellent. Darcy laughed and drank champagne and ate a little bit of everything as the afternoon turned into evening. When the dance music switched to slower songs, she grabbed the little ring bearer, who was all of two years old, and held him tight until the band took a break.

"That was very cute," Finlo told her as she returned the young boy to his mother. "But I do expect a dance or two before the night is over."

Darcy laughed and patted his cheek. "I just need to excuse myself for a minute," she told him, heading towards the loos, forcing herself to forget about the look she'd seen in Finlo's sapphire blue eyes. They were not getting back together, even if they did have to work together.

"You are not getting back with Finlo," she told her mirrored reflection sternly as she washed her hands.

"No, you aren't," Lisa agreed from the doorway. "He's not good enough for you, and you know it."

Darcy laughed. "Perfect timing," she told her friend.

"I thought you might need to talk," Lisa told her. "You and Finlo appear to having a wonderful time together."

"Well, we aren't, so no worries there," Darcy assured her. "I am having fun," she added quickly as Lisa frowned. "But I'm done with Finlo and ready to move on with my life. I think I may have to find a new job, though. I'm not sure working with Finlo is still manageable."

Lisa grinned. "I've been telling you to find a new job for years," she reminded her friend. "You're many talents are being wasted as an air hostess."

"I don't know about that," Darcy replied. "But I do know I'm ready for a change."

"Are you going to give in your notice, then?" Lisa asked.

Darcy shrugged. "I guess so, maybe on Monday."

"I wish I were going to be here," Lisa said slowly.

Darcy laughed. "Don't you dare wish that," she said. "You go and have a lovely honeymoon and don't worry even a tiny bit about me. I'll be fine and I'll catch you up on everything the minute you get back."

Lisa looked doubtful, but Darcy didn't give her time to argue. "I must get back. I promised Finlo a slow dance," she told her friend with a wink. Darcy was out of the room before Lisa could protest.

Halfway down the corridor, Andy was leaning against the castle wall.

"I was starting to think you slipped out a different door," he said, crossing to her.

"There aren't any other doors," Darcy replied, taking a step backwards when he reached her.

"I miss you," Andy said, reaching a hand out and touching her cheek.

Darcy stared into his deep blue eyes and sighed. "That's nice to hear, but it isn't nearly good enough," she told him.

Andy shook his head. "We should try again," he suggested. "Let's go on a cruise for six months. How does that sound?"

"Magical," Darcy admitted. "But what happens when it's over? You're retired and have plenty of money, but I need to work for a living."

"I'll take care of you," Andy said softly.

"But you won't marry me," Darcy replied.

Andy shrugged. "I don't really believe in marriage," he replied. "But we can have lots of fun together."

Darcy shook her head. "It was fun while it lasted," she said sadly. She took a step forward to walk around him, but he grabbed her arm.

"You'll regret it if you just walk away," he told her.

"I'll regret it more if I don't," she replied. She brushed past him and then sighed. Finlo was standing at the end of the hallway, glaring at them.

"Come along, darling. I owe you a dance," she said lightly when she reached him. She pulled him away after he'd given Andy another hard stare.

As yet another slow love song began, Darcy let Finlo pull her into his arms. After a few seconds, she felt herself melting into the familiar embrace and she rested her head on his chest.

"This just feels right, doesn't it?" Finlo asked quietly.

"It feels familiar," Darcy countered. "But that doesn't make it right."

"We should try again," Finlo told her in a low voice. "I truly did miss you."

"But you found lots of other women to keep you company while I was dating Andy," Darcy reminded him. "And you'll find plenty more after today."

"We were so good together," Finlo said, his eyes staring into hers.

He pulled her closer and Darcy sighed. The intimate look in those gorgeous blue eyes almost changed her mind, but she took a deep breath and smiled at him. "Is that a proposal?" she asked, raising one eyebrow.

Finlo's jaw dropped. "Pardon? I mean, I was just, that is, I thought we could start dating again, that's all. You know I'm not looking to get married, not now and probably not ever."

Darcy laughed lightly, even though she felt as if her heart was breaking. "Yeah, I know that," she told him. "But you know what? I'd like to get married some day, maybe even start a family. Dating men like you is just wasting my time."

She pushed away from him and headed for the bar. Another glass of champagne was exactly what she needed. Finlo followed, but Darcy ignored him.

"I don't want to fight," he hissed at her as she smiled at the bartender, who was quick to pour her drink for her.

"We aren't fighting," Darcy countered. "I would never fight with you at Lisa's wedding. The last thing I want to do is cause a scene and spoil her perfect day."

She thanked the man behind the bar and turned, glass in hand, to face the crowd. Finlo was at her elbow, frowning at her.

"Why don't we take this conversation somewhere more private?" he suggested. "My flat isn't far away and I have a bottle of champagne on ice there."

"Which part of no are you not getting?" Darcy asked him, working hard to keep her voice low.

"But we have so much fun together," Finlo said.

"We did have fun together," Darcy agreed. "But life isn't always all about having fun. I'm just starting to appreciate that."

"Nonsense," Finlo laughed. "Life is all about fun. When did you get so serious? I liked you better before."

Darcy shook her head. "Some people grow up, at least a little bit," she told him. "But let's not get too serious about this. I know you'll stop listening if I try to explain how I feel anyway. For today, let's just have fun."

"Excellent," Finlo replied. He grabbed his own glass of champagne and downed it in one gulp. "Come and dance," he said, dragging Darcy back onto the dance floor.

For another two hours Darcy sipped champagne and laughed and danced with Finlo as if she hadn't a care in the world. She fought temptation every time he whispered yet another sexy suggestion in her ear, sternly reminding herself that she deserved better. When Finlo took a short break, she danced with Andy, ignoring his attempts to woo her back as well.

It was nearly midnight when the bridal pair finally slipped away. They'd be spending the night at a hotel near the airport before flying off on their month-long honeymoon the next morning. As she stood with the crowd, waving and watching their car disappear down the road, Darcy let out a huge sigh of relief. As soon as she was certain that Lisa was truly on her way, Darcy pulled out her phone.

"Who are you ringing?" Finlo asked as he slipped an arm around her.

"A taxi," Darcy replied, ducking away from him. "I'm tired and I'm going home."

"I'll take you home," Finlo told her. "Or back to my place."

"Thanks, but I'd rather just get a taxi," Darcy replied. "It's time for me to stand on my own two feet and stop relying on my looks to get me what I want."

"Why?" Finlo asked bluntly.

Darcy chuckled. "I want my own happily ever after," she replied. "And if that means staying single, then I'll make that work for me. What I'm not doing is spending any more time with men who don't properly appreciate or respect me."

"I respect you," Finlo protested.

Darcy shrugged. "Not enough."

The taxi arrived a few minutes later. Finlo held the door for her, helping her into the car.

"If you change your mind, ring me," he said in her ear.

Darcy had the car drop her off at Lisa's little house in Douglas. She'd agreed to watch the house for her friend and Lisa had told her she could stay there whenever she wanted. Now Darcy let herself in and headed straight for the guest room. A few tears escaped as she buried her face in the pillow. It was time for some big changes, and change was difficult and scary.

2

"What do you mean, you're giving notice?" Finlo demanded, waving the paper she'd just given him in the air. "You can't quit."

"I can and I just have," Darcy told him, keeping her voice calm even though she felt slightly ill. She sat down in the chair on the opposite side of the desk from him. His office wasn't huge, but today it felt almost claustrophobic.

"But I need you," Finlo said. "And besides, what will you do? Don't tell me you're going back to work for the local carrier? They don't pay as well as I do and you don't get to go to as many interesting places."

"I'm not going back to my old job," Darcy replied.

"Is this about more money? I suppose I could give you a little bit more, but you're already my best paid member of staff, aside from the pilots, of course."

Darcy shook her head. "This isn't about money," she assured him. "It's about making changes. I'm going to find a new job that has more sensible hours and might allow me to have a proper relationship."

Finlo frowned. "This is all about finding a husband, isn't it? Just because Lisa got married doesn't mean you have to do the same."

"It isn't at all about getting married. I don't even know if I want to get married, but it would be nice to find a guy who isn't afraid of commitment and actually wants to spend time with me. It's hard to find men like that when I'm constantly flying here, there and everywhere."

"I want to spend time with you," Finlo told her. His mobile phone beeped. When he glanced down at it, Darcy saw the look on his face as he read the screen.

"Who is the text from?" she asked.

"Oh, no one," Finlo told her. "A friend."

"Really?" Darcy laughed. "I'll bet she's twenty-five, gorgeous and you're having dinner with her tonight."

Finlo flushed. "You didn't want to get back together," he reminded her.

"No, but even if I did, you'd still be seeing other women behind my back."

"I never did anything behind your back," Finlo argued.

Darcy nodded. "I suppose that's true. You never bothered to hide all of the other women from me. What was stupid was my staying with you in spite of them. I won't make that mistake again."

"I'll cancel dinner with Debbie if you want me to," Finlo offered.

"Gosh, thanks," Darcy replied. "What about tomorrow night?"

"I'm having dinner with an old friend," he told her, not meeting her eyes.

"And you won't cancel that one?"

"Jane's flying over just to see me. It's her birthday. I can't really cancel that."

"It's always something and it's always other women," Darcy said with a sigh. "But we were finished personally a long time ago. Now I'm ending our professional relationship as well. I'll work out a month's notice if you want, but that's all."

"You're very good at what you do. I don't want to lose you."

"I'm sorry, but I won't change my mind," Darcy replied firmly. "You know you won't have any trouble replacing me. You must have a file full of applications."

Finlo nodded. "I pay better than the other carriers and we go to much more interesting places."

"Exactly. You'll have me replaced before lunch."

In the end, they agreed that she'd work through the rest of the current schedule, which meant through the end of the month. She could only hope most of her flights would be with pilots other than Finlo. While she knew she was doing the right thing, she still found him incredibly tempting.

As she wasn't due to fly until late afternoon that day, she headed for her flat near the airport. Finlo did pay well and she had been far less extravagant lately than she used to be. She could probably survive without a job for five or six months, but that wasn't her plan.

At home, she fired up her laptop and dug out her CV. By the time she needed to head back to the airport, it was polished and ready to go. Tomorrow, when she got home, she'd start sending it off in response to any jobs that looked at all appealing.

The next few weeks flew past for Darcy. While she'd had good intentions, she never did manage to reply to any job postings. Finlo did his best to persuade her to change her mind, assigning her to his flights to Paris and Rome and then insisting on dragging her around the sights. When she worked his trip to Ibiza, he insisted they stay an extra day and just lie on the beach, soaking up sunshine.

"You're going to miss this," he told her after they'd had dinner together at a restaurant on the sea.

"I know," Darcy said with a sigh. "It's been fun, but I really am ready to move on. I worked hard at university to earn my degree in business management. It's time to use it."

On her last day, when she'd flown home from Barcelona with Finlo and Jack, her favourite co-pilot, she found they'd arranged a small surprise party for her. When she looked around at the people she'd worked with for the last few years, she felt teary, but resolute.

"You can still change your mind," Finlo told her when he drove her back to Lisa's house. "I'll take you back, both professionally or personally. Just say the word."

That made Darcy laugh. "I know I'm doing the right thing," she told him. "I just don't know what I'm doing next."

Darcy rarely drank when she was alone, but if ever there was a night for having a glass of wine, this was it. She filled up the bathtub in the guest bathroom and sank into the bubbles with her wine and a historical romance book she'd found on Lisa's bookshelf. An hour later, the water was cold and Darcy was crying as the heroine had her heart broken by the villain of the piece. The sound of the telephone had her jumping out of the tub, grabbing a towel and rushing to the kitchen.

"Hello?" she asked a bit breathlessly.

"I hope I'm not interrupting something," Lisa's voice came down the line. "I rang your flat and your mobile, but you didn't answer either. This was my last resort."

Darcy laughed. "It's so good to hear your voice," she told the woman who'd been her best friend since early childhood. "But you're supposed to be on your honeymoon. Ringing me can't be a good thing."

"It's all good," Lisa assured her. "But darling hubby actually has to do a bit of work this evening so I thought I would ring you and we could catch up. Should I start by asking why you're at my house?"

"My flat is cold and feels empty and your house feels warm and inviting," Darcy replied after a moment's thought. "And I want to keep an eye on everything and keep your plants watered and whatever."

"And are my plants watered?"

Darcy flushed. She'd kind of forgotten about the plants, but she would sort that out after she hung up. "Of course," she said, pulling the watering can out from under the sink to remind her later.

"Or they will be, after this call," Lisa suggested.

"Exactly," Darcy agreed with a giggle.

"Well, I'm glad my house feels like home for you," Lisa told her. "I should just sell it to you."

"I might be interested," Darcy replied thoughtfully.

"Hubby and I need to talk about what we're going to do with the house," Lisa replied. "I'll let you know what we decide. It isn't terribly convenient for the airport, though."

"Which doesn't matter a bit, as I quit my job," Darcy said. She pulled the phone away from her ear as Lisa shrieked.

"You what?" Lisa demanded.

"I quit my job," Darcy repeated herself. "You should be happy; you've been nagging me to do so for years."

There was a long pause before Lisa spoke again. "I did want you to quit your job," she agreed. "I just worry about you. Do you have a new job lined up yet?"

"Nope, not a thing," Darcy replied cheerfully. "I'm sure it will all work out."

"Of course it will," Lisa replied robustly. "If you haven't found anything by the time I get back, I'll help you. But I bet you'll find something really quickly. You're smart and beautiful and wonderful and any company would be lucky to get you to work for them."

"So I can use you as a reference?" Darcy asked, laughing. "Seriously, though, today was my last day at Quayle Airways. Tomorrow I start job hunting in earnest. Or maybe Monday."

"Let me know if I can do anything to help," Lisa told her. "We were supposed to be back in another fortnight, but we're going to be away a little bit longer than expected. Hubby was offered a chance to speak at a conference and he can't turn it down. I can probably help from here, though, if you need anything."

"I need you to enjoy your honeymoon," Darcy replied. "I'll worry about me for the next three weeks. You worry about keeping your new husband happy."

"Oh, he's happy," Lisa assured her. "We're both stupidly happy all the time."

Lisa told Darcy all about the sights she'd seen and the places she'd been so far. Then Darcy told Lisa about Finlo's attempts to get her to stay in her job.

"Honestly, I've been to all my favourite places in the world since you've been gone. Finlo tried hard to change my mind, but he couldn't stop himself from looking at every pretty woman that strolled past us, either. I know I'm better off without him, even if I am little bit lonely tonight."

"Read a book," Lisa advised. "Fall in love with a fictional character. Book boyfriends are much more reliable than real ones."

"Says the newly-married woman," Darcy teased.

"My husband is an exception, of course," Lisa added hastily. "And he's just walked in, so I'd better go."

"Don't ring me again," Darcy ordered her. "Enjoy your time away. You can sort out my life when you get back."

Darcy felt both better and worse after her phone call. She finished her glass of wine and watered Lisa's plants. Then she curled up with the book and finished it, shedding more tears as the heroine fell into the loving embrace of the book's hero in the final pages. As she dropped off to sleep she decided that she'd give herself the weekend to relax, but Monday morning she was going to start pounding the pavement, looking for her dream job.

3

"**I**'m sure you'd be the perfect personal assistant," the balding man behind the desk told her with a leer. "But I don't think my wife would be very happy if I hired you."

"You wouldn't want to upset her," Darcy replied sweetly. "I can't imagine you'd ever be able to replace her."

The man blinked and Darcy was sure she could see him trying to figure out if he'd been insulted or not. She got to her feet.

"Thank you for your time, anyway," she told him. "I'll see myself out."

As she exited the tiny office, she glanced back to see that his eyes were firmly fixed on her bottom. She sighed. Working as a personal assistant to the managing director of a very small manufacturing company wasn't exactly her dream job, but she'd been out of work for over a fortnight and this was only her second interview.

The first one had been worse, she reminded herself as she climbed into her car and drove steadily away from the remote industrial estate. She'd actually been offered that job, as an assistant to the manager of a small retail chain. She'd been tempted to accept until he'd wrapped up the interview with: "I know you used to work with, and date, Finlo Quayle. I do hope we can come to some sort of a similar arrangement."

When she'd politely told him that she wasn't interested in mixing business and pleasure, the job offer had disappeared. The man, who wasn't unattractive, had been surprised when she'd refused to have dinner with him anyway.

Her next interview, some hours later, started off promisingly. The hiring manager at the small retail store was an older woman who asked a great many questions about Darcy's work experience.

"And what was it like working with Finlo Quayle?" she asked eventually.

"He's a very talented pilot," Darcy replied smoothly.

"Is that a euphemism? I bet it is," the woman said, giving Darcy a wink. "I know I'm a bit old for him, but he's just about the most gorgeous man I've ever seen. Do you still see him often? Do you think you could introduce me to him? Do you think I'd have a chance with him?"

Darcy swallowed a sigh and forced herself to smile. "He's gay," she told the woman as she stood up to leave.

The woman's jaw dropped, and Darcy left the room while she was still speechless. Darcy didn't really want to work in retail, anyway, but especially not for a woman who was nurturing a crush on Finlo.

Darcy headed for Lisa's house, only just resisting the temptation to bang her head against her dashboard. She hadn't realised how exhausting and frustrating job hunting was going to be. It was Wednesday and Lisa was due back from her extended honeymoon on Sunday. Darcy had really hoped she'd already have a new job in place before Lisa returned.

She picked up some Chinese takeaway on the drive, treating herself to all of her favourites. When she pulled up in front of the small house, she frowned. Finlo's fancy sports car was already parked at the kerb. She climbed out of her car, her boxes of food in hand.

"I thought I'd find you here," Finlo said as he stood up from the small bench near Lisa's front door. "I stopped by your flat first, but the welcome mat was dusty."

"I don't have a welcome mat," Darcy replied, trying to get past him on the short and narrow walkway to the door.

"You should," he countered. "It would make your guests feel more loved."

"What do you want?" she demanded, circling around him across the grass.

"I was hoping you'd like to have dinner with me," he answered, following her to the door. "But I see you've already sorted dinner out. I don't suppose you got enough for two?"

"Nope," Darcy lied. She'd bought extra so she could have some for lunch the next day. She didn't want to share her feast with Finlo.

"How's the job hunt coming?" he asked.

"I've had three interviews this week," Darcy answered. "One man was afraid his wife would object to his hiring me, a second wanted to date me as well as work with me and the third, a woman in her late forties, just wanted me to introduce her to you."

Finlo laughed heartily while Darcy dug out her keys. She pushed the door open and stepped inside, turning quickly to shut the door in his face. He was quicker than she was, and he caught the door before it shut.

"Put the food in the refrigerator and come and have dinner with me," he suggested. "We can go anywhere you like."

Darcy thought about it. Finlo was great company and she'd had a terrible day. But dinner could only be thought of as a date, and she wasn't going back there.

"Sorry, Finlo, but I don't think that's a good idea," she said, surprised at just how reluctant she was to send him away.

He stared at her for a moment and then sighed. "I don't suppose you want your old job back, either, do you?"

That was even more tempting, but Darcy shook her head. "No, thanks," she replied. "Ask me again in a fortnight, though," she added impulsively.

Finlo grinned and then leaned forward and kissed her gently. "I'll do that," he whispered. "For the job and for dinner."

Darcy stood in the doorway and watched him walk away. She had to bite her tongue to keep herself from calling him back.

You're just lonely because you're used to having a boyfriend, she told herself as she piled food onto a plate in Lisa's kitchen. And even when she didn't have a boyfriend, she'd always had Lisa. That relationship was bound to change though, now that Lisa was married. Darcy felt tears forming and she swallowed hard and then poured herself a large glass of wine.

"To new possibilities," she toasted by herself. The food was delicious and the wine cheered her up slightly. Once she'd finished eating and done the washing up, she fired up her laptop and clicked through the long list of job postings that she'd seen every day since she'd handed in her notice. Tonight a new listing caught her eye.

Event Planner. *We are seeking a creative, hard-working, hands-on manager to plan a very special event on the island to be held later this year. We offer competitive pay for the right person, including performance-related bonuses. Degree in business management and event planning experience required.*

Darcy read it several times. She had a degree, but her event planning experience was limited to planning lively themed birthday parties for herself and her friends. Still, she could probably spin that into something that sounded like a real skill. There was nothing else new in the pages of listings. Darcy knew Lisa would worry if she hadn't found a job by the time Lisa's honeymoon was over. Now she wrote a quick email reply to the posting and attached her CV.

After she'd pushed send, she curled up with another romance from Lisa's shelf and read until she was tired enough to sleep.

Her working hours when she was flying regularly were erratic, so now she'd established a routine for herself. When her alarm went off at seven, she rolled out of bed, did a quick workout and then took a shower. As she had nothing on her schedule for the day, she threw on casual clothes before she turned on her laptop to get back to the job hunt.

After deleting all of the junk emails, Darcy was left with two new messages. The first was a follow-up from her second interview.

Just wanted to let you know that I'd still like to have dinner with you. If you change your mind, ring me.

Darcy hit delete and opened the second message.

I'm intrigued by your CV and your work experience. Finlo Quayle is an acquaintance and he had very nice things to say about you when I contacted him. I'd like to discuss the event planner position with you today. Your flight to London (on Quayle Airways) leaves at two this afternoon and there will be a car at the airport to collect you. I'll see you in my office at four. I suggest you pack an overnight bag, as we have a lot to discuss. Alastair

Darcy read the message a dozen times, uncertain of exactly what to think. The ringing telephone interrupted her indecision.

"Good morning," Finlo's voice came down the line. "Alastair Breckenridge rang me last night. Did you really apply for a job with him?"

"I don't know," Darcy replied. "I applied for a job as an event planner and I received an email from someone called Alastair this morning in reference to it, so I guess I did."

Finlo chuckled. "That sounds like the Alastair I know," he told her.

"He sounds mysterious, demanding and a little creepy in his email," Darcy told him.

"He's not really any of those things, except probably demanding," Finlo said. "He's a very successful businessman from old money. We went to university together for a while, although he did business and economics. We've not really kept in touch, but he has a few business interests over here. He always uses my service when he wants to come across."

"So he's your age?" Darcy checked.

"He is, and he's good-looking and filthy rich. Darcy, my dear, he's perfect for you."

Darcy laughed in spite of Finlo's harsh tone. "I'm not looking for a man, I'm looking for a job," she reminded him.

"Your flight is at two," Finlo said. "You should be here by one."

"I will," Darcy replied. "But what sort of event does he need planning?"

"He didn't say," Finlo answered before he hung up.

Darcy spent her morning trying on and discarding a dozen different outfits. She wanted to look professional and efficient, but when she looked at herself critically everything she owned seemed to show off her curves. By midday she was ready to cancel the interview and go back to bed. In desperation, she raided Lisa's wardrobe. There she found a dozen conservative suits in dark colours.

Knowing her friend wouldn't mind, Darcy borrowed a black skirt and jacket, adding her own green silk blouse that matched her eyes. She bundled her long hair into a neat knot at the back of her head and then carefully applied a minimal amount of makeup. Slipping on low-heeled black shoes that had also come from Lisa's collection, Darcy was on her way to the airport with about a minute to spare.

She was the only passenger on the chartered flight. Once they were airborne, Finlo joined her in the cabin.

"Who's flying the plane?" Darcy demanded as he dropped into the seat next to her.

"Jack's up there," he assured her. "He could fly to Heathrow in his sleep."

"So tell me all about Alastair Breckenridge, please."

Finlo shrugged. "His family owns a couple of mid-sized retail chains." He named a few high street shops that Darcy knew well. "He got his degree in business and then moved to the US for a few years. He came back with an MBA from some obscure university in Texas and a penchant for doing things on a grand scale."

"He didn't give you any hint as to what he's planning for the island?"

"No. He just asked for a reference."

"What did you tell him?" Darcy asked nervously.

Finlo laughed. "I told him you were hard-working, incredibly sexy and, as far as I know, single."

Darcy shook her head. "Did you at least list them in that order?"

"I can't remember," Finlo replied.

Darcy frowned. "I'm not looking for a man," she reminded him. "I need a new job. Why did my looks or my relationship status even come up?"

"It wasn't a formal request for a reference," Finlo said. "He just rang me up, as an old friend, to ask about you, that's all. If he wants a proper report on your job performance, you know I'll be happy to give him one."

Darcy nodded and then looked out the window. Her looks were

always an issue. She was hugely grateful that she was attractive, but it seemed to mean that no one took her seriously. She was determined to make Alastair Breckenridge see her as more than just a pretty face. If he hired her, she'd make his event the most successful one ever held on the island.

"If it doesn't work with Alastair, you know I'll have you back," Finlo told her as he stood up. "And he's not the settling down type, either, just so you know."

Finlo was gone before Darcy could reply. She sat back in her seat and flipped through a magazine from the seat pocket. It wasn't like she wanted to settle down necessarily, she told herself. What she wanted was to feel like she was loved so much that no one else mattered. She'd been cautious with Andy, not letting herself fall for him until she was sure that he was serious. As he wasn't, that turned out to have been a good choice. Her flight landed in London before Darcy managed to figure out exactly what she wanted.

After years of flying daily, Darcy knew exactly how to get through the airport quickly. She walked into arrivals and looked around for her ride. The uniformed man holding the sign with her name on it was staring straight ahead, his face blank.

"Hi, I'm Darcy," she introduced herself, holding out a hand and smiling brightly.

"Good afternoon," he replied, bowing rather than taking the offered hand. "I'll be your driver for today. You can call me James."

He took her bag from her hand and then led the way out of the building. Darcy wondered, as she walked, whether his name was really James or if that was just what he was called. It didn't really matter, but she thought he looked like a George, or maybe a Harold.

The black limousine was parked nearby. James ushered her into the back. "Help yourself to beverages and snacks," he told her, bowing again before shutting the door.

Darcy opened the small refrigerator. Bottles of champagne took up nearly every inch of space. While they were tempting, she reminded herself that she was there for a job interview, not a party, and pulled out a can of fizzy drink instead. She sipped it slowly as they made their way from the airport into London. Traffic was, as always, heavy, but

Darcy enjoyed watching the scenery go by. After a short time, a bell chimed and then the driver's voice filled the space.

"I've notified Mr. Breckenridge that we are being delayed by traffic. He has adjusted his schedule in order to accommodate the delay."

"Thanks," Darcy replied, wondering if the man could actually hear her.

Forty-five minutes later, they pulled up in front of a shiny glass and steel skyscraper in central London. A uniformed doorman opened Darcy's door and helped her from the car.

"Ms. Robinson? Mr. Breckenridge is expecting you," he told Darcy, ushering her into the cool and dimly lit foyer of the building.

"My bag," Darcy said, turning back towards the car.

"James will bring it up," the doorman assured her. The doors to the lift were open. Once Darcy was inside, he pushed the button labelled "P" and then stepped back. "Mr. Breckenridge's assistant will meet you at the top," he said.

Darcy used the mirrored wall to check her hair and makeup. After years of flying, she was an expert at fixing both so that she looked as fresh on arrival as she had on departure. The lift rose unhurriedly and Darcy had a smile in place when the doors finally slid open.

"Ms. Robinson? I'm Jennifer, Mr. Breckinridge's personal assistant. If you'll follow me, please?"

Darcy nodded and followed the sophisticated-looking blonde in the tight red dress down the short corridor. The carpet was incredibly thick, making Darcy glad she'd worn low heels. She wasn't sure how Jennifer could walk across it in the six-inch gold stilettos she was wearing.

"Mr. Breckinridge will be right with you," the woman told her after Darcy had followed her into a huge room. "Help yourself to a drink, if you'd like." She gestured towards a bar that was in one corner of the space, then turned and left, shutting the door behind her.

Darcy looked around the room. It had more of the same plush carpeting and several comfortable looking couches and chairs arranged in an arc that faced the huge windows that overlooked the city. Along one wall was a long table with eight chairs around it. She walked over to the nearest window and looked down at the busy street below. Several deep breaths did little to calm her nerves.

You've worked with wealthy men for your entire career, she reminded herself. And you've dated more than a few as well. Alastair Breckinridge is just another person.

Another person who might just be able to give me my dream job, a little voice interjected. Darcy looked around the beautifully appointed space and sighed. There was no way she had enough relevant experience to get a job with a man who could afford offices like this. She was just considering getting herself a drink when the door swung open.

"Ah, you must be Darcy," the man who entered said with a dazzling smile. "I must say, we would have stunning children, wouldn't we?"

Darcy flushed and her mind went blank. She could only stare at the man, who was now holding out his hand. His hair was shoulder-length and blond, artfully cut to look casually tousled. Perfectly straight, very white teeth flashed at her, but when she looked into his eyes she felt mesmerised. They were a bright green that almost matched her own, but as he got closer she could see tiny flecks of brown in them. She took his hand and felt a rush go through her. Alastair Breckenridge was one of the most attractive men she'd ever met.

"Come and sit down and let's talk," he said now, releasing her hand and taking her arm. He escorted her to one of the couches. She sat down, her brain feeling muddled.

"Can I get you a drink before we get started?" he asked.

"No, I'm fine," she murmured without thinking.

"Excellent." He sat down next to her on the couch, just inches away from her. "I'm Alastair, by the way," he said, turning to face her. His knee brushed against hers and Darcy found herself sliding backwards as her stomach lurched.

"It's nice to meet you," she said after she'd swallowed hard. Maybe a drink would have been a good idea, she thought now. Her mouth was dry, and she wouldn't mind having something to do with her hands, either.

"I can't believe we never met before. I fly with Finlo a couple of times a year at least," he replied. "But you were never on my flights. I definitely would have remembered you if you had been."

"I would have remembered you as well," Darcy told him honestly.

He smiled. "Good to know," he said softly. "When can you start?"

Darcy gasped. "I think I need to know a bit more about the job before we have that conversation," she said after a moment.

Alastair laughed. "I'm a bit desperate," he told her. "Everything was going very well and then my man on the island had a bit of an issue with the owner of the event location, and now it's all a bit of a mess. I need to get someone in there fast who can not only negotiate, but also charm the land owner."

"I see," Darcy said slowly, her mind racing. "What's the problem with the land owner, exactly?"

"It was just a personality clash," Alastair told her with a wave of his hand. "We originally worked with someone called William Kewley, but now we have to work with his son, Kerron, and Kerron didn't like my representative, that's all."

"What happened to William Kewley?" Darcy asked.

Alastair shrugged. "I don't know, maybe he died," he said casually. "Which would be sad," he added quickly. "But I still have an event to put on and a lot of money already invested."

"What is the event? I don't recall hearing anything about any special events coming up on the island." Darcy told him.

"We haven't made any announcements yet," Alastair told her. "Press releases and publicity are all part of the job description, but not until closer to opening day."

"I did some promotional work with Quayle Airways, but mostly at events. You know, passing out brochures and little sets of wings to children. I've never written a press release, although I did take a couple of classes in public relations as part of my degree."

"I'm sure you'll manage," Alastair replied.

"But what is the event?" Darcy smiled to hide her frustration. She couldn't commit to anything until he answered that very basic question.

Alastair grinned. "You mustn't tell anyone about this," he cautioned her. "We don't want word getting out before we're ready."

"That's fine."

He stood up and offered his hand. Darcy took it reluctantly, bracing herself for the sparks that raced up her arm. Alastair led her across the room to the large table and then let go of her hand. He opened a wall cupboard and pulled out a large board that seemed to have some sort of model on it.

After putting the model on the table, he turned to Darcy with eyes shining with excitement. "This is it," he said. "Manx Christmas World."

Darcy looked at the large rectangle. It was covered in fake snow and had numerous small buildings dotted across it. A large building that resembled a castle was at the very centre.

"That's Santa's castle, of course," Alastair told her. "We might call it Father Christmas's castle, I haven't decided."

Darcy nodded. "He was Father Christmas when I was growing up, but I know Santa is gaining ground."

"Anyway, these are the pens for the reindeer and this is the elf workshop where they make the toys," Alastair pointed to different sections of the model. "There will be a train to take visitors all around the site and a few other gentle and child-friendly rides, all for an additional fee, of course. And then, over here is the café and the gift shop."

"It sounds like an expensive day out," Darcy commented dryly.

"The standard admission ticket will include all of the exhibits, and even a visit with Santa. Photos with Santa will be a bit extra, of course. But you get to meet Santa, pet a reindeer and watch the elves make toys, all for one low price."

"Until the kids see the train, the rides and the gift shop and you have to take out a second mortgage on your home," Darcy countered.

Alastair laughed. "I'm a businessman," he told her. "Of course I'm hoping to make a lot of money from the thing. I've already spent a fortune on leasing the land, and tents and supplies aren't going to be cheap. Do you know how much fake snow costs?"

Darcy shook her head. "I'm not sure I want to," she muttered.

"Don't say that," Alastair said. He took her arm and led her back to the comfortable couch. "I'm going to be totally honest with you," he said as they both sat back down. "I've only had a handful of applicants for the position and yours is the only one from an Isle of Man worker. I don't have the time to wait for a work permit to come through the system. I need someone on the island now, getting everything organised. I have a team here to handle the financial details and worry about cost overruns. I just need an on-site manager."

"I don't know," Darcy told him. "It isn't really like anything I've done before."

"In your email you said you were looking for a new challenge," Alastair said. "It's a short-term contract. I'd need you from now until early January. If all goes well, once it's over I might be able to offer you a different position in my organisation or I might want to keep you on staff to start planning the next Manx Christmas World. At this point, I just don't know. Think of it as a great adventure."

"I think 'great' might be a bit optimistic," Darcy said with a small smile.

Alastair handed her a sheet of paper. "Here's the offer, in writing," he told her.

Darcy glanced at the numbers and struggled to keep her face from reflecting her surprise. The base salary was generous, with an almost ridiculously lavish bonus scheme based on hitting various targets over the coming months.

"As you can see, I believe in rewarding excellence," Alastair said. "I'm confident that everything on that list is achievable. The position could be very lucrative for you."

Darcy nodded. "I really need to think it over," she replied.

Alastair frowned. "Did I mention I'm desperate?" he asked. He patted her knee. "You think if you need to. While you're thinking, maybe we could get some dinner? There's an excellent restaurant on the roof of this building."

Darcy found herself nodding, even as her mind was racing. She was feeling overwhelmed by the job offer and by the man himself, but she was also feeling hungry. Dinner would help take care of at least one of her problems.

"I could use a minute to freshen up," Darcy said as they both rose to their feet.

"Certainly." He crossed to the table and pressed a button. A moment later the door swung open. "Jennifer, please show Darcy where she can freshen up and then ring and get us a table upstairs, please."

Jennifer nodded and then ushered Darcy down the corridor.

"How is he to work for?" Darcy asked the woman.

"Mr. Breckenridge is a wonderful employer," Jennifer told her. They stopped in front of a door. "You can freshen up in there," she told Darcy.

Darcy walked into the large room, her mind still racing. She found it slightly worrying that Jennifer hadn't met her eyes when she'd responded to the question. In front of the large mirror, Darcy took her hair down. She brushed it thoroughly with the brush in her bag and then pulled back just the front to keep it out of her eyes. She added a bit more eye makeup and a fresh coat of lipstick to her face. Finally she removed the jacket from her suit, letting the green blouse take centre stage.

"That's as good as it gets," she muttered to herself before heading back down the corridor. Apparently she hadn't done too badly, as Alastair's eyes seemed to light up when he saw her.

"You look stunning," he remarked. "Shall we?"

They rode the lift the short distance to the roof, where a tuxedoed host showed them to a small table in a quiet corner of the elegant restaurant.

"Wine or champagne?" Alastair asked her.

"Either is fine," Darcy replied, picking up her menu, as much to hide behind as to consult. Alastair was overwhelming her at the moment and she felt as if she needed to catch her breath.

"Champagne, then," he told their waiter, requesting a bottle that Darcy knew was very expensive.

"What would you recommend?" she asked after a moment of studying the choices.

Alastair made a couple of suggestions and by the time the waiter had poured the champagne, she was ready to order.

"So, tell me all about you," Alastair said when the waiter had gone. He put his hand over Darcy's and then squeezed it gently.

"What do you want to know?" Darcy asked, working hard to keep her voice level as her pulse raced.

"What's the story with you and Finlo?"

Darcy laughed lightly and then took a sip of champagne. "We worked together for a few years," she answered. "And then we dated for a short time as well. He's a committed bachelor, so it was never going to be more than just a bit of fun, though."

"So, is there a man in your life now?"

Darcy flushed and took another sip of her drink. "Not at the moment," she replied.

"Excellent." Alastair smiled at her. "I may have to apply for that position."

Darcy chuckled. The waiter arrived with their starters before the conversation could continue. Over dinner, Alastair kept Darcy entertained with stories from his extensive travels. While she'd flown all around Europe as a flight attendant, he'd been all over the world, including many trips to destinations that seemed exotic to Darcy.

"Is there anywhere you haven't been?" she asked eventually, over pudding.

"Lots of places," he laughed. "I feel very fortunate to have been born to parents who see travel as life-enhancing and mind-expanding, rather than simply a pleasurable pursuit. Even better, I've plenty of money to allow me to travel much of the time."

"How very nice for you," Darcy murmured, hoping she didn't sound as jealous as she felt.

"I do love to work, though," he added. "I love making money at least as much as I love spending it. Which is lucky, I suppose."

Darcy declined coffee after the meal, feeling as if it wouldn't go well with the rather large amount of champagne she'd drunk.

"The night is still young," Alastair told her in the lift on their way out of the building. "Shall we go dancing?"

Darcy shook her head. "I hate to admit it, but I'm quite tired," she told him. "I think I need some sleep."

Alastair's car pulled up to the kerb as they emerged from the building and Alastair helped Darcy climb in before following her inside.

"We could go back to my place for coffee," Alastair suggested. He looked over at Darcy and then took her hand. "Let's cut through the word play, okay? I'd love for you to spend the night with me."

Darcy pulled her hand away. "I don't mix business with pleasure," she said, annoyed with how stiff her tone sounded.

"What was dinner about, then?" Alastair demanded.

"Food?" Darcy suggested.

Alastair laughed. "I'm rushing you," he said. "We can take things at whatever pace works for you."

"I'm more interested in working for you than going to bed with you," Darcy said with a frankness that surprised her almost as much as it did Alastair.

He laughed again. "Let's just take it slowly and see what develops," he suggested.

A few moments later the car pulled up at a luxury hotel. Alastair escorted Darcy inside and got her room key for her.

"You could invite me up," he suggested, pulling her into his arms.

"But I won't," she answered, trying to step away.

"Just one good night kiss, then," Alastair murmured.

He stared at her for a moment and Darcy felt herself being drawn into Alastair's gorgeous eyes. For a moment nothing happened and then Alastair leaned forward and kissed her lips very gently. Sparks raced around Darcy's body as Alastair slowly but steadily increased the pressure. For a moment Darcy let herself get lost in the kiss.

"We could get more champagne from room service," Alastair whispered in her ear.

"Not tonight," Darcy told him. "What time do you want to meet tomorrow to discuss the job?"

Alastair shook his head and then sighed. "Nine? I'll make you my first appointment of the day."

"Perfect," Darcy replied. "I'll read over the papers you gave me and be ready with questions."

"I hope you'll say yes," he told her as he turned to go. "I really think you'll be perfect for the job. But if you say no, I still want to see you again."

"We'll talk tomorrow," Darcy said firmly, turning to head for the lift.

"We will indeed," Alastair replied.

She didn't allow herself to turn around until she'd boarded the lift and selected her floor. When she glanced back to where she'd left Alastair, he gave her a wink and a jaunty wave. She felt colour rush into her cheeks as the lift doors slid slowly shut.

4

After a restless night, Darcy felt tired and slightly grumpy the next morning. She ordered fruit and yoghurt from room service and they, along with a lot of coffee, helped improve her mood. While she'd been tossing and turning rather than sleeping, she'd reached one conclusion. Getting romantically involved with Alastair would be a mistake.

A car collected her at half eight for the trip back to Alastair's office. In the backseat, Darcy went over her notes. She wanted to be absolutely certain she was ready for the interview ahead and that she was focussed and strictly professional with Alastair. It turned out she needn't have worried about Alastair.

"I'm terribly sorry," Jennifer told her with a bright smile, "but Mr. Breckenridge has been called away. He's arranged for you to meet with Mr. Stuart, one of his business managers, instead."

Jennifer led her to a small conference room, furnished with a long table and several chairs. The man sitting at the head of the table rose to his feet when Jennifer ushered her in. He was older than Darcy had expected, probably in his fifties, with dark eyes and brown hair sprinkled with grey.

"Mr. Stuart, this is Ms. Robinson," Jennifer said. As Darcy moved forward to take the hand he offered, Jennifer left the room, shutting the door behind her.

"It's very nice to meet you," Darcy said.

"Likewise. I just hope you can sort out this project. Alastair has full confidence in you," the man replied. He gestured towards the chair next to him. "Have a seat and let's get started."

Darcy sat down, feeling confused. It sounded like Mr. Stuart thought she'd already accepted the job.

"Obviously, the first issue is the parking situation, but once that's arranged, we have a lot of other things that need doing fairly quickly," he sighed. "I'm afraid the gentleman that was handling things for us on the island has left things in rather a mess. We have some ground to make up, as it were, if we're going to get Christmas World up and running on time."

"Perhaps we should start by figuring out if I'm actually taking the job or not," Darcy replied.

The man sat back in his chair with a frown on his face. "Alastair told me he'd hired you yesterday," he told her. "He said you were coming in this morning to go over everything, ready to fly back at midday and start work, including meeting with Mr. Kewley." He glanced at his watch. "Unfortunately, Alastair is out of reach until later today."

Darcy shook her head. "He offered me the job yesterday, but I was meant to come in today to discuss it further. I certainly had no intention of starting today, even if I did decide to take it."

"Could you start today?" Mr. Stuart asked. "I don't know how much Alastair told you, but I don't mind telling you that we're a little bit desperate. The man who should be dealing with all of this had a huge disagreement with the landowner. That was over a week ago, and every day we're falling a little bit further behind our schedule. We sent someone else, but, well, she didn't have any luck. We need Mr. Kewley brought back on board and then all of the other issues worked out. As you can imagine, getting everything over to the island is something of a logistical nightmare and at the moment, once it gets there, we don't have anywhere to put it. We need someone on the island to start sorting things out today."

Darcy sighed. "I have a lot of questions about the job," she told the man.

He smiled. "Let me order up some coffee and muffins and let's see if we can work through them."

An hour later, full of lots of black coffee and far too many mini muffins, Darcy was feeling much better about the job. Mr. Stuart, who'd told her to call him Michael after a while, seemed to be an expert at his job.

"So, what else are you concerned about?" Michael asked eventually.

"I think that was it," Darcy replied, looking over her written list of questions. It was now nearly illegible, as she'd taken note of every answer the man had given her.

"I think it's a good offer," Michael told her. "The salary is fair, even if the working hours will be longer and non-traditional as the event gets closer. The bonus scheme is very generous, and even with the current setbacks, every target is still achievable. I know Alastair thinks you're the perfect person for the position, but ultimately, it's your decision, of course."

Darcy nodded. "I'll take it," she replied, feeling impulsive.

"Excellent, let's get down to work, then," Michael told her with a smile.

Two hours later, Darcy was in the car on the way back to the airport, her head swimming with information overload. She read back through her extensive notes as they went.

At the airport, she made her way to the Quayle Airways check-in desk, smiling and greeting the woman working behind it, who she knew well. "Sarah, how are you?" she asked.

"Darcy? It's wonderful to see you again. What are you doing here?" the young and pretty blonde answered.

"Flying home," Darcy replied. "Mr. Breckenridge arranged my flight."

"Oh, really?" Sarah winked at her. "Dating the gorgeous Alastair, are you now?"

"Actually, I'm not. I'm working for him," Darcy replied.

"Doing what?" Sarah demanded.

Darcy laughed. "I'm not able to answer that. You'll find out eventually, I suppose, but for now, it's all top secret."

Sarah giggled. "That sounds terribly exciting," she said. "I don't suppose you need any help?"

"I thought you liked your job here," Darcy replied.

"I guess," Sarah said with a shrug. "But if there were something more exciting on offer...." She trailed off, looking hopefully at Darcy.

"Unfortunately, I'm not hiring anyone at the moment," she told the other woman. "And when I am hiring, it will only be temporary positions."

Sarah shrugged. "Never mind. I guess I'll keep working here until my knight in shining armour arrives."

"Knights are overrated," Darcy replied. "You need to make your own happily ever after."

The flight back was uneventful. The pilot was one that Darcy only knew slightly, and he didn't do more than say a quick "hello" as she boarded. As it was a small plane and she was the only passenger, there was no cabin crew. Darcy helped herself to a fizzy drink, and few small packets of biscuits. That would have to suffice as lunch. Michael had rung Kerron Kewley and arranged for Darcy to meet with him at three o'clock. By the time she arrived back on the island, she was already behind schedule.

After half an hour of driving, Darcy pulled over to the side of the road and looked at the map Michael had given her. She'd followed his directions exactly, but they seemed to have led her to the middle of nowhere. Douglas, where she'd grown up, seemed a million miles away from the endless fields that now surrounded her. With only the one road to follow, she sighed and carried on. Eventually she would find the Kewley farm or she would reach the sea, and considering how long she'd been driving, she felt certain the water's edge was just around the next corner.

Instead, another mile along the winding dirt road, she spotted a sign for the Kewley farm. She turned up the driveway, which had tall pine trees growing along both sides at seemingly random intervals. After another mile or more, she came to a large farmhouse. The building looked quite old, but seemed to be in excellent condition.

Darcy parked in front of it and climbed slowly out of her car. She frowned as her heels sank into the muddy ground. Feeling as if she was squelching with every step, she made her way to the front door and climbed the handful of stone steps. Not able to find a doorbell, she knocked sharply on the painted wooden door. After a full minute she knocked again.

"I'm coming. Be patient," a voice shouted from somewhere.

At least another minute passed before Darcy could hear movement on the other side of the door. The lock clicked and the door slowly began to open. Darcy forced a bright smile onto her face.

"We aren't buying anything," the woman who had opened the door told Darcy firmly. The woman looked to be in her late sixties. Her hair was grey and had been gathered into a messy pile on top of her head. She had wrinkles and laugh lines, which she hadn't bothered to cover with makeup. Darcy could see blue eyes that were assessing her behind the woman's thick glasses.

Darcy just managed to keep the fake smile in place as she replied. "I'm not selling anything. Alastair Breckinridge sent me. I'm his new on-island representative for the event being held here."

"Christmas town?" The woman made a face. "Overpriced nonsense for spoiled children and their materialistic, status-obsessed parents. I told Mr. Kewley what I thought of the scheme, but all he saw were pound signs. Young Mr. Kerron, he agrees with me, but his dad's signature is on the paperwork, so he's stuck."

"Mr. Breckenridge's office rang. I have an appointment with Mr. Kewley at three," Darcy said in her friendliest voice, choosing to ignore everything the woman had said rather than argue.

"Mr. Kerron is out in the fields, doing his job," the woman told her.

"But he's expecting me," Darcy replied.

The woman shrugged. "He'll be back eventually. I guess you can wait."

With that, she turned her back on Darcy and started to walk away. After a moment's indecision, Darcy followed, wishing she knew whom Michael had spoken to at the farm. It seemed quite possible that Kerron Kewley didn't even know she was coming.

The farmhouse was light and airy, and as Darcy slowly followed the woman through it, she couldn't help but admire the beautiful crafts-manship of the old building. At the back of the property, the large and very modern kitchen might have felt out of place, but it had obviously been designed to blend modern conveniences with the same rustic feel as the rest of the home. Darcy loved to cook and bake and she was immediately impressed with the layout of the room.

"This is wonderful," she said as she turned slowly to inspect the entire space.

"Mr. Kewley just had the addition built last year," the woman replied. "It cost a fortune, it did, but it's much nicer to work in than the old kitchen was."

"I'm sure," Darcy said, running a hand along a length of granite countertop. "I'm sure I could make amazing meals in a kitchen like this."

"Harumph," the woman muttered under the breath. "I suppose you're going to be underfoot all afternoon, then? Waiting for Mr. Kerron?"

Darcy nodded. "As I said, we have an appointment."

The woman glanced at the wall clock, which showed that it was a few minutes past three. "Guess Mr. Kerron forgot," she said, sounding quite satisfied with the thought.

"I can wait," Darcy said with forced cheer. "I'm Darcy Robinson, by the way."

"Marion Christian," the woman replied, with a small nod in Darcy's direction.

"But I don't want to be in the way. Is there somewhere I can wait that won't inconvenience you?" Darcy asked.

Marion shook her head. "Can't leave you on your own, now can I? I don't know anything about you."

Darcy bit her tongue before a sharp reply could burst out. "I'll just sit here quietly, then," she said through clenched teeth. She dropped onto a stool that was placed to allow seating at the long peninsula of granite that ran along the centre of the kitchen. Sliding herself as far into the corner as she could, she gave the woman another tight smile. "I hope my arrival didn't interrupt anything important," she said.

Marion shrugged. "I was just thinking about starting some dinner for Mr. Kerron. It's steak and kidney pie tonight."

Darcy debated her reply for a moment and then threw caution to the wind. "Can I help?" she asked. "I'm good at pastry, or I can peel and chop things, whatever you need."

The woman studied her a moment and then threw back her head and laughed. "You know something, polished and professional-looking businesswoman? I'm going to take you up on that. Let's see what you can do."

An hour later, Darcy had made the pastry and rolled it out. She'd peeled and chopped carrots and onions while the older woman prepared the rest. When the pie finally went into the oven, Marion looked over at Darcy and shook her head.

"Okay, you aren't at all what I was expecting," she admitted. "Women who look like you can't normally cook."

Darcy laughed. "I know I can't get by on my looks forever," she replied. "Besides, I like to eat and there's something very satisfying about creating delicious food for yourself."

"So how did a nice woman like you get mixed up with Alastair Breckenridge and his Christmas nightmare?"

Darcy sighed. "The job was advertised in the local paper," she explained. "But I don't think it's going to be a nightmare. I think it sounds lovely."

The woman laughed. "Look, you seem like a nice enough person and I really do appreciate your help with the pie, but Mr. Kerron doesn't want to have this Christmas World thing here. His dad was the one that agreed to have it, and Mr. Kerron isn't happy about it. My best advice would be to find a different location as quickly as you can. We're awfully remote up here, anyway. I can't imagine why Mr. Breckenridge thought this location would work, anyway."

Darcy thought quickly before she answered. She knew exactly why Alastair had selected the Kewley farm for Christmas World. William Kewley had agreed to provide a great deal of space at a fairly reasonable rental rate. The farm was remote enough that parking shouldn't have been a problem and besides those things, no other farmer on the island had even been willing to talk to Alastair's representative about the idea.

"As I had nothing to do with the original negotiations, I can't possibly comment," she said eventually. "I'm just here to make sure things continue to move forward."

"Good luck with that," Marion laughed. "If Mr. Kerron has anything to do with it, Christmas World won't be happening."

Darcy frowned. Michael had told her that there were a few issues with the contract, but he hadn't suggested that there was any chance the whole event might be cancelled.

"Perhaps...."

Before Darcy had a chance to say more than that, a loud bang seemed to echo through the house.

"That'll be Mr. Kerron," Marion told her. "I suggest, if you want him in a good mood, you wait to talk to him until he's had a chance to eat his dinner."

"I've already been waiting for him since three o'clock," Darcy said. "I have to say that his not being here for our appointment wasn't very professional of him. What sort of man makes an appointment and then doesn't bother to show up?"

"The sort that is hoping that the annoying woman sent to plague his life will just go away if he avoids her," a deep voice from the doorway said.

Darcy spun around and felt her breath catch. The man who was casually leaning against the door was gorgeous, with hair so dark it was almost black. His eyes were blue and Darcy was sure they looked amused by her scrutiny. It seemed as if he'd taken a quick shower before he'd joined them. His hair was still damp and he smelled of soap and some spicy aftershave. He took a step forward and offered his hand.

"I'm Kerron Kewley," he said smoothly. "I thought, after I made the fluffy blonde Alastair sent cry, that he was done sending beautiful women to negotiate with me. I was sure this time he'd just send his solicitor."

Darcy rose from her stool and reached out to take his hand. She was tall and wearing heels, but the man towered over her. His shoulders were broad and he looked as if he worked out regularly. His hand-shake was firm and businesslike, and Darcy ignored the butterflies that fluttered through her stomach as their hands touched.

"I'm Darcy Robinson," she replied, working hard to keep her voice steady. "I've been given a long list of issues that need to be cleared up as quickly as possible. I'd like to get started."

Kerron's smile nearly took her breath away. "Is that steak and kidney pie I smell?" he asked, his eyes never leaving Darcy's.

"Yes, sir, Ms. Robinson made the pastry and chopped the veggies for me," Marion answered.

"Did she now?" Kerron asked. He raised an eyebrow. "A beautiful woman who can cook? Wherever did Alastair find you?"

"If you'd like to see a copy of my CV, I'm sure I can arrange that," Darcy replied. "I'd rather get on with the things that need doing, however."

Kerron laughed. "Frightfully professional," he commented. "I'm sure that isn't all that Alastair sees in you, though."

"Perhaps you'd like to save your speculation about my private life for after I've gone," Darcy said dryly.

Kerron laughed again, a sexy sound that sent shivers through Darcy. "This is going to be far more interesting than I expected," he said. He finally looked away from Darcy, smiling at Marion. "Is there enough pie for Ms. Robinson to join us for dinner?" he asked.

"Sure, if you don't want any warmed over tomorrow," she answered.

"Tough choice," Kerron said. He seemed to think for a moment and then shrugged. "I suppose the polite thing to do is invite her, especially if she did most of the work."

"Not most of it," Marion argued.

"I know you hate making pastry," Kerron replied. "I suppose I should be grateful to her for taking on that job. Not having to do it has left you in a better mood than normal on pie nights."

Marion chuckled. "You aren't wrong," she admitted.

Darcy looked from Kerron to Marion and back again. She was frustrated by her lack of progress and very conscious that the day was getting away from her. "If we could just talk about parking," she began, but Kerron held up a hand.

"Let's eat," he said. "I'm too hungry to concentrate anyway. Please, join us for dinner. I'm sure Marion can come up something for pudding as well. When I'm stuffed and unable to move, it will be easier to get me to agree to things."

Darcy felt like arguing, but she needed the man to work with her. Having wasted the entire afternoon, another hour was only a minor inconvenience.

"Wine?" Marion offered.

"I'm driving," Darcy demurred. "And it's a long way home from here."

Marion pulled the pie from the oven and spooned generous portions onto plates. Kerron picked up his plate and a second one and nodded to Darcy.

"If you grab that one and follow me, I'll show you to the dining room," he said.

Darcy picked up the last plate and followed him through a side door. The dining room had a large table that would seat a dozen people. Kerron put a plate at the head of the table and the second at the place on his right, then held out the chair for the place on his left.

"Here you are," he said.

Darcy set her plate down and slid into the seat. Marion followed, carrying a tray with glasses and a pitcher of ice water with lemon on it.

"I can make you tea or coffee if you prefer," she told Darcy. "But it's such a warm night, I thought iced lemon water would be refreshing."

"It sounds wonderful," Darcy agreed.

For a few moments everyone ate quietly before Kerron spoke.

"You said home is a long way away. I do hope you aren't flying back to London tonight."

"I don't live in London," Darcy replied. "I live just outside Castletown, although I'm staying at a friend's house in Douglas as the moment."

"You're from the island?" he asked in surprise.

"My family moved to the island when I was in primary school," Darcy replied. "My parents moved back across when my father retired, but I love it here."

"Interesting," Kerron said, looking thoughtful. "Perhaps I underestimated Alastair. You're a much better choice to head up this project than the last two people who tried."

"Thank you," Darcy said. She took a bite of her pie and smiled at Marion. "This is delicious. I don't suppose you'd share the recipe?"

Marion looked at her for a moment and then shrugged. "I guess I could," she said grudgingly. "Your pastry is better than mine."

Darcy chuckled. "My mother hated making pastry, so she taught me how to do it at a very young age. My father loves pies, both sweet and savoury, so I got a lot of practise over the years."

"Your father sounds like mine," Kerron remarked.

"Ah, yes, Alastair said that your father had recently passed away. I am sorry," Darcy said.

Kerron and Marion exchanged glances and then they both began to laugh. Darcy put her fork down and took a sip of water. Clearly Alastair was mistaken, she thought as she waited for one of them to explain their mirth.

"My father is absolutely fine," Kerron said, after drinking some water himself.

"So why am I dealing with you rather than him?" Darcy asked. "I understand he signed the original contract."

"He did," Kerron agreed. "And then he took the generous deposit that Alastair paid him and used it as a deposit on a villa in the Algarve."

"The Algarve?" Darcy echoed.

"He just up and declared himself retired and off he went," Marion told her, her tone suggesting that she hadn't approved.

"Leaving me with a farm to manage and Alastair Breckinridge to deal with," Kerron added. It was clear he definitely didn't approve.

"I see," Darcy said, her thoughts racing. If Kerron's father had already spent the large deposit Alastair had paid, he'd put Kerron in a difficult position. No matter how much Kerron hated the idea of the event, unless he could find the money to repay Alastair, he was going to have to let it go ahead.

"That doesn't mean I'm stuck with you," Kerron told her, almost as if he could read her mind. "Or rather, it doesn't mean I have to agree to anything else. You have your contract to have your event, and I won't stop you. But I don't intend to make it any easier for you, either."

Darcy took a deep breath and then smiled as brightly as she could at the man. "I'm sure we can work things out," she lied. "We'll just take them one thing at a time."

They ate silently for a while and then Darcy sat quietly while Kerron and Marion discussed several issues from around the farm, from livestock to fences to farm machinery. After everyone finished their pie, Darcy helped Marion clear the dishes.

"I'll just put some pudding on plates and then leave you and Mr. Kerron to your chat," Marion told her as she loaded the dishwasher. A short time later she served large slices of Victoria sponge onto two plates and then added them to a small tray. A teapot with cups and cream and sugar were already on the tray.

"Here, you take this in and enjoy," Marion told Darcy. "Once Mr. Kerron's had some cake, he'll be in a better mood."

"Thanks," Darcy said with a smile. "I hope so."

Back in the dining room, Darcy passed Kerron his cake and served the tea. Then she sat down and began to eat her own generous portion.

"So, let me guess why Alastair sent you," Kerron began after a moment. "Because he needs a car park and he forgot to negotiate one."

Darcy took a sip of tea and then smiled at the man. "Not exactly," she said smoothly. "The original contract covers the rental of the space we need for, well, let's call it Christmas Town for now, as a working title."

"You can call it whatever you like," the man told her. "I'm still not renting you any more land."

Darcy shrugged. She reached into her large handbag and pulled out the paperwork Michael had given her. One of the sheets was the map of the site, which Darcy laid on the table in front of her.

"This is how we envision using the site," she told the man. "Clearly, we're using nearly every square inch for the various attractions. When Paul Hanson first discussed things with your father, I believe he was imagining something somewhat smaller, with a parking area on the west side."

Darcy pointed on the map. "As we are now planning to use that area for food tents, obviously it can't be used as a car park. What we'd like to do is rent this field here," Darcy pointed again. "It's adjacent to the site we're already using and we estimate it's just about the right size to accommodate parking for our guests."

"This is where the argument between Paul and I began," Kerron told her, looking amused. "He was shouting at me within two minutes."

"I won't shout at you," Darcy said calmly. "I've spent far too many years dealing with drunk and disorderly passengers to let a little thing like this upset me."

"Passengers?"

"I was a flight attendant for a while," Darcy explained. She felt her cheeks flush as Kerron raised an eyebrow.

"Really? Is that where Alastair found you?"

"No," Darcy replied. She smiled sweetly, but said nothing further.

After a moment, Kerron laughed. "Paul seemed to think I was being unreasonable," he said, returning the conversation to the business at hand. "Or that I was holding out for an unrealistic sum of money for the extra plot of land."

"And are you?"

"No," Kerron replied. "I'm simply refusing to even consider it. I don't want you here. My advocate says I can't break the contract without repaying the deposit and a large penalty as well, which I also won't consider. So, you can go ahead and have your event, but I won't let you use any more land than my father has already agreed to."

Darcy nodded. "I'm sorry you feel that way," she said as she tried to think.

"This is where the pretty blonde that Alastair sent last week started to cry," Kerron told her. "She seemed to think that her tears would persuade me to change my mind."

"She wasn't a good judge of character, then," Darcy said.

Kerron laughed. "Not very, but she was lovely and she cried beautifully."

"And yet, here we are," Darcy replied. "No closer to a solution."

"Indeed. Perhaps it's time for you to find a new location for your event."

"If we break the contract, you still have to pay back the deposit,"

Darcy told him. She'd read the entire contract, including the very tedious fine print, on the plane back to the island.

"I would," he agreed. "But I would have a year to do so and without any penalties. I think I could just about manage that."

Darcy nodded. "I guess that leaves us at something of an impasse," she said, keeping her voice level. She gathered up the various papers and put them back into her handbag and then stood up.

"I'll be in touch after I've done some checking into things," she said.

Kerron stood up, a surprised look on his face. "That's it? You aren't going to argue with me or try to change my mind?"

"Would it be worth my time to do so?" Darcy asked.

"Well, no," the man admitted. "But I still expected you to try."

Darcy grinned. "I see very little point in wasting any more of my time today. It's Friday night, after all. You probably have a hot date. I definitely do. Let's meet again in a week or so and see if we can't find some common ground."

"Just as things were getting interesting," Kerron said with a sigh. "She dashes off for a hot date with some incredibly lucky guy. Never mind, how about a week on Monday? What time works for you?"

Darcy tapped on her phone and looked at the calendar. There was nothing on it, but Kerron didn't need to know that. "How about three o'clock?" she asked.

Kerron shrugged. "Sure, why not?"

"It would be helpful if you could actually turn up on time," she said tartly.

"Yes, ma'am," he replied.

Darcy was annoyed to see that she'd amused him. "And thank you so much for your time and for dinner tonight," she said in a sugary sweet tone.

"It was my pleasure," he replied. "I'll walk you out."

He offered an arm and Darcy took it, hiding her reluctance. She also hid her reaction to the rush of electricity that his touch sent through her. He walked her down the porch steps and over to her car. Darcy frowned as her heels sank in the mud again.

"Those aren't great shoes for spending time on a farm," Kerron remarked.

"I'd just about figured that out for myself," Darcy shot back. "I'll wear something more sensible on Monday."

"They are great shoes, though," Kerron told her.

Darcy felt her face flush as his eyes moved from her shoes slowly up her body.

"I don't think they'll come in your size," she told him, unlocking her car and quickly climbing behind the wheel.

"I probably couldn't walk in them anyway," Kerron said with a laugh. "See you next Monday at three."

"You will indeed," Darcy replied. She started her car and drove away slowly across the muddy and uneven car park. Even if it had been big enough for more than a few cars, there was no way they could let Christmas Town's guests park there, she thought. Not in the state that it was currently in.

Back at Lisa's house, Darcy carefully cleaned her muddy shoes and then took a long shower. She'd only been back in the work force for a few hours and she was already exhausted. Saturday she needed to clean the house, ready for Lisa's return, but on Sunday she was going to start making a few phone calls. Kerron Kewley wasn't going to defeat her that easily.

🦂 5 🦂

Darcy had the best of intentions, but she didn't get very far in cleaning the house the next morning. First she overslept, and then she had a few errands to run and some shopping to do. She needed to get ready for a new week, a week when she expected to be working more or less full-time. Finally back at Lisa's after a quick lunch at one of her favourite cafés, Darcy was just about to start the vacuum when her mobile rang.

"How's my favourite new employee?" the sexy deep voice asked when Darcy answered.

"I'm fine," Darcy replied automatically.

"I'm flying over this afternoon to take you out for dinner," Alastair said. "Where will I find you when I arrive?"

"I have a million things to do today," Darcy said, her mind racing. "I've been staying with a friend and I need to get her house tidied up before she gets home tomorrow."

"Surely you can hire someone to do that," Alastair said.

Darcy bit her tongue and counted to ten before she replied. "I'm perfectly capable of dusting and running a vacuum around," she said eventually. "Besides, I wouldn't want a stranger in my friend's house."

"But I want to see you." Alastair's tone suggested that he always got what he wanted. When Darcy didn't reply immediately, he spoke again.

"I was so disappointed when I was called away yesterday. I rearranged a dozen things on my calendar for today, just so I could fly over to spend some time with you. You've made quite an impression on me, you know."

"I don't want to mix business with pleasure," Darcy reminded him.

Alastair chuckled. "So let's start out as friends," he suggested. "Then, after Manx Christmas World is over, we can take things further."

"I don't think that's a good idea," Darcy told him honestly. "I don't think you'll be happy with just being friends for months on end."

"You could be right," Alastair conceded with a laugh. "But won't it be fun while it lasts?"

Darcy laughed in spite of her uncertainty. "You're very persuasive," she admitted.

"And I'm not even really trying yet," he told her. "Give me an address and I'll pick you up at six. I've made a booking already. I'd hate to have to cancel it."

When he named Darcy's favourite restaurant, she found she couldn't say no. "Just as friends," she reminded him. "I can let you know how my meeting with Mr. Kewley went yesterday."

"Or we can talk about more pleasant things," Alastair suggested. "I'll see you at six."

Darcy disconnected and looked at the clock. She only had a few hours to get Lisa's house in order, drive home and get changed for her date. At half four she stopped and looked around. Every surface had been dusted and the entire house had been vacuumed. Darcy had cleaned the loos and the kitchen, and she'd finished the job by arranging a vase full of fresh flowers that she put on the coffee table in the middle of the sitting room. She'd left a loaf of bread and some fresh milk in the kitchen, along with a box of Lisa's favourite chocolate truffles.

As she drove south to her flat near the airport, Darcy felt a bit melancholy. She was looking forward to Lisa coming home, but she knew that their relationship would be different now that Lisa was married. Darcy wouldn't be able to just drop in unannounced and drag Lisa off to parties like she used to. Maybe spending some time with Alastair was just what she needed, she thought as she parked her car.

After a quick shower, Darcy slid on one of her favourite little black dresses. She debated over what to do with her hair, eventually deciding to leave it down, just pulling a small section from either side of her face back in a sparkly clip. She did her makeup with care, but years of experience meant it took very little time. With one last spray of perfume, she felt ready to go at almost exactly six. As she crossed to the sitting room window to look outside, her doorbell rang.

"You look gorgeous," Alastair told her.

Darcy flushed as she took the huge bouquet of red roses from him. "You shouldn't have," she muttered as she shut the door behind him.

"Why not?" he demanded.

Darcy carried them into the small kitchen area in one corner. She found a vase and filled it with water while she tried to figure out how to reply.

"It just seems like a romantic gesture," she said after she'd put the vase in the centre of the small dining table next to the kitchen. "And we're just friends."

Alastair laughed and crossed to her. "You're beginning to sound like a broken record, my dear. Let's just take things as they come and stop worrying about defining things precisely, okay?"

Darcy looked at him, ready to argue, but found herself getting lost in his incredible green eyes. He raised his hand and ran a finger down her cheek.

"You're far too beautiful," he said softly. "I could just sit and stare at you for hours."

Darcy felt herself blushing. She shut her eyes and turned away. "I'm also starving," she said, which was true. "Maybe we should get going?"

"Absolutely," Alastair replied. He offered his arm. "Shall we?"

Darcy ignored the offer, instead crossing the room to pick up her handbag and fish out her keys. She followed Alastair from the room and then locked her door behind them. Another couple in the lift meant that she didn't have to make conversation on the way down.

When they emerged from the building, Darcy wasn't surprised to see a limousine waiting for them.

The car whisked them towards Douglas quietly and smoothly. Alastair had champagne chilling in the back and he poured Darcy a glass as soon as she was seated.

"Just one," she muttered as she took the champagne flute.

"Or maybe two," Alastair said, winking at her.

"I had a meeting with Kerron Kewley yesterday," Darcy began after a sip of her drink.

"Good," Alastair said with a shrug. "I trust you'll have everything sorted out with him in no time. Let's not talk about work for now, though. Tell me all about you instead."

"What do you want to know?" Darcy asked.

"If you could go anywhere in the world, where would you go?" Alastair asked.

Darcy took another sip of champagne while she thought about her answer. "There are so many exotic places I haven't been," she said after a moment. "But I'm not sure I'd cope well without running water and electricity. Really, I've always wanted to visit the US. You see so much of it on telly. I'd love to see some of it in person."

"I travel to New York quite a bit," Alastair told her. "It's definitely different."

They arrived at the restaurant before Alastair could tell her more. The driver held the door for Darcy and helped her from the car. Alastair followed and then offered his arm. This time Darcy took it, handing her empty glass to the car's driver as she went.

They were shown to a small table in a quiet corner in front of the huge windows that showcased the Douglas promenade.

"What an amazing view," Darcy said as she sank into her chair.

"It is breathtaking," Alastair agreed.

Darcy studied her menu. She'd eaten at this restaurant several times and everything had always been delicious. The waiter's arrival interrupted her.

"The wine list, sir," he said, handing the list to Alastair.

"Would you like to choose?" Alastair asked Darcy.

"I'm sure you know more about wine than I do," Darcy replied. "But I was thinking I might just have a soft drink."

Alastair shook his head. "Gourmet meals need wine," he told her firmly. After a brief discussion with her and then the waiter, Alastair ordered.

"I hope you'll like my selection," he told Darcy as the man walked away. "It's one of my favourites."

"I'm sure it will be wonderful," Darcy answered. It was clear that Alastair knew a great deal about wine and also that he had expensive tastes. There was no doubt whatever he had selected would be excellent.

The waiter returned with the bottle and he took Alastair through the usual tasting ritual. Once that was completed, Darcy took a cautious sip.

"It's gorgeous," she said. "I love it."

"I'm so glad," Alastair told her. "Now let's hope we do as well with the food."

Darcy glanced back at her menu, but looked up when she heard approaching footsteps. Expecting the waiter, she felt herself blushing when she met Finlo's eyes.

"Darcy, what a lovely surprise," he said, clearly amused.

"Finlo, I didn't expect to see you here," she muttered.

"I might say the same," Finlo replied. "When I flew Alastair across this afternoon, he didn't mention he was planning to see you."

Darcy glanced at Alastair and then back to Finlo. "I don't suppose Alastair has to keep you up-to-date on his personal life," she replied.

Both men chuckled.

"So what brings you here tonight?" Darcy asked Finlo.

"My cousin William's wife is away for a few days, so I thought I'd buy him dinner to cheer him up," Finlo told her, gesturing to a table across the room.

Darcy looked over and then smiled and waved at William, whom she knew slightly.

"Well, enjoy your evening," Alastair said, his tone brusque.

Finlo just laughed. "Likewise," he said. With one last smile for Darcy, he turned and walked away.

Alastair watched until Finlo sat back down beside his cousin. "He's a good pilot, but I don't like the way he looks at you," he told Darcy.

"We've been friends for a long time," Darcy said airily.

"You were more than friends," Alastair argued.

"And you and I are just work colleagues," Darcy reminded him. "Whatever happened between Finlo and me, you have no reason to be getting jealous."

The waiter interrupted the awkward silence that followed Darcy's words. Once their orders were placed, Alastair smiled at Darcy.

"Sorry, when I want something I go after it. And when I feel like someone is in my way, it bothers me."

Darcy opened her mouth to speak, but he held up a hand. "Please don't remind me that we're just working together or that you don't mix business with pleasure," he said. "For tonight, let's just enjoy each other's company and get to know one another better. Let me tell you about New York and Texas."

For the next hour, over several delicious courses, Alastair kept Darcy entertained with stories about his various trips to New York City and his years as a student in Texas. He was an excellent storyteller with great comic timing and Darcy found herself hanging on every word. By the time pudding arrived, Darcy felt like she was in over her head.

"I'll have to take you with me the next time I'm going to the Big Apple," Alastair told her in between bites of crème brulee. He covered her hand with his. "We can take a carriage ride through Central Park and visit the top of the Empire State Building."

Darcy sighed. "It will have to be after Christmas," she said. "I won't be going anywhere between now and then."

Alastair laughed. "Now, now, don't let me turn you into a workaholic," he protested, squeezing her hand. "I'm sure we can figure something out."

As the waiter cleared the dishes, Darcy excused herself. In the enormous and luxurious loo she sat at a mirror and touched up her lipstick.

"He's your boss," she said to her reflection.

"So was Finlo," a little voice whispered in her head.

"And look where that got me," she told the little voice grumpily.

"He's gorgeous and very, very rich," the voice said. "Think of the fun you'd have."

"I have a job to do," she reminded herself. "And I'm going to do it well and surprise everyone."

A new arrival to the room ended the conversation, and Darcy reluctantly headed back towards her table. She just hoped she was strong enough to ignore the powerful attraction she felt towards Alastair.

"You can do better," a voice said just before she reached the dining room.

"Like maybe you?" Darcy asked Finlo sarcastically.

The man flushed. "Look, I know I didn't always treat you right, but I really do care about you," he told her. "And I've known Alastair for a long time. He isn't looking for anything more than a bit of fun. He'll soon grow tired of you."

"Just like you, then," Darcy suggested.

"I'm not even close to tired of you," Finlo told her. "I keep asking you for another chance, but you won't listen."

"Because I know you too well," Darcy replied. She shook her head. "Don't say anything," she told him. "I need to get back to Alastair." She turned and walked away before Finlo replied. Alastair was staring at her as she crossed the room, and she could see his frown.

"What did Finlo want?" he demanded as Darcy sat back down across from him.

"He's worried you'll break my heart," she told him lightly.

"I think it's rather more likely you'll break mine," he told her, staring into her eyes.

Darcy smiled nervously back at him, unsure of how to reply.

"Shall we?" Alastair asked, rising to his feet.

Darcy stood up and took the arm he offered. They made their way out of the restaurant. Darcy resisted the temptation to turn and glance back at Finlo as they went. Outside, the limousine driver was quick to open the car door for them. The drive back to Darcy's flat was a silent one, but not uncomfortably so. Darcy was busy trying to figure out how to convince Alastair that she truly did just want to be friends. What Alastair was thinking about, Darcy couldn't guess.

"I'll only be a minute," Alastair told the driver as he followed Darcy out of the car.

Darcy was glad it was dark, as that hid her surprise at his words. As they walked into the building, Alastair took her hand, but he didn't speak in the lift. At her door, she dug her keys out of the bottom of her bag.

"Thank you for a lovely evening," she said once she'd opened the door.

"You are very welcome," he replied. He slipped an arm around her and pulled her close. "Just one kiss," he murmured before his lips claimed hers.

Darcy thought about arguing, but she was lost in a maelstrom of emotions before she had a chance to object. When Alastair finally lifted his head, Darcy couldn't quite remember why she didn't want to get involved with the man.

"I don't want to push you into anything," he told her, his eyes burning into hers. "So I'm going to let you set the pace. I can be very patient when I really want something."

Darcy blushed. "Thank you," she said eventually.

Alastair laughed. "I hope you won't make me wait until Manx Christmas World opens," he teased. "December is a long way off."

"We need to do something about that name," Darcy said, changing the subject. "I'm going to work on that."

"It seems like you have a lot to work on," Alastair said. "I suppose it's a good thing I have to fly home early tomorrow. If I were staying another day, I'd just be a distraction."

Darcy hoped the disappointment she felt didn't show on her face as Alastair's words registered. "Have a safe journey home," she said. "I'll email you a summary of meeting with Mr. Kewley and my thoughts on possible solutions to our problems with him."

"Make sure you copy everything to Michael Stuart. He's the one who is handling things from my end," Alastair told her. "I can put him totally in charge if you prefer. Then you won't be mixing business with pleasure when we're together."

"I couldn't possibly tell you how to run your business," Darcy said, feeling annoyed with the man. He didn't seem at all interested in what she was doing for his company.

Alastair just laughed. "Sleep well, my dear," he said. He leaned down and gave her another quick kiss. This one was soft and gentle and confused Darcy even more than the first one had. She stood in her doorway and watched Alastair as he headed back towards the lifts. He turned around and waved to her as the lift doors closed. Darcy sighed and went into her flat.

After having spent nearly all of the last month or so at Lisa's house, Darcy's flat felt cold and lonely to her. Lisa had spent a lot of time and effort making her house into a warm and cosy home. As Darcy had previously spent most of her life flying around Europe, she had never bothered to do much with her small flat.

She kicked off her heels and pulled the clip out of her hair. For a moment she considered having a hot bath, but it seemed like too much effort. In her small bedroom, she changed into fleecy pyjamas. She washed her face and smoothed on moisturiser and then made a face at herself in the mirror.

"No more cosy nights drinking wine at Lisa's house," she told her reflection. "Lisa's married now and her husband won't want you hanging around all the time."

She tried to make a silly face at herself, but instead she found that her eyes were filling with tears. "You're a little bit drunk," she told herself sternly. "You'll feel better in the morning."

While this was undoubtedly true, it did little to cheer Darcy up at the moment. She climbed into bed and snuggled down under the duvet, switching on the television more for company than anything else. A satellite channel was showing a James Bond marathon, and Darcy finally drifted off to sleep as Sean Connery turned into Roger Moore.

Darcy slept late on Sunday, finally rolling out of bed not much before midday. She did feel quite a bit better and very determined to get to work on her problems with Kerron Kewley. She decided in the shower that Alastair was best simply ignored, at least for now.

After she'd treated herself to brunch at a nearby favourite restaurant, she started ringing people, working her way through the many contacts she had made over the years she'd worked for Finlo. As it was the island's only charter air service, just about every businessman or woman on the island flew with Finlo, at least once in a while. Darcy had met many of the island's most influential professionals over the years and some of them, the more frequent flyers, she'd become friends with. Now she used those connections to her advantage.

She had just taken a break from her calls when her phone rang.

"Darcy? We're back. Thank you so much for the flowers and the milk and bread," Lisa's voice came down the line. "And especially for the chocolates."

"Welcome home," Darcy replied. "I wasn't sure if you'd be staying at your house or not, but I assumed you'd at least stop there." Lisa's husband had a home of his own, but Darcy had guessed that Lisa would be eager to see her beloved little house.

"Of course we stopped here," Lisa replied with a laugh. "We're even going to stay for a few days. We still have to figure out exactly what we're going to do with my house."

"I want first refusal if you decide to sell," Darcy told her.

"Naturally," Lisa agreed. "But tell me how you are. How is the job hunt going?"

"I started a new job on Friday," Darcy replied.

"Come on then, tell me everything," Lisa demanded.

An hour later Darcy had done just that, sharing every last detail of the job, and her incredibly sexy new boss, with her friend.

"He sounds exactly like your type," Lisa said.

"I can hear the disapproval in your voice," Darcy replied with a laugh. "I don't intend to get romantically involved with the man, and he knows it."

"I just don't want to see you get hurt," Lisa said. "Tell me more about Kerron Kewley, though. You said he was gorgeous, too."

"Gorgeous and stubborn and impossible," Darcy told her with a sigh. "He's doing everything he can to get the whole event cancelled."

"But you're not going to let him get away with that," Lisa said firmly.

Darcy laughed. "No, I'm not." She told Lisa all about her plans for working around the obstinate Mr. Kewley.

"I'm impressed," Lisa said when Darcy had finished. "If anyone thought you were just a pretty face, they're in for a surprise."

Darcy glanced at the clock on the wall and gasped. "We've been talking for over an hour," she exclaimed. "Your poor husband will be furious with me."

"He's curled up with a good book and couldn't care less," Lisa told her with a laugh. "We had a wonderful month together, but I think we're both happy to have a bit of space to ourselves at the moment."

"But everything is good with you two, right?" Darcy asked tentatively.

"Everything is wonderful," Lisa replied.

Darcy could hear the sincerity in her friend's voice, and though she was happy for Lisa, she felt a momentary pang of jealousy.

"Now we just have to find you the perfect man," Lisa said. "After you did such an, um, interesting job in fixing me up with all those blind dates, I think I need to repay the favour."

"No, no, no, thank you, but no," Darcy replied quickly. "I already have too many men in my life. Besides, I quit my job with Finlo to focus on a new career. This isn't the right time for me to meet a new man. I want to make Manx Christmas World an event to remember. Maybe I'll start looking for a new man in the New Year."

"You need a better name," Lisa told her. "Manx Christmas World is lame."

Darcy laughed. "I'm working on that as well," she assured her friend.

After the call was over, Darcy didn't feel like working any more. As her meeting with Kerron wasn't for over a week, she decided she had plenty of time to ring the rest of the people she wanted to talk with. They would still have plenty of time to get back to her if she waited until the working week began. Instead, she filled her bathtub and added extra bubble bath to the water. She poured herself a glass of wine and relaxed in the tub until the water began to cool.

A pizza from her freezer and a second glass of wine made the perfect evening meal, and once she'd eaten, Darcy crawled back into bed and switched the telly back on. By now, Pierce Brosnan was James

Bond and Darcy was happy to watch him chase down bad guys for a short time before she drifted off to sleep.

Darcy had set her alarm for seven and she got out of bed with more enthusiasm for her new job than she'd expected. She showered, ate breakfast and then got dressed in one of her favourite black suits. Feeling as if she at least looked like she knew what she was doing, she sat down at the small table in her flat and made a few more phone calls.

By the time she was ready for lunch, she felt as if everything was now moving forward quickly. She fixed herself a sandwich and ate it while looking out her window at the airplanes on their way in and out of the airport. She'd become a flight attendant because she loved to travel, and for the first time since she'd handed Finlo her notice, she felt as if she missed her old life.

A few chocolate truffles improved her mood, and once she'd tidied up her kitchen, she sat down and sent off a long email to Alastair and Michael. She briefly mentioned her meeting with Kerron Kewley, only mentioning the points that were relevant and leaving out details, such as the fact that she'd had dinner with the man. Then she explained her plans for moving things forward, with or without the farmer's cooperation. She pushed "send" and then sat back and sighed, wondering what the men would think of her plans.

Only a short time later, her computer beeped with an incoming message.

It appears that Alastair was right to have confidence in your abilities. I look forward to hearing how your meeting with Mr. Kewley goes. I've no doubt you'll win the day. In the meantime, I'll provide whatever you need in terms of contracts and paperwork. Regards, Michael.

Darcy smiled. It seemed she'd impressed him, at least so far.

The rest of the week seemed to fly past as Darcy spoke to several different people and made various arrangements. Michael was true to his word, sending her the necessary contracts and forms for her backup plan. By the time the day for the meeting arrived, Darcy was torn between feeling confident it was all going to work and terrified that it was all going to go badly wrong.

The following Monday afternoon she paced anxiously around her flat for several minutes; going over what she intended to say repeatedly until she felt as if her head might explode. Standing in front of her bedroom mirror, she pulled her hair into a twist and then added an extra layer of lipstick.

"He's going to say something you aren't expecting and all your planning will have been for nothing," she told herself. "If he's even there," a little voice added. Darcy stuck her tongue out at the little voice and then squared her shoulders.

"Here goes nothing," she muttered.

✼ 6 ✼

Before she left, Darcy changed out of her preferred stilettos and into a pair of black flats that would more easily cope with the muddy parking area at the Kewley farm. Even though she'd only been there once before, the drive felt almost familiar as she made her way north. She put a favourite album of pop music on in her car and turned the volume up as loud as she could, choosing to sing along loudly to prevent herself from endlessly rethinking her plan.

She'd just climbed out of her car when she heard her name being called.

"Darcy? Hurry up, can you? I don't have all day."

She turned around and smiled brightly at Kerron Kewley, who was walking towards her. He looked gorgeous in the afternoon sunshine. Wearing tight jeans and a T-shirt that might have been white once, but wasn't anymore, he nearly took Darcy's breath away. The shirt clung to his broad shoulders and emphasised his flat stomach.

She took a deep breath. "It isn't quite three yet," she told him.

He gave her a dazzling smile. "Sorry, but my livestock manager just rang and I need to head over and check on a few sheep. I waited for you so you could come along and we could talk on the way."

Darcy felt her smile falter. This wasn't the way she'd envisioned their business meeting happening.

"You can wait here, if you'd rather," Kerron told her now. "But I need to get down there."

"Let's go," she said, feeling instantly like she'd made the wrong choice.

Kerron just grinned and then led her to another parking area behind the house. "Hop in," he suggested.

"It's a tractor," Darcy said flatly.

"Well spotted," he replied. "I suppose we could take your fancy car, if you prefer, but I can't promise it will get where we're going and back again."

Darcy thought about a dozen different replies and discarded them all. Instead, she pulled open the tractor door and carefully climbed up into the machine. Kerron climbed in on the driver's side.

"All set?" he asked.

"It's a bit, um, basic," she said, glancing around the small space. The seat was uncomfortable and there seemed to be levers and knobs just about everywhere. She was almost afraid to move in case she bumped the wrong thing and sent the machine crashing into a wall.

"It's perfect for its job," Kerron said, shrugging. "It doesn't need to be fancy."

"It could do with being clean," Darcy muttered as she shuffled her feet across the muddy footwell.

"Clean isn't a priority for farm machinery," he replied. "Especially with the amount of rain we get."

He started the tractor's engine, which ended any chance of a conversation being held. When he pulled out of the car park and headed down a dirt road, Darcy found that she didn't really feel like chatting anyway. She was too busy holding on for dear life as they bounced their way across the farm.

For Darcy, the journey seemed to take hours, but it was only a few minutes later when Kerron pulled up next to a large barn.

"You're very quiet," he remarked after he'd switched the tractor off.

"Actually, I ran my entire proposal by you on the journey," Darcy said. "Since you didn't object, I'll just assume you're on board."

Kerron looked at her and then grinned. "Cute," he said. He stared at her for a while and then reached across and ran a finger down her cheek, catching a stray hair. He pushed it behind her ear gently, his eyes never leaving hers.

Darcy felt her heart skip a beat and then race from the contact. She was suddenly very aware of how incredibly sexy the man was.

"Boss?"

The man standing next to the tractor looked amused as Darcy jumped. She hadn't heard his approach. He looked to be somewhere in his sixties, with a weathered face that suggested he'd worked outdoors his entire life. His jeans and T-shirt covered a body that still looked muscular in spite of his age.

"Ah, Don, what's the big emergency, then?" Kerron asked. He opened his door and jumped out of the tractor.

Darcy opened her door to follow. Don quickly came around and held out a hand.

"It's a long way down if you aren't used to it," he told Darcy as she climbed down.

"Thank you," she said, grateful to the man for his kindness.

"She works for Breckenridge," Kerron told the other man.

"We all have our faults," he replied easily.

"Darcy Robinson, this is Don Kelly. He's the farm manager and he has a weakness for redheads."

Darcy laughed. "It's a pleasure to meet you, Mr. Kelly," she replied. "I do hope nothing is seriously wrong."

"Oh, you must call me Don," he replied. "As for the trouble, I think I overreacted in ringing the boss. A couple of the sheep were having a bit of a disagreement, but it all seems to have settled now."

A loud crashing noise in the barn behind them made Don frown. "Or maybe not," he said.

The trio walked towards the barn door, with Darcy making sure she was well behind the two men. She needn't have worried, as all of the animals were in enclosures within the structure.

"They're Manx Loaghtan," she said, as a pair wandered into view.

"Aye, they are," Don replied. "We have one of the largest flocks on the island."

Darcy couldn't resist getting a closer look at the nearest sheep. His brown wool and four horns made him look quite different to the fluffy white animals she imagined when someone mentioned sheep.

"We've some little guys down here," Don told her, gesturing further into the barn.

Darcy followed him down through the centre of the barn to a small pen. The young lambs instantly captivated her. "How old are they?" she asked as she watched one suckle.

"A couple of months," Don told her. "Most of the lambs arrived in early April. We'll be weaning them in another couple of months."

One lamb wandered over to the fence and "baa'd" plaintively at Darcy. She found herself stroking its tiny head. "Aren't you lovely?" she cooed. "Your mum must be very proud of you."

"Ah, that one's mum wasn't impressed with him at all," Don said. "She had triplets and didn't have enough milk for all of them. We've been feeding that one, as she won't."

Darcy swallowed hard. She felt terrible for the poor little lamb, but this was meant to be a business meeting. Showing how she felt simply wouldn't do.

"I suppose that's nature," she said, instead.

"It is, aye," Don replied. "But Mr. Kerron makes sure all our livestock thrives, no matter what nature thinks."

Darcy nodded and then gave the small lamb another pat.

"I've checked on Larry and Moe and they seem fine," Kerron said now as he joined Darcy and Don. "I think they're just having fun bashing at the fence posts. Tomorrow I think we'll shift them across to the other barn and do some repair work where they've been particularly persistent."

"Sounds good," Don agreed. "Sorry to drag you all the way down here for nothing, then."

"It's fine. This way Darcy got to see the lambs," Kerron replied.

Darcy smiled tightly. "But we do have a lot to go over, so maybe we should head back."

Kerron nodded. "Back we go, then."

"It was a pleasure to meet you," she told Don, offering a hand.

He looked amused again as he shook it. "Likewise, I'm sure," he replied.

Outside the barn a light rain had begun to fall. Darcy frowned as she scrambled into the tractor. She didn't dare look at her shoes, which were undoubtedly ruined.

Kerron had taken his time walking back, talking with Don along the way. As he climbed into the tractor, Darcy couldn't help but notice how his soaking wet T-shirt now fit him like a second skin. While the men Darcy usually dated were the type to work out regularly in a gym, Kerron's muscles looked to have been earned through hard work rather than pointless repetition.

She took a deep breath and then sighed. Kerron Kewley was about as far from her type as a man could get. There was nothing wrong with admiring his good looks, but there was no way she was going to get romantically involved with a farmer.

Not that he'd shown any signs of being anything other than amused and irritated by her, she thought to herself. He'd even felt the need to warn Don Kelly that she worked for Alastair. Clearly the man didn't like her.

While her mind was racing, Kerron had started the engine and turned the tractor around. Again, Darcy held on as they drove across the uneven dirt road. Back at the house, Kerron parked the tractor and smiled at Darcy.

"I need a few minutes to clean up," he told her. "I'll leave you with Marion, if that's okay."

"I think I could do with a bit of cleaning up myself," Darcy muttered, looking down at her muddy shoes. Her legs were speckled with mud that had splashed up as she'd rushed through the rain to get back to the tractor.

"That can be arranged," Kerron replied.

As he climbed down, Darcy opened her door and looked at the ground. It seemed a long way off and she hesitated without Don's support.

"Come on, then," Kerron said as he walked around the back of the machine. He held out a hand and Darcy took it gratefully. As she jumped down, he stepped slightly closer to her, so that when both of her feet touched the ground, she was pressed tightly against him.

Kerron released her hand, and then both of his arms encircled her. "Steady now," he whispered into her hair.

The light rain was heavier now, but for a moment Darcy didn't care. She was caught up in the electricity that was racing between her and Kerron. There was no doubt in her mind that if she looked up he would kiss her, Darcy felt frozen with indecision. After a moment that might have been one minute or twenty for all Darcy knew, Kerron chuckled.

"Let's get out of the rain," he suggested. He stepped away from her and Darcy suddenly felt the rain and the cold. She followed Kerron to the front door, shivering slightly in her light suit jacket.

"Fancy dragging her around in the rain," Marion scolded Kerron as the pair went into the house. "I can't imagine what you were thinking. Those sheep could have waited until after your meeting."

"I'm going to go and get cleaned up," Kerron said as a reply. "I believe Ms. Robinson would like to do the same."

He was gone before either woman replied. Marion looked at Darcy and shook her head.

"He could have at least offered you a coat," she said. "Come on then, there's a loo down the hall you can use."

In the small bathroom, Darcy did her best to dry off and clean up. Marion provided her with a flannel and several towels, so Darcy washed the mud from her legs and feet as well as she could. Marion had insisted on taking her shoes away.

"I'll see what I can do with them," she told Darcy. "I'm not sure if they can be saved or not, though."

Darcy nodded. "I'll need them back, anyway," she'd replied. "I don't want to drive home barefoot."

Now Darcy took her hair down and patted it dry, then she twisted it back up on top of her head. She took off her sodden jacket. The shirt underneath was nearly dry, so she decided to leave the jacket off for the meeting with Kerron. She assumed she looked less professional, but she preferred that to feeling cold and wet. After retouching her makeup, she padded barefoot towards the kitchen, assuming she'd find Marion there.

"I've done my best with your shoes," Marion told her. "They're just in the airing cupboard to dry out."

"Thanks," Darcy replied. "I wish the rest of me could go in there, too."

Marion laughed. "How about a nice cuppa instead? Warm you up from the inside out."

"Perfect," Darcy agreed.

When the tea was ready, Marion sat down with Darcy. "Have a biscuit," she suggested, pushing the plate that was piled high with them towards Darcy.

"Just one," Darcy agreed. They were fancy chocolate-covered ones, and Darcy didn't have enough will power to refuse after her soaking.

"I thought you were saving those for a special occasion," Kerron's voice came from the doorway. "You wouldn't let me have any of them earlier."

Darcy looked up and then, when her eyes met Kerron's, back down at the table. His hair was wet from the shower and Darcy inhaled the delicious soapy and spicy scent he brought into the room with him as he entered.

"You're not special," Marion said with a laugh. "Oh, go on and have one, then," she conceded. "But not more than two or you'll spoil your dinner."

"Yes, ma'am," Kerron replied. "And may I fix myself a cup of tea, as well?" he asked.

"Oh, you sit down and have your meeting with Darcy. I'll make you a cuppa," Marion told him, getting to her feet.

"I can't see what we have to discuss," Kerron said as he dropped into a chair opposite Darcy. "I think I've made my position perfectly clear."

"You have," Darcy agreed. "But that just means we have a great deal to discuss."

"I'll just eat my biscuits and drink my tea. You go ahead and talk all you like," Kerron told her.

Darcy bit back an angry reply and forced herself to smile. "Excellent," she said brightly. She opened her enormous handbag and pulled out the folder of paperwork inside, grateful that the folder had managed to stay dry.

Putting the map of the farm in the centre of the table between them, she began.

"As we discussed previously, this is the area that will make up Manx Christmas World or whatever we end up calling the event," she pointed to the map. "This section here, what are you currently using it for?" she asked, pointing to a large section that was adjacent to the planned event area.

"Oats," Kerron replied.

"And when do you harvest those oats?"

Kerron shrugged. "Autumn."

Darcy took a sip of tea while she counted to ten. She'd expected a little more cooperation that this, but she wasn't going to let him upset her.

"So the field will be empty when we would want to use it? Probably late November until early January."

"Yep."

Darcy laughed. She couldn't help herself. The man was clearly trying to be annoying, but she knew she had the upper hand, even if he didn't.

"So, I'd like to rent that field from you, and here's what I'm willing to pay," Darcy said, handing him a slip of paper with a number on it.

Kerron glanced at the sheet and raised an eyebrow. "Paul offered me more," he said, letting the paper drop back down onto the table.

"You should have taken it," Darcy told him.

"But I didn't," Kerron replied. "And I won't take your offer, either. This has been fun, though. Thanks for coming by."

It's about to get fun, Darcy thought to herself. "I think you're making a big mistake," she said. "Give me a minute to explain where I got that number from and then see if you don't agree with me."

Kerron chuckled. "Go ahead, then," he said, his tone challenging.

Darcy grinned to herself. The conversation was playing out almost exactly as she'd planned. Don't get overconfident, she reminded herself sternly. Things might still go wrong.

She patted the folder that she'd pulled from her bag. "I won't bore you with every single detail," she said. "But I have signed agreements here from two gentlemen with small landholdings in Douglas. They've both agreed to rent me space to use for car parking during Christmas World."

"You expect everyone to walk here from Douglas?" Kerron asked incredulously.

"Not at all," Darcy replied smoothly. "I expect everyone to take the Father Christmas Express from Douglas."

"The Father Christmas Express?"

"Did you know the island's main tour bus company takes half its buses out of service in the winter months?" Darcy asked him. "And those buses just sit around in the bus garage, taking up space."

Darcy could see that Kerron was beginning to see where she was going.

"My friend, George, at the tour bus company, was happy to provide a very reasonable quote for providing a round-trip continuous service from Douglas to here and back again for the entire duration of Christmas Town," she told him.

"People aren't going to like having to take buses back and forth," Kerron said.

"They won't just be buses," Darcy replied. "They'll be part of the whole Christmas World experience. There will be elves on board on the way here to help the children write their letters to Santa. On the way back, there will be special games and activities, hot chocolate and mince pies. The buses will be decorated and each one of the four I think we'll need will have its own special theme."

"I don't want buses going back and forth all day," Kerron said grumpily.

"The original agreement includes a provision for unlimited access to the site for both staff and visitors. It doesn't limit in any way what sort of vehicles are allowed."

"I see," he replied.

"The offer I made for renting the car parking space from you is more or less the same amount as renting the two spaces in Douglas and hiring the buses. The decision you have to make is whether you would rather have that money yourself or see it go to other people. Christmas Town, World, whatever, is going to happen on your land anyway. Why not make as much money from the event as you possibly can?"

Kerron shrugged. "That's a good point," he said after a moment.

Marion clattered a few pots behind Kerron's head. "Sorry about that," she said when both Kerron and Darcy looked at her. "I just thought I ought to get dinner started."

"You should, indeed," Kerron replied. "I'm starving. What are we having?"

"Spaghetti Bolognese."

"Can you make enough so that Ms. Robinson can join us?" Kerron asked.

"Of course I can," Marion said. "And it'll go faster if you get out of my kitchen while I'm working. Take Ms. Robinson down and show her the foals."

Darcy was going to object, but Marion caught her eye. "All this talk about business is fine," she said, "but you need to give Mr. Kerron time to think. Go look at the horses while he does some thinking."

"I'll need my shoes back," Darcy said, hoping the rain had finally stopped.

Marion laughed. "Oh, aye, I forgot about them."

She disappeared around a corner. Darcy glanced at Kerron, but he quickly stood up and walked to the nearest window.

"The rain seems to have stopped, at least for now," he told her. "The horse barn is close by. We can probably just walk."

"If my shoes have dried out," Darcy said.

Kerron laughed. "That would help."

Marion was back a moment later. "Here you go," she said, handing the shoes to Darcy. "They aren't completely dry, but they'll do."

Darcy swallowed a sigh and slid her feet into the damp shoes. She pulled on her still damp jacket and gave Kerron a forced smile. "Let's go see these horses, then," she said with as much enthusiasm as she could muster.

Outside, the sun was struggling to warm up the late afternoon air. There were puddles everywhere as Darcy followed Kerron along the muddy path to a nearby barn. She was going to have to buy Wellington boots for future trips out to the farm, she decided as she slipped and nearly fell in the mud.

"Careful now," Kerron said, taking her arm. "We can't have you falling and hurting yourself."

Darcy was about to pull away when her foot slipped again. This time she stumbled even closer to Kerron, who smiled and slid an arm around her.

"Steady on. You need Wellies."

Darcy was too worried about falling to pull away. At least that's what she told herself as she felt the delicious warmth radiating from Kerron's body, which was now pressed against hers.

They walked the last few yards to the barn, where Kerron released her to open the barn door. She followed him inside the large space, which felt airy and smelled much better than she'd been expecting.

"Our newest arrival is down here," Kerron told her. He took her arm and led her to the last stall on the left.

Darcy couldn't help but smile at the small foal standing next to its much larger mother.

"He's adorable," she said. "Unless it's a girl. If it's a girl, then she's adorable."

Kerron laughed. "It is a girl," he told her. "We've called her Aalin, which is Manx for beautiful."

"It suits her," Darcy said. The two horses stood and stared back at their visitors for a moment before the larger of the pair returned to eating. Her baby was more curious and took a few cautious steps towards Kerron and Darcy.

"Hello, Aalin," Kerron said quietly. She walked over and nuzzled against the man. He stroked her head and murmured things to her while Darcy watched.

"Come and get a cuddle," Kerron suggested, holding out a hand.

Darcy hesitated.

"She won't hurt you," Kerron told her.

Darcy smiled. She wasn't worried about the horse; she was worried about getting closer to its owner. There was no way she was going to admit that to Kerron, of course. She took a step forward, ignoring Kerron's hand in favour of reaching up to stroke Aalin's nose.

Aalin stared steadily into Darcy's eyes for a moment and then shook her head and sneezed. Darcy jumped while Kerron laughed.

"Bless you," Darcy said as Aalin turned and wandered back towards her mother.

Kerron introduced Darcy to the rest of the horses in the barn, taking a few minutes to give each one a pat and a bit of conversation.

"They all have Manx names," Darcy remarked after she'd met them all.

"Aye, Marion's in charge of naming the animals. At least the ones that aren't going to be eaten."

Darcy frowned. The thought of any of the adorable lambs she'd seen earlier ending up on someone's dinner plate upset her.

"We raise sheep and cattle for food," Kerron told her, his tone matter-of-fact. "We don't name those animals."

"What about Larry and Moe?"

"We keep the Loaghtan for wool. We have a larger herd of other sheep for the supermarkets."

Darcy nodded, looking at the ground. Kerron chuckled.

"If you think that's sad, wait until I tell you how we treat the oats," he said. He took her arm and set off walking slowly across the still muddy ground.

Firmly pushing the animals out of her mind, Darcy focussed on why she was there. "You still haven't said what you want to do about parking," she reminded him.

"Traa-dy-liooar," he replied. "We can talk after dinner."

Darcy thought about arguing, but decided it wasn't worth the effort. Besides, she was starving and didn't want to argue her way out of more of Marion's excellent cooking.

The conversation was general and light while the threesome ate their spaghetti and garlic bread. Darcy found herself laughing at Kerron's stories about life on the farm.

"That was truly wonderful," Darcy said, washing her last bite down with the single glass of wine she'd allowed herself.

"There's tiramisu for pudding," Marion told her. "I will confess that I bought it, though. It takes more fussing than I have time for."

Darcy grinned. "Whoever made it, I'm sure it will be delicious."

"Now you see our guest out while I get on with the washing up," Marion told Kerron when they'd finished the final course.

"I can help," Darcy offered.

"I'm just going to pile everything into the machine," Marion replied. "Besides, it's getting late. You'll be wanting to get home."

Darcy nodded, gathering up her handbag and checking that all of her paperwork was back inside it. For some reason she felt strangely reluctant to leave the cosy kitchen. The long drive back to her lonely flat held no appeal.

Kerron stood up. "Let's go then," he suggested. "Whatever Marion says, she'll want me back to help with the tidying up as soon as possible."

Darcy followed Kerron through the house and out to her car. He walked quickly and she felt as if she were rushing to keep up with him. Luckily the ground had dried out a bit while they'd been eating. Now she managed to negotiate her way around the remaining puddles without slipping in the mud.

"You still haven't said what you want to do about the car park," she reminded the man, who had stopped next to her car.

"Oh, I'll take the money," he said causally. "Congratulations, as much as I hate to admit it, you were right. I might as well get as much of Alastair Breckinridge's cash as I possible can."

Darcy forced herself not to smile too broadly, though in her head she was dancing and waving her arms in the air. "Excellent," she said crisply. "I'll have the necessary paperwork drawn up immediately. I'll be in touch soon and we can make arrangements for getting it signed."

"You do that," Kerron said softly.

Darcy pushed the button to unlock her car and then reached for the door handle. Kerron caught her hand in mid-air.

"I'm sure Alastair won't mind if I have a bit more of his money," he said, stepping closer to Darcy. "How would he feel if I make a play for you?"

"I don't mix business and pleasure," Darcy said stiffly, even as her pulse raced.

"Does that mean you aren't romantically involved with Alastair?" Kerron asked.

"I am not romantically involved with Alastair," Darcy repeated.

Kerron's hand caught her chin and tipped her head up. Their eyes met and Darcy felt a flood of emotions that seemed to culminate in a single thought. Just hurry up and kiss me, her brain shouted.

"That's good to know," Kerron whispered.

He lowered his head and brushed his lips across Darcy's. She caught her breath, afraid that he'd stop there and even more afraid he wouldn't. Kerron lifted his head slightly and their eyes met again.

"So beautiful," Kerron muttered.

Then he kissed her properly and the world melted away.

Someone was coughing. Darcy felt herself being pulled out of the world that was just her and Kerron and their kiss by the sound. The noise grew louder until Kerron finally lifted his head.

"What do you want?" he growled at someone behind Darcy.

"You wanted to go through that paperwork on the cattle tonight." Don Kelly sounded as if he were trying not to laugh.

Darcy flushed and pulled open her car door. Kerron let her go and she slid into the driver's seat and jammed her keys into the ignition.

"Ring me when you have that paperwork ready," Kerron reminded her as he pushed her door shut for her.

"I will," she replied, not looking up to meet his eyes.

She waited until he'd taken a few steps away from the car before starting the engine, then she drove very slowly and steadily away from the farm. When she was sure she was out of sight, she stopped the car and sat back in her seat, covering her face with her hands.

What had she been thinking, kissing the man like that? Okay, he was gorgeous and sexy and he smelled amazing, but she truly didn't want to get involved with anyone she worked with, especially not someone like Kerron Kewley. Farmers were not her type, she reminded herself. Her brain didn't seem to be listening, however. It seemed to want to replay that amazing kiss over and over again as Darcy drove slowly home.

Back in her flat Darcy kicked off her ruined shoes and ran a bath. She wanted to ring Lisa and talk through everything that had happened, but Lisa's home phone went unanswered and Darcy was reluctant to ring her mobile. Lisa was probably spending time with her husband and Darcy didn't want to interrupt.

Instead, after her bath, she fired up her computer and sent a quick email to Alastair and Michael, filling them in on the results of the meeting. Only moments later she had a reply.

You're amazing! Ring Quayle Airways and book yourself a flight to London for Friday. We'll sort out the formal agreement for the rental and I'll buy you dinner to celebrate. You can fly home on Saturday with all the documents. Yours, Alastair.

Darcy sighed. As if the kiss with Kerron hadn't complicated her life enough.

❧ 7 ❧

Tuesday morning Darcy got up and headed out to do some shopping. Her first stop was in downtown Douglas to look for Wellingtons. While the pink and purple ones tempted her, she bought the sensible black pair.

"They're a bit boring," the shop assistant commented as she rang up the sale.

"I need them for work," Darcy explained. "They need to go with my black business suits."

"You're going to wear Wellies with a business suit?" the girl asked.

"Yes, I am," Darcy replied.

She spent the rest of the week working on a few other little jobs that Michael had given her, making sure she had the right contacts at the various media outlets ready for when she started the publicity campaign. Her other job was securing a Douglas location for temporary storage.

By Friday she was ready for a change of scenery, even if a meeting with Alastair wasn't her first choice for that change. In her flat, she packed her overnight bag with care. She had no idea what Alastair had planned for the evening, so she put three different outfits into the bag, from casual through to formal wear. Whatever he suggested, she'd be ready, she thought with grim satisfaction.

At the airport, she was grateful to learn that Finlo was in Munich and not due back until Monday.

"He's doing more flying at the moment than normal," the girl behind the desk explained. "Pete's gone to work for one of the commercial airlines, so the boss is short a pilot."

Darcy knew from experience that it could take a while for Finlo to find a suitable replacement. It was likely that Finlo would be very busy for the foreseeable future. When they had been dating, such things were upsetting for Darcy, but now she was grateful that the man wouldn't be around to complicate her life.

The flight to London was uneventful, and Darcy was met by another of Alastair's staff and whisked into central London almost before she had time to think.

"Mr. Stuart has been waiting for you," Alastair's assistant told Darcy as soon as she emerged from the lift.

Darcy just smiled and followed the woman down the corridor to Michael's office.

"Ah, there you are," Michael said, standing up as Darcy entered. "London traffic is unpredictable. I wasn't sure when to expect you."

"The driver did his best," Darcy replied.

"I'm sure he did. Anyway, congratulations on getting Mr. Kewley to agree to the car park. That was some excellent work."

Darcy flushed. "Thanks."

"Our solicitor is drawing up the relevant paperwork. You'll just need Mr. Kewley's signature."

"Not a problem," Darcy said with far more confidence than she felt. It seemed like Kerron had given in too easily, and Darcy could only hope he wasn't planning to refuse once the paperwork was in front of him.

"Now that you're here and you've started, I have a great deal for us to go over," Michael continued. "Please have a seat."

For the next hour the pair discussed every aspect of the planned event, going over a number of things that Darcy hadn't had time to consider yet. When they took a tea break, Darcy couldn't help but bring up the issue that had been nagging her for the past half hour.

"It seems like we should have gone over a lot of this when I first took the job," she said tentatively.

Michael chuckled. "I wasn't sure how committed you were to the project," he told her. "A lot of what we've discussed today is confidential. I didn't want to share every last detail of Manx Christmas World with you and then have you quit after the first day."

Or you didn't think I was competent, so you didn't want to bother, Darcy thought. She simply sipped her tea and chatted about the weather, rather than challenge the man. Whatever he'd thought of her initially, he clearly had more confidence in her abilities now.

After their break, they spent more time going over even more of the details. By five o'clock Darcy was feeling exhausted and a little overwhelmed.

"It's a lot to take in," she said when Michael finally told her they'd finished for the day.

"There's a lot to do," he replied. "I was handling as much of the advance planning as possible after Paul left, but I really don't have the time. It's also almost impossible for me to manage things from here. You're much better placed to make the necessary arrangements."

Darcy nodded. "You've done a great job so far," she told the man. "I'm looking forward to taking things from here."

A buzzing noise interrupted their conversation. Michael picked up his phone.

"Yes, Alastair?"

Darcy collected the piles of paperwork that were spread across the desk while Michael said little more than "yes" and "no" on his end of the phone call. By the time he hung up, Darcy was putting her share of the paperwork back into her handbag.

"The boss is ready to see you now," Michael said after he put the phone down.

"Or I could just grab a flight home tonight," Darcy suggested.

Michael shook his head. "Alastair has plans for you tonight," he told her.

"That's what worries me," Darcy muttered under her breath.

She was surprised when Michael laughed. "Women are usually thrilled when Alastair shows any interest in them," he told her. "I usually have to, well, let's say, discourage them."

Darcy shrugged. "He's wealthy and gorgeous. What's not to like? But I'm really trying to keep my personal life and my professional life separate. This job really matters to me and I don't want to mess it up."

Michael nodded. "I think you're doing a great job so far," he told her. "But when Alastair sees something he wants, he goes after it. And he very rarely fails to get it."

"I'll take that as a warning," Darcy said dryly.

"I meant it as one," Michael replied.

He escorted her to Alastair's office, knocking once and then opening the door for her. "In you go. He isn't interested in seeing me."

"Thank you so much for everything," Darcy told him. "I'm really enjoying working with you."

"It's my pleasure."

Darcy turned and walked into Alastair's office, a bright smile firmly fixed on her face.

"Sorry I wasn't free earlier," Alastair said from his desk. "I hope Michael kept you suitably entertained."

"We went through a lot of the details for Manx Christmas World," she replied. "Although I want to change the name."

"Talk to Michael," Alastair replied, waving a hand. "He's dealing with all of that for me."

"I will do," Darcy assured him.

"Anyway, I was hoping to take you out for a very romantic dinner tonight, but I've just been reminded that I have to go some charity auction thing instead."

Darcy felt a genuine smile bubble up. "That's okay," she said quickly. "I'll ring the airline. Maybe they can get me back to the island tonight."

"Oh, goodness no," Alastair said with a laugh. "I want you to come to the auction with me. It's a dinner as well, so you'll get fed."

Darcy couldn't think of an excuse fast enough. She opened her mouth, but nothing came out.

"Seriously, I need a beautiful woman on my arm tonight," Alastair told her. "We can tell everyone that we're just work colleagues, if you like, and I'll be on my best behaviour."

Darcy sighed. "I'm sure it will be fun," she lied.

"I promise it will be fun," Alastair replied, looking delighted at her capitulation. "I'll even buy you a little something from the auction. I'm sure there will be jewellery or maybe a new car?"

Darcy shook her head firmly. "I don't want anything," she said a little more loudly than she intended. "I'll only go if you promise not to buy me anything."

"Really? I don't understand women," Alastair said, shaking his head. "No woman has ever said anything like that to me before."

"I'm not most women," Darcy told him.

"No, you aren't," he replied, looking at her with a thoughtful look on his face.

"What time does this thing start?" Darcy asked, wondering how soon she had to be ready.

"Seven. I'll have someone run you to your hotel so you can get changed. As I rather doubt you've brought an evening gown with you, feel free to shop at the hotel boutique and have whatever you want billed to your room. It's the least I can do."

"It's fine, actually," Darcy told him. "I have just the right outfit in my bag."

Alastair raised an eyebrow, but didn't question her. Instead he picked up his phone. "Ah, Jennifer, I need a car for Ms. Robinson, please."

Alastair walked Darcy to the lifts. "Your car will be waiting for you outside," he told her. "I'll pick you up just a few minutes before seven. The party venue is quite near your hotel."

In the car, Darcy flipped through her papers, forcing herself to concentrate on work rather than think about the evening ahead. Once in her luxurious hotel room though, her thoughts focussed on Alastair. He'd been friendly but distant when they'd met in his office. Maybe he was actually going to respect the boundaries she'd set.

Darcy took a quick shower and then climbed into the stunning emerald green evening gown she'd brought. It was perfectly cut to showcase her curves and the colour worked beautifully with her hair.

She slid on strappy silver stilettoes and then worked on her hair and makeup. Years of experience meant she was ready with time to spare.

Sitting in a comfortable chair, staring out at the London skyline, she found herself wondering what Kerron Kewley was doing. She could picture him in the farmhouse's cosy kitchen eating something wonderful that Marion had prepared.

And you're going to a glamorous charity fundraiser with a gorgeous millionaire, she reminded herself. Six months ago she lived for invitations to events like this and dates with wealthy men. Tonight, she couldn't help but feel as if dinner at the Kewley farm would be more enjoyable.

Alastair was only a few minutes late and she was quick to grab her handbag and get out of the hotel room. The sooner the evening finished the better, as far as she was concerned.

Their car pulled up at the nearby hotel only a few minutes later. A red carpet was in place and as Darcy stepped from the car flashbulbs began to light up the night.

"Alastair? Who is she?" someone called from the small group of photographers and reporters who were clustered along the edge of the red carpet.

"A business associate," he answered with a smile.

"Yeah, right," was the reply.

Darcy forced herself to smile. She strolled down the red carpet, holding Alastair's arm, as if she hadn't a care in the world. Her head was starting to ache and she knew it was going to be a long night.

"You don't look happy," Alastair remarked as they crossed the hotel lobby.

"I have a bit of a headache," Darcy admitted.

"What do you take for them? I'll get something brought over for you."

Darcy thought about arguing, but there was no point in suffering. Alastair stopped the first hotel staff member he saw and requested the tablets Darcy needed.

"Let's just wait here for them," he suggested, gesturing towards a small seating area in a corner of the lobby. "Otherwise we'll get lost in the crowd."

Darcy agreed and sank down into one of the couches gratefully. "Thank you for this," she said as Alastair sat next to her.

"It's no problem," he assured her. "I just wish we could use your headache as an excuse to skip the whole thing. But I'm expected to bid generously and often and it is a really good cause. If you don't feel better soon, though, there's no reason you have to stay."

"I'm sure I'll be fine," Darcy replied, feeling somewhat better already as her nervousness about the evening began to fade. Alastair was being far kinder and more attentive than she expected and she felt herself relaxing in his company.

"I'm sure this isn't your idea of a fun evening out," Alastair said now. "But I do feel that it's important to support charities, and fortunately I have sufficient funds to give generously."

A man bearing a bottle of headache tablets and a glass of water interrupted Darcy's reply. She gratefully swallowed two tablets and put the rest of the bottle in her handbag.

"Thank you," she told the man, who bowed before he disappeared into the crowd.

"Do you want to wait out here until the tablets can start working?" Alastair asked.

Darcy had been watching the steady stream of people making their way into the ballroom. "I think we'd better not," she said reluctantly. "We don't want things getting underway without us."

Alastair stood up and offered her his arm. Darcy took it and they crossed the lobby to the ballroom entrance. The space was incredible, with huge crystal chandeliers and large sections of mirrored walls. There were a number of fountains spaced around the room, dispensing wine, champagne and exotic drinks.

Within seconds several different people were rushing to speak to Alastair, and Darcy felt herself being swept up into the crowd. Alastair introduced her to everyone and Darcy could see that no one believed that they were anything other than a couple. The proprietary arm that Alastair kept around her waist throughout the next half hour did little to dispel that notion.

"Let's see what's up for auction, shall we?" he asked after a while.

They crossed the room to the large exhibit table and Darcy caught her breath as she looked at the glittering display. There was an amazing assortment of beautiful jewellery, the keys to three different luxury automobiles, a solid silver tea set, several "celebrity" lots with auto-graphed memorabilia and a large board listing a dozen luxury holidays to exotic destinations.

"Wow, this is incredible," Darcy said.

"I know Suzanne, who organised it. She did an amazing job in getting donations," Alastair told her.

"Alastair, there you are," a loud voice shouted.

"Speak of the devil," Alastair muttered. He turned around, gently pulling Darcy along with him. "Suzanne, you've done your usual incred-ible job," he said.

"I do try," the woman simpered, leaning in to give Alastair an extended embrace.

When she finally released him, Alastair pulled Darcy closer to him. "Darcy, this is Suzanne Martin. She's a very dear friend of my parents' and an expert organiser."

"It's a pleasure to meet you," Darcy said, offering her hand to the other woman, who although dressed far more sexily than Darcy, must have been somewhere in her fifties.

Suzanne took it, frowning. "Where did you find this one?" she asked Alastair, after barely touching Darcy's fingers.

"She's working on a project for me," Alastair replied.

"What sort of project?" Suzanne demanded.

"A top secret project," Alastair replied with a laugh. "We aren't ready to announce anything yet. You know how things work in busi-ness. I announce my big plans and then some other guy comes along and does the same thing."

"If you needed something planning, you should have called me," Suzanne said, batting her heavily mascaraed false eyelashes at Alastair. "I could have helped you out."

"I'll keep that in mind for next time," Alastair said. "But where's Jason tonight?"

Suzanne shrugged. "He'll turn up eventually," she said in a bored voice. "In the meantime, I'm going to have fun."

"So are we," Alastair said, pulling Darcy even closer. "I'm just having Darcy pick out a little present. Something I can give her as a bonus for all of her hard work."

Darcy laughed throatily. "I told you I don't need a bonus," she cooed. "I love my job."

Suzanne rolled her eyes and then glanced around. "Winston," she shouted over the crowd, "there you are."

As she rushed away, Darcy sighed. "She's rather horrible," she whispered to Alastair, who laughed.

"She is, indeed," he replied. "She's miserably married to a very stupid but very rich man. They can barely stand one another, but neither is willing to pay for a divorce."

"She didn't seem to like me," Darcy said wryly.

"She probably figured out that I brought you as protection," Alastair whispered. "She isn't happy if she has to sleep alone and she likes variety in her bedroom."

"But she's old enough to be your mother," Darcy suggested.

"Not quite, and anyway, she prefers younger men. She'll probably take at least one of the waiters home at the end of the night."

Darcy shuddered. "The poor, unhappy woman," she said softly.

"She is brilliant at arranging things," Alastair told her. "She would have been better off having to work for a living instead of marrying for money at a very young age."

The next hour passed in something of a blur for Darcy, as Alastair introduced her to many more people while they made their way around the huge room. The tables for dinner were set up in one corner of the space and Darcy was relieved when it was finally time to eat. She was starving and she hoped some food would help with the headache that was still irritating her.

The food was excellent and the other couple at their small table were friendly and interesting. Darcy found that, by the time the last of the pudding plates had been cleared, she felt much better.

"Show time," Alastair whispered as he shifted his chair closer to hers. The lights around the room were dimmed and a spotlight illuminated a small stage where a podium was centred. Suzanne Martin took her place behind the podium.

"Okay, now everyone is full and a little drunk, let's get started," she said. After some brief remarks, she turned the evening over to the auctioneer, who was quick to remind everyone of the good cause the auction was supporting. Then the bidding began and Darcy just sat back to watch.

Several of the larger tables clearly had groups of work colleagues at them and they seemed to be egging each other on to bid higher and higher as the evening progressed. Alastair bid on a few things here and there, but didn't win any of them.

One of the last items was a month-long holiday in Lanzarote at a five-star luxury resort.

"Spend the entire month of January in the sunshine of Lanzarote," the auctioneer announced.

Alastair grinned at Darcy. "How about it? Want to spend the month of January with me in the Spanish sunshine?"

Darcy grabbed her wine glass and took a big swallow while she tried to think of an appropriate answer. Before she managed one, the bidding began and Alastair's attention shifted to the auctioneer. A few minutes later, he'd bid an outrageous amount for the trip.

As the crowd cheered, he gave Darcy a hug. "We'll have a wonderful time," he whispered in her ear. "You'll be done working for me by then. It will be perfect."

Unsure of how to answer, Darcy simply took another sip of her drink. The rest of the evening passed uneventfully and Darcy was relieved as the night began to wind down to a close.

"I think we can safely sneak away now," Alastair said after the room had begun to empty. "I just need to go and pay for our holiday first."

Darcy nodded and then sank down into a quiet corner to wait for his return. She was half asleep when he returned several minutes later.

"Sorry, I got held up with things," he told her. "Are you okay?"

"Just tired," Darcy admitted.

"Let's get you back to your hotel, then."

Alastair was quiet on the short journey back to Darcy's hotel. He insisted on walking her to her room.

"I won't try to convince you to invite me in for a nightcap," he told her, stroking her cheek. "You look completely done in."

"I'm sorry. I have this new job that's really stressful," she replied, laughing when he looked concerned. "I'm kidding," she said quickly. "But I am really tired."

"And you're flying home early tomorrow, aren't you? I won't get to see you again this trip."

"My flight is at nine, so I'll have to be at the airport by eight or so," she said.

"When will you be back?"

Darcy shrugged. "When I need to be, I guess," she said. "I have a lot to get done on the island, though."

"And I'm swamped here, so I won't be able to come over to see you any time soon," Alastair said, sounding frustrated.

"I'll keep you up-to-date via email," Darcy replied.

"Email is somewhat less satisfying," he said, sliding his arms around her. "Actually, it's not satisfying at all."

He lowered his lips to hers and Darcy let herself enjoy the friendly kiss. When he shifted to pull her even closer, she resisted.

"I'm really tired," she reminded him as he lifted his head.

"And you don't mix business and pleasure," he teased.

"I would rather not," Darcy answered, aware that it wasn't as strong an answer as it should have been.

"So, take good care of yourself and work hard on Manx Christmas World. Just remember that January is our holiday. I'm already looking forward to that."

He turned and walked away before Darcy spoke. "I haven't agreed to go," she said softly to no one.

Back in her room, she got ready for bed and took a second dose of the headache medicine. Her sleep was restless, and her dreams were full of Christmas elves in bikinis and lambs wearing tiny Wellington boots and chasing each other in the mud. She was relieved when her alarm finally went off and she could start her new day.

❄ 8 ❄

Darcy decided on the flight home to give herself the weekend off. She waited until Monday morning to ring the Kewley farm.

"Mr. Kerron's out in the field," Marion told her. "I'll tell him you called."

Darcy had to be satisfied with that. She set up her laptop and began working through the list of tasks that she and Michael had identified. Arranging tents and marquees wasn't all that difficult. Very few people were looking to rent such things for November and December. She made a preliminary booking for what she thought she would need from the island's largest rental company and moved on.

Next, she rang a few people she knew, trying to find the right people to build the central "Santa's Castle" building. She wanted something more substantial than the tents that would house the smaller exhibits. If she could find the right builder for the job, she might even have him build a few smaller structures and do away with some of the tents. Tents would be cold and damp in the chilly and wet winter weather. The better built the structures were, the warmer and more comfortable they would be for everyone.

Michael had given her a very strict budget, so she knew exactly what she could afford and what she couldn't. She just had to find a way to get what she wanted within that budget.

"Ah, Darcy, I'm sure I could do something for you," a builder she knew said. "Winter's our quiet time. Send me the basic specs for what you want and I'll give you a quote."

And that was pretty much what everyone she spoke to told her. Most of them were happy to look at her specifications and provide a quote for what she needed constructing. Darcy had never really thought about the seasonal nature of things like construction, but clearly it was going to work to her advantage.

By the time she stopped for dinner, she'd accomplished a large portion of what she thought she was going to need the entire week to get through. She sent off a quick note to Michael and Alastair to update them and then shut her computer down. Tomorrow she'd get all the building specs sent out to the people she'd spoken with today and then start thinking about advertising and ticket sales.

Too tired to think about cooking anything elaborate, she fixed herself a simple omelette with the various scraps in her refrigerator. She'd just slid the perfectly cooked omelette onto her plate when the phone rang.

"Hello?"

"Am I ringing at a bad time?" The voice was warm and sexy, and Darcy nearly dropped her plate.

"Ker, er, Mr. Kewley?"

A soft chuckle prefaced the reply. "I think you can call me Kerron," he said. "Although I can call you Ms. Robinson if you prefer."

"No, Darcy's fine," she replied, feeling far more flustered than she felt she should.

"So, am I ringing at a bad time?" he repeated himself.

"I was just sitting down to an omelette," Darcy said.

"Marion made shepherd's pie tonight," he told her. "With apple crumble and custard for pudding."

"Okay, you win," Darcy said with a laugh. "I don't even have a pudding."

"I suppose, after your fancy dinner last Friday, you're happy with something plain tonight."

"What do you mean?" Darcy asked.

"I saw some great photos of you and Alastair Breckenridge heading into some posh party the other night," he explained.

"Where?" Darcy demanded.

"They're all over the internet," Kerron told her. "The man is one of London's most eligible bachelors. He's photographed everywhere he goes."

"And you just stumbled across them while you were looking for replacement parts for your tractor?" Darcy asked tartly.

Kerron laughed. "Marion finds the man intriguing," he told her. "She met him when he came to meet with my father several months ago, when the whole Christmas Town thing was first mentioned. She's been keeping an eye on him ever since."

"I see," Darcy said slowly. While she was thinking about his words, she put a bite of her dinner into her mouth.

"Anyway, she was surprised to see you with him and she showed me a few of the pictures."

"I went over to get the paperwork for the car park arranged," Darcy told him, annoyed with herself for feeling defensive.

"You look great in green," Kerron replied. "That was a terrific dress."

"Thanks," Darcy replied around another bite. The omelette was delicious and she wasn't going to let it get cold while she talked.

"So, was the food good?" Kerron asked.

Darcy frowned at the phone. "It was fine," she said. "Why do you care?"

"I suppose I don't, really," he replied with a chuckle. "I was just making conversation. I'm trying to figure you out. You told me you aren't involved with Alastair and then, less than a week later, I see photos of you hanging on his arm on your way to some glamorous society event."

"I spent the day meeting with one of his business managers, discussing Manx Christmas World. After we were done, Alastair asked me to accompany him to the charity auction, as he didn't want to go on his own. We may have looked like a couple, but we aren't." Darcy took a sip of wine, wondering why she felt like she had to explain things to the man. They weren't a couple, either.

"You rang earlier. Should I guess it was to discuss that paperwork, then?"

"It was," Darcy confirmed. "I'll have the contract for the car park ready for your signature in about a fortnight's time. When would it be convenient for you to sign it?"

"Can it wait until the eleventh of September? I know that's more like four weeks, but we have a lot going on at the moment. If you come up around five, you can join me for dinner and I'll sign the papers for you."

"I'll have them sent to your advocate as soon as I get them," Darcy told him. "He or she can look them over before we meet."

"That's not necessary. I trust you," Kerron said quietly.

The words echoed in Darcy's head after the call was finished. After all the questions about her evening with Alastair, she wasn't sure she believed that he trusted her at all. But the words, as they replayed in her mind, gave her a warm feeling even as they worried her. Michael had told her the contract was fair, but what if it wasn't? She intended to read it through several times once it arrived, but perhaps she didn't know enough to be certain.

With the contract still on her mind, she headed to bed several hours later. After tossing and turning for a while, she switched on the telly and found an old movie to watch. She finally drifted off to sleep and found herself dreaming in black and white.

The next morning she rang her advocate. "Doncan, I need you to look over a contract for me. I should have it by the twenty-fourth, so any time after that and before the eleventh of September, please," she told the man.

"I can fit you in on the Tuesday the eighth," he told her after a moment.

"I guess that will work," Darcy replied. "What time?"

"How about midday? You bring us lunch from somewhere and I'll look over the contract while we eat."

His suggestion told Darcy that he was making room in his calendar for her, even though he didn't really have time to see her. She was quick to agree.

The weeks that followed seemed to fly past as Darcy visited builders to look at plans and spent time tracking down a small herd of reindeer that could be happily moved to the Kewley farm for the month of December.

When the contracts arrived from Alastair's solicitors, Darcy read them through and then put them aside, grateful that she was going to be able to have Doncan go through them. On the appointed day, Darcy arrived at his office in Douglas with enough Chinese food to feed ten people. Breesha, Doncan's long-suffering assistant, laughed as Darcy carried in the huge box full of small take-away containers.

"Who are you expecting at this lunch?" she asked as Darcy set the box down.

"Just Doncan," Darcy said. "But he's doing me a huge favour, so I wanted to be sure he has enough to eat."

"He hasn't eaten that much in one meal since he was a teenager," Breesha told her. "But I'm sure he'll appreciate the effort."

A few minutes later Breesha escorted her into Doncan's office.

"So good to see you," he told Darcy. "I didn't tell you that you had to feed the whole of Douglas, did I?"

Darcy laughed. "This way I'm sure I have something you'll like," she replied.

While they ate, they chatted easily about nothing much. Once they'd cleared away their plates and put the many boxes of leftovers into the office refrigerator, they got down to business.

Darcy handed him the contract. "I'm working for Alastair Brecken-ridge," she explained. "His solicitor drew this up and I want to make sure that it's fair for both parties."

Doncan raised an eyebrow. "It doesn't sound as if you trust your boss," he said mildly.

"I guess I don't trust his solicitors," Darcy countered.

Doncan laughed and then quickly read through the contract. Then he read it through very slowly. After that he read it one more time. Darcy tried to hide her impatience as she looked around the room, studied her nails and then counted the books on the shelves that covered one wall.

"Really, Mr. Kewley should have his own advocate go over this," Doncan began after he put the document down. "His advocate should be protecting his interests."

"I did suggest that," Darcy told him.

"And what did he say?"

"That he trusts me."

Doncan laughed. "Which is why you're here. Because you are trustworthy and you're looking after his interests even if he isn't."

"So, what's wrong with the contract?" Darcy asked.

"Actually, as far as I can tell, nothing," Doncan replied. "It's very straightforward and there wasn't anything in it that raised any red flags for me."

"Really?" Darcy asked, surprised.

Doncan laughed. "Most advocates and solicitors are pretty honest people," he told her. "We don't deliberately try to trick or cheat anyone. I'm sure Mr. Breckenridge's solicitor expected Mr. Kewley's advocate to go over this with a fine-tooth comb. I can't find anything to question."

Darcy blew out a long breath. "That's wonderful," she said with real relief. "Thank you so much."

"Happy to help," Doncan told her.

Back at her flat, Darcy wondered if she could add Doncan's bill to her expense account with Alastair, but decided against it. She would rather pay Doncan herself than explain to Alastair why she felt the need to consult him.

She spent the afternoon making more phone calls. She had the details for three different companies in England that could supply the handful of fairground-type rides they wanted for the site. Now she rang two local companies that she thought might do something similar. She was happy to find that one of them could probably supply her with exactly what she wanted at a much more reasonable price than what the English companies had quoted. Removing the cost of transporting things across the Irish Sea was significant.

At four o'clock she shut her computer down. She was ahead of where she needed to be and she wasn't meeting with Kerron until Friday. That gave her a few days to relax and think about some of the other changes she might want to make in her life. The first thing she did was ring Lisa.

"Can you take a day off work tomorrow or Thursday and go shopping with me?" she asked her best friend.

"I wish I could," Lisa replied. "I'd love to see you, but I'm swamped at work at the moment. What are you shopping for?"

"Either things to make my flat feel more like home, or a new house, I'm not sure which," Darcy replied.

"It will probably be at least a month before I can take any time off during the week," Lisa said, disappointment evident in her voice. "But let's get together for dinner soon. I'll ring you."

Darcy decided that she'd just have to tackle the shopping on her own. She spent Wednesday chasing the few quotes she was still missing and looking at houses on the Internet. There was nothing for sale that made her feel like selling her flat, though. The few properties in Douglas that were within her budget were either on modern housing estates or in need of expensive renovations. Little houses like Lisa's were apparently few and far between.

By Thursday morning Darcy had given up, at least temporarily, on the idea of moving, and was getting excited about redecorating her current home. She drove into Douglas with a long list of things she was looking for, everything from pillows and bedding to new dishes and even some artwork for her walls.

When she drove home many hours later, she was exhausted and her car was packed full with just about everything on her list. She'd shopped almost nonstop, aside from a quick lunch break at midday. Now she fixed herself a meal in front of the telly, before answering a few emails and then having an early night. She spent most of Friday figuring out how best to display her new purchases. By mid-afternoon her bed was remade with new sheets and a new duvet cover, several pieces of artwork covered her sitting room wall, and her kitchen cupboards were full of new dishes, cups and glasses.

Standing in the middle of her sitting room, Darcy turned slowly, looking around the space. It was beginning to feel more like a home.

Now she started to think about the evening ahead. After the sizzling kiss that had ended her last visit with Kerron, she was both excited and terrified at the thought of seeing him again.

"It's just business," she told her reflection as she touched up her makeup and sprayed on a bit more perfume. She checked that she had all of the relevant paperwork in her bag and then headed out to her car. Again she turned up the volume on a CD, rather than let herself do any serious thinking. She was pretty sure where her thoughts would go and she didn't really want to feel any more worried about the evening ahead.

She reached the farm a few minutes before five. Grabbing her bag, she slid out of the car and headed for the farmhouse door. As she was wearing her new Wellies, she splashed happily through the various puddles that dotted the car park. The skies were grey and it looked as if they were going to get a storm.

After she knocked, she turned and watched the clouds rolling in. Summers were usually quite mild, but it was now the middle of September and as the wind picked up the air began to feel quite cool to Darcy. She knocked again, wishing Marion would hurry up. A few moments later large raindrops began to fall. Darcy thought about knocking again and then changed her mind and ran back to her car instead.

By the time she'd opened her door and climbed back inside, she was pretty well soaked. Torrential rain was pouring down and Darcy could only watch as the puddles around her car grew. With a deep sigh, she pulled out her mobile phone and rang the number she had for the Kewley farm. She let it ring a dozen or more times, but no one answered.

"Great, now what?" she asked herself. It was raining too hard to even think about trying to drive home, so she settled back in her seat and spent a few minutes catching up on social media. Then she sent a long email to Lisa, telling her, in all uppercase letters, just how frustrated she was about sitting in her car in the rain at the farm.

The rain finally began to taper off after half an hour or so and Darcy decided to head for home. She was just about to pull away when a large tractor came down the road, heading for the car park. A moment later she saw Kerron waving at her from the driver's seat.

He pulled up next to her car and motioned for her put her window down. She did so reluctantly, as the rain was still coming down.

"Sorry, I got held up. Give me a minute to park this and I'll come get you with an umbrella," he shouted. He was driving away before Darcy could argue.

For a moment she considered simply leaving, but she did need his signature on the papers in her bag.

When Kerron came back, he was holding a huge umbrella that looked as if it was going to blow inside out any second. Darcy opened her door and climbed out of her car as quickly as she could. With only one umbrella between them, she had little choice but to move close to Kerron.

He laughed as a huge gust of wind almost yanked the umbrella from his hands. "This isn't helping much," he said. He slid an arm around her and pulled her close. "Let's get inside," he said in her ear.

In spite of the cold rain and wind, Darcy suddenly felt warm all over. They headed for the farmhouse door, squelching through the thick mud of the car park. At the door, Kerron quickly inserted a key and then stepped back.

"In you go," he said.

Darcy dashed inside, leaving Kerron to fight the umbrella closed and follow. They were both dripping wet and Darcy wasn't sure if she wanted to laugh or cry.

"Come on, I'll show you where you can dry off," Kerron told her. "I think I'd better find something else for you to put on or you're sure to catch cold."

Darcy was too cold and wet to disagree. Leaving their muddy boots by the door, he led her up the stairs and into a small bedroom.

"The en-suite is there," he told her, pointing. "I'll be back in a minute with something for you to wear."

Dripping her way over to the bathroom, Darcy slowly removed the light jacket she'd worn. She hung it on a hook near the door and then looked in the mirror. When she'd left home, her hair had been in a tidy twist, now it hung around her face in sodden clumps. Her mascara wasn't nearly as waterproof as advertised, she discovered as well.

"I'm sorry, but this is all I could find," Kerron said from behind her.

He was holding out a pair of jogging bottoms and a T-shirt. Darcy took them gratefully. Anything was better than being cold and wet.

"I'm going to grab a shower, so take your time. Dinner can wait," he told her.

"Thanks," she replied. As soon as he'd gone, she shut and locked the bathroom door and peeled off her clothes. A hot shower helped warm her up, and then she climbed back into underwear that she'd blasted with the hair dryer she'd found in a drawer. She needed to tighten the drawstring waist on the joggers as tightly as it would go in order to keep them up, and the T-shirt went past her knees, but at least they were dry.

After blasting her hair as well, she pulled it back into a ponytail and then washed her streaky makeup off. She only habitually carried lipstick with her, so now she applied a coat of that and then shrugged. There was no way she could possibly have looked any less professional, she thought, but that wasn't going to interfere with her getting her job done.

She hung her wet clothes along the shower curtain rail and then slipped on the shoes she'd put in her bag. The Wellies were just to get her to the front door; she'd brought some black pumps to go with the black suit she'd been wearing. Glancing down, she felt a little ridiculous. Black leather pumps didn't really go with navy jogging bottoms and a grey T-shirt, but bare feet were hardly businesslike.

Leaving the shoes on, she headed for the door. Back downstairs, she walked towards the back of the house, expecting Marion to intercept her as she went. When she reached the kitchen, wonderful smells hit her nose. Darcy could see a casserole dish bubbling away in the cooker, but there was still no sign of Marion. Outside, the rain seemed to have settled into a slow and steady rhythm. Craving a cup of tea, Darcy filled the kettle and switched it on. If Kerron or Marion didn't like her making herself at home, they should have been there, she told herself.

The kettle hadn't boiled yet when she heard footsteps on the stairs. A moment later Kerron joined her.

"Ah, thanks for putting the kettle on," he said as a greeting.

"No problem," Darcy replied. "But where is Marion?"

"Oh, she usually takes Friday nights off," he answered as he began taking plates from the cupboard. "She left us a beef stew and there's ice cream in the freezer."

"But I thought she lived here," Darcy said.

"She does, but she often stays with her sister in Douglas on a Friday night. They like to play cards until the wee small hours and she doesn't like to drive in the dark."

"You didn't mention that when you invited me," Darcy said, feeling flustered.

"I also didn't mention that I'm an axe murderer," he said, winking at her. "I figured it would be more fun to spring that on you as well."

"Very funny," Darcy said grumpily. "I just assumed Marion would be here, that's all. She was here on a Friday the first time I came out."

"Her sister was away for a fortnight in July, so Marion didn't bother taking those Fridays off," Kerron explained. "Did you need her to sign the papers, too?" he asked.

Darcy flushed. This is a business meeting, she reminded herself. As long as Kerron was here, it didn't matter who else was around. "Sorry, I think the weather has rather thrown me for a loop," she muttered.

"I have to say, I never thought to wear fancy shoes with my jogging bottoms," he told her. "It's an interesting look."

"My feet were cold," Darcy said defensively.

"I should have given you socks," Kerron replied. "Sorry, I didn't think. Here, you serve up the stew and I'll go and find you some."

Darcy took the serving spoon from him and tried to ignore the spark she felt when their hands touched. She scooped out generous helpings of the meaty stew in its thick gravy, only just resisting the urge to try a bite. Kerron was back as she finished.

"I thought you'd prefer black," he told her in a teasing tone. "Just like your shoes."

Darcy sat down and slipped the shoes off. The socks were warm and thick and they felt much better on her feet than the pumps had.

When she stood back up, though, she felt shorter and somehow disadvantaged.

Kerron grinned at her. "You look warmer and more comfortable," he said softly. "Do you need a sweatshirt or are you warm enough?"

"I'm fine," Darcy replied. "It's quite toasty in the kitchen."

Kerron carried the plates to the table and then opened the refrigerator. "There's a big bowl of salad if you want some," he told her. "And some fresh bread."

He pulled the loaf of bread from its container and sliced it, putting the slices onto another plate. Grabbing a block of butter from the refrigerator, he added them to the table and then held out a chair for Darcy.

"Sit. I'll make some tea and then join you," he told her. "And go ahead and start eating while it's hot."

Darcy thought about objecting, but hunger won out over social convention. She took a bite of the hearty stew and sighed. It was as delicious as it smelled.

"Marion is a wonderful cook," she said after her third bite.

"She is. I know I'm lucky to have her," Kerron agreed. He put a mug of tea next to her on the table and then sat down.

For several minutes neither of them spoke as they enjoyed their meal.

"Did you want some salad?" Kerron asked suddenly.

"I probably should," Darcy replied. "But I really don't. This is lovely and hot and salad doesn't sound the least bit tempting."

She buttered some bread. "The bread is really good, too," she said after her first bite.

"Marion makes it herself," Kerron told her. "She's spoiled me completely. I hate when I have to eat supermarket bread."

"I'd weigh three hundred pounds if I had access to this bread all the time," Darcy said with a sigh.

"I'd weigh a lot more if I wasn't out working in the fields every day," Kerron admitted. "I'm lucky my job is so physical."

"Maybe I need a new job," Darcy said lightly.

"I'd agree with that," Kerron muttered. "Or at least a new boss."

Darcy flushed. "Alastair is okay," she told him. "And Manx

Christmas World is going to be a fun day out for families all over the island."

"A fun and very costly day out, I reckon," he replied.

"It isn't going to be cheap," Darcy conceded. "But I'm doing my best to pack as much into the space as possible. Then I just have to convince Alastair to include it all in the admission price."

"Good luck with that," Kerron said. "Although you're probably much better at persuading him than I was."

Darcy laughed. "It's actually one of his business managers that I'm working with mostly," she told him. "And he's very reasonable, really."

They'd both cleared their plates, and Darcy felt ready for a long nap.

"How about some ice cream?" Kerron suggested. "We have vanilla, chocolate, butterscotch or mint chocolate chip."

The temptation was too much. "Just a very small scoop of butterscotch," she said. "I haven't had ice cream in ages."

"I love ice cream," Kerron said in a sheepish voice. "I'd have it every day if Marion would let me."

Darcy laughed. "As it's your house, I can't see how she stops you."

Kerron shrugged. "She's been working here since I was a baby and pretty much brought me up after my mum left. I still feel like I need her permission to eat treats."

It would have felt rude to ask questions about his mother, but Darcy was very curious about her. She took a bite of ice cream and tried to think of a casual way to pry.

He dropped into the seat next to her, his own bowl piled high with scoops of ice cream.

"Before you ask, my mum decided that life on a farm in the middle of nowhere wasn't the life for her. She left when I was tiny." Kerron's voice was flat and devoid of emotion as he spoke.

"I'm surprised she didn't take you with her," Darcy said before she'd taken the time to think.

"Yeah, well, life as a mum wasn't really for her, either. Having a small child underfoot didn't fit in with her new lifestyle. She wanted to live in a big city and to go out dancing and partying every night. I was just another reminder of the life she hated on the island."

Darcy wasn't sure what to say. She put a hand on his arm. "I'm sorry," she said softly.

He looked at her for a long moment and then sighed. "Dad did a great job on his own," he told her. "And, of course, I had Marion."

"You seem to have turned out quite well," Darcy said, earning herself a small smile.

"What about you? Did you have a happy childhood?" he asked.

Darcy nodded. "My parents are still together, happily retired and driving each other crazy. They wouldn't have it any other way."

"So you have papers for me to sign?" Kerron asked.

Darcy blushed. She was enjoying herself far too much. This was meant to be a business meeting, and she should have been making sure they got down to business.

"Of course," she said. She pushed her empty bowl towards the centre of the table and picked up her bag. The paperwork was near the top.

"This is the contract for the field in question," she began. "If you'll just read it over...."

She stopped because Kerron was shaking his head. "I'm sure it's all in formal legal language that I won't understand," he told her. "As I said on the phone, I trust you."

"But you don't trust Alastair," she reminded him.

"No, but you won't let him cheat me," he said.

Darcy wished she had as much confidence in her abilities as he seemed to have. "I'm going to try hard to make sure he doesn't cheat anyone," she replied.

Kerron nodded and flipped through the pages of the contract. "Where do I sign?" he asked.

Darcy showed him, and he scrawled his name on the line.

"Did we have anything else to go over?" he asked her as she put the papers back in her bag.

"We need to discuss site access," Darcy said. "I know it's only September, but I'd like to start having things delivered to the site soon. I know we can't actually start using it until November, but I'd like to have a space to start storing things, if possible."

"I'll think about it," Kerron replied. "This is a working farm. We tend to try to use every square inch of the farm for something productive. I can't promise I'll be able to find room for storage, at least not yet."

"See what you can do," Darcy said. "I'll be getting the quotes in for Santa's Castle in the next few days. I believe that's going to be built in large pieces for assembly on-site. Once the pieces are together, we'll need to put them somewhere until they're needed. I have some temporary storage arranged in Douglas, but the sooner we can get things up here, the better."

"Why not wait and have the castle built closer to opening day?"

"I'll sleep a lot better knowing it's done," Darcy told him. "The last thing I want to do is open on December first with a half-finished castle for our most important staff member."

"I think the rain has stopped," Kerron told her as he loaded the dishwasher. "Let me walk you out."

Darcy stood up, suddenly feeling reluctant to leave. The house was warm and cosy, and even without the rain, the night was dark and windy.

"I should change," she said.

"Your clothes won't be dry yet," Kerron pointed out. "You may as well stay in those things for now. You can get them back to me the next time you have to come out."

Darcy ran up to the small guest room and gathered up her clothes. Kerron was right, everything was still wet. She threw them all into the plastic bag he'd given her and then went back down the stairs. Kerron was waiting for her at the front door.

"Keep the socks as well," he suggested. "They should fit inside your Wellies without any trouble."

Darcy slipped on her boots and then checked that she had everything.

"I'll walk you out," Kerron told her.

Outside the rain had stopped, but a strong wind was blowing. Darcy gasped as an empty plastic bag flew past her head. Kerron grabbed it out of the air and crumpled it in his hands.

"Drive carefully," he told her as he held her door while she climbed into her car.

"I'll take it slow," Darcy replied.

Kerron looked at her for a long time. Darcy thought he was going to kiss her, but instead he reached out and stroked her cheek. "See you soon," he said softly before gently pushing her door shut.

Darcy watched him cross back to the house before she started her engine. She made her way down the long driveway, driving slowly and carefully. She was nearly to the main road when she heard a loud cracking noise. Instinctively, she hit the brakes. A moment later one of the large pines that edged the drive crashed to the ground in front of her, missing the bonnet of her car by mere inches.

9

Later, Darcy was surprised that she hadn't screamed as the tree fell, but at the time she was too preoccupied with surviving. As the wind howled around her, Darcy turned her car around and headed back for the farmhouse. Her heart was pounding so loudly that she couldn't hear the music she was playing. When she reached the car park, she parked haphazardly and ran to the front door, desperate to get out of the weather. She pounded on the door, tears streaming down her face.

When Kerron finally opened the front door, after what felt like hours, Darcy threw herself into his arms.

"Darcy, what's wrong?" he demanded as he held her tightly.

"Big tree," she stammered, her teeth chattering as adrenaline coursed through her body. "On the road."

Kerron tightened his grip and pushed the door shut. He stroked her back and murmured meaningless words into her ear. For several minutes Darcy struggled against the panic that was overwhelming her. As her heart rate finally began to slow and she began to regain control, she suddenly realised how inappropriately she was behaving.

She drew a long and very shaky breath and then tried to pull away.

Kerron relaxed his hold slightly, but not much. Darcy took another deep breath.

"I was going along your drive towards the road and one of the big pine trees on the side suddenly crashed down into the road in front of me," she said, pleased to find that her voice only shook slightly as she spoke.

"Did it do any damage to your car?" Kerron asked, looking concerned.

"I didn't inspect every inch of it, but I think it just missed the front bumper," Darcy replied.

"And you're okay?"

"I think so," Darcy replied. "I'm sorry about the hysterics, but it was such a huge shock." She took a step backwards, and this time he let her go.

"I'll ring Don. He can run down and have a look," he told her. Darcy still felt shaky as she watched Kerron. He picked up the phone that was on a nearby table and frowned when he put the receiver to his ear.

"Looks like the wind took out the phone lines," he said. "At least we still have power."

The words were barely out of his mouth when the lights flickered a few times and then went out.

"Famous last words," Darcy muttered.

"Just stand still for a minute," he instructed. "If the power doesn't come right back on, I'll find a torch."

A moment later the lights flickered again and then came back on. Kerron had his mobile phone out.

"Don, Darcy was just leaving and a tree came down across the drive. Can you check it out?"

"I'm not sure he should be out in this weather," Darcy said when Kerron had disconnected.

"Someone needs to take a quick look right away," Kerron argued. "We need to know what we're dealing with so we can start figuring out what needs to be done."

The lights flickered again and Darcy jumped.

"You're still overwrought," Kerron said. "Come in the kitchen."

Darcy followed him back into the kitchen, trying not to overreact to every sound. She felt as if her emotions were on a knife edge.

"Tea or scotch?" Kerron asked Darcy.

"Tea," she replied firmly. She was having enough trouble with her emotions without adding alcohol to the equation; besides, she needed to be able to drive later.

"Sit down. I'll have it ready in a minute."

Darcy sank down at the table. She felt shaky and slightly sick. A sudden blast of noise made her jump and shriek. Kerron raised his eyebrows at her as he pulled his mobile from his pocket. She blushed scarlet, embarrassed by her reaction.

The conversation took a while, and by the time Kerron had disconnected, the kettle had boiled. He served her tea and biscuits, taking the seat next to hers after delivering everything to the table.

"Don reckons we're going to need a crew with chainsaws to get rid of the tree," he told her. "He's going to try to get one put together for first thing in the morning."

"So how do I get home?" Darcy asked. "Is there another way out to the road?"

"Yes and no," Kerron replied. "There's another road, but it's more of a path than a road. It's fine for the tractors and farm machinery, but I don't think your car would make it."

The wind howled and the lights flickered again. Darcy's tea spilled as she flinched.

"Besides," Kerron said, watching her closely, "I don't think you should be driving tonight. You can stay in the guest room."

Darcy shook her head. "That's very kind of you, but I want to go home," she said insistently.

"Unfortunately, I don't think that's a possibility," Kerron replied. "I certainly don't intend to start trying to get a chainsaw through that tree tonight. I suppose I can lend you the equipment if you want to give it a go, though."

Darcy took a deep breath. "I'm sorry. I'm not myself. I appreciate the offer, and of course I'll stay in the guest room tonight. Thank you."

"In that case, how about that scotch?" he asked, running a finger along her arm.

"Oh, I'm not sure that's a good idea," Darcy stammered, suddenly very aware of the electricity that was humming between them and the fact that they were alone in the house. "Where does Don live?"

"He has his own little house near the sheep barns. Why?"

Darcy shook her head. "I was just curious," she answered.

The wind roared again, and Darcy flinched and then shook her head at her reaction.

"How about popcorn and a movie?" Kerron asked. "I have a collection of old US Westerns that is the envy of absolutely no one."

"It beats listening to the wind," Darcy said fervently.

"I can't argue with that," Kerron replied.

Darcy tidied up the tea things while Kerron threw a bag of popcorn in the microwave. As the kitchen filled with the warm, buttery smell, Darcy felt herself beginning to relax. Kerron poured the popcorn into a large bowl and handed it to Darcy.

"You carry this and I'll bring the wine," he told Darcy.

"Wine?" Darcy echoed.

Kerron winked at her and pulled a bottle of wine from the refrigerator. He grabbed two glasses from the cabinet near the door and then led the way down the corridor to a cosy room at the end of the hall. There were two large couches angled in front of a huge television. Kerron set the glasses on the table between the couches and then opened the bottle of wine.

"Why don't you go through the movies and find something you'd like to watch?" he suggested. He pulled open a cupboard door to reveal more DVDs than Darcy had ever seen outside of a video store.

"Where do I start?" she asked.

"They're arranged by category and then alphabetically," he told her. "All of the action and adventure films are on the top two shelves, then the comedies and lastly, the westerns. There are probably a few dramas or whatever on the very bottom shelf as well."

Darcy set the bowl of popcorn on the table and then ran her finger along the top row of movies, scanning the titles.

"I've never seen this one," she said, pulling out a heist movie full of Hollywood stars. "It's supposed to be very good."

"It was okay," Kerron told her.

"Have you seen everything on the shelves?" Darcy demanded. "Because if you would like to choose something you haven't seen, that's okay with me."

Kerron shrugged. "I've probably seen just about all of them," he told her. "The farm needs a lot of looking after, so even when my dad was here I tended to stay home at night and watch telly, rather than go out."

"So is there something here you'd like to watch?"

"That one's fine," he told her. "I don't mind seeing it again. It will cover up the sound of the wind just as well as anything else."

Darcy wasn't really happy with that, but she didn't argue. Instead she handed him the DVD and sank down into one of the overstuffed couches. She tucked her feet up underneath herself and picked up the glass of wine Kerron had poured for her.

Kerron loaded the DVD into the player and then turned, armed with the remote. He handed Darcy the bowl of popcorn, picked up his own wine glass, and then dropped onto the couch next to her.

Darcy was instantly aware of his leg resting against hers. She tried to shift away from him, but every movement seemed to send her sliding closer to Kerron rather than further from him. She sighed and then shoved the bowl of popcorn onto the couch between them. Kerron chuckled and pushed play on the remote.

When the credits ran ninety minutes later, Darcy was feeling warm and secure. She'd drunk half a bottle of wine, eaten half a bowl of popcorn and grown used to the low hum of energy that was flowing between her and Kerron.

"It's getting late," she murmured as he switched over to a television channel that was showing repeats of an old panel comedy show.

"And the wine is empty," Kerron said, making a face. "I could get another bottle."

Darcy shook her head. "I think I've had enough," she said, frowning at the lack of conviction she heard in her voice.

"No more popcorn?" Kerron asked.

"I'm good," Darcy said softly. "I think I could just sleep here, though."

"That's a tempting thought," Kerron said, stretching his arms above his head and then settling one across Darcy's shoulders. "Maybe we should both just stay here?"

Darcy let herself enjoy the warmth that flooded through her for a long moment and then sighed deeply. "I should go to my room, then," she said, standing up slowly.

Kerron stood as well and then put his hands on her shoulders. "My room is more comfortable," he told her in a low voice.

Looking up at him, Darcy opened her mouth to reply, but Kerron lowered his mouth to hers before she could speak. The room, the storm, the world vanished as Darcy felt herself getting lost in their kiss. Several minutes later, Kerron lifted his head and smiled at her.

"My room?" he suggested.

Darcy closed her eyes tightly so that she wouldn't get lost in his. "I don't think so," she said after a moment. "But thank you for the offer."

Kerron laughed lightly. "The offer stands. If you change your mind in the middle of the night, or any time, just let me know."

Nodding, Darcy forced herself to take a small step backwards. Kerron did nothing to stop her. As she turned to leave the room, she felt sad and lonely.

"Before you rush off, I want you to have a look at something," Kerron said behind her.

Darcy turned back, slightly apprehensive as to what he might be talking about.

"Come with me," he said, holding out a hand.

Darcy took it cautiously, and then followed him out of the room and then out a door at the back of the house. The wind had died down, having blown the thick clouds away. Darcy breathed in the fresh night air as they took a few steps away from the house.

"Look up," Kerron suggested.

Darcy tipped her head back and gasped. The sky was alight with what looked like millions of stars. Feeling as if she could see entire galaxies from where she was standing, Darcy just stared.

"I don't think you can see all of this from Douglas," Kerron said. "There's too much light pollution."

"You can't see this much by the airport, either," Darcy told him, thinking of the car park for her flat, with its well-illuminated spaces.

She never really bothered to look up at the sky when she was there, unless she happened to notice a full moon. If her view there was as spectacular as this, though, she'd take the time to look at it more often.

"It does make me feel rather insignificant," Kerron told her.

Darcy nodded. She'd never really thought about the vastness of space before, but here it was, spread out in front of her and seemingly endless.

The pair stood together, just watching the sky for several minutes, before the cool breeze began to make Darcy shiver.

"I should let you get to bed," Kerron said, turning back towards the house.

"Thank you for showing me this," Darcy told him. "It's gorgeous."

"My pleasure," he replied.

Inside, she headed for the stairs, not wanting to risk spending time with the increasingly appealing Kerron Kewley.

In the small guest room, she brushed her teeth with the small travel brush she kept in her handbag and ran a comb through her hair. She pulled off the jogging bottoms that Kerron had lent her and slid into bed in only the oversized T-shirt.

It took her a long time to fall asleep, and her sleep was restless as her brain insisted on replaying her near-miss accident and her passionate kiss with Kerron, one after another, all night long.

She felt groggy and out of sorts when she finally gave up on sleep and climbed out of bed. A shower did little to wake her or lift her spirits, and having to get dressed in the same clothes she'd slept in did little to help. She made her way down the stairs, perking up slightly when she smelled coffee.

"I was just leaving you a note," Kerron told her as she entered the kitchen. "I need to get to work, but I thought you might sleep in a bit longer."

"I didn't sleep very well," Darcy admitted, pouring herself a cup of coffee.

"You should have come and joined me," Kerron said, giving her a suggestive smile.

"Maybe next time," Darcy replied, flirting almost automatically. She blushed when she realised what she'd said.

Kerron smiled. "I might just hold you to that," he told her.

Darcy sipped her coffee and thought about the best possible reply. "Any idea when the road will be clear?" she asked, clumsily changing the subject.

"Don's got a crew down there now working on it. If you take your time over a bit of breakfast, you can probably head down after that."

"Great," Darcy replied unenthusiastically. She had a lot of work waiting for her at home, but Kerron's house was cosy and comfortable, and going back to her flat to deal with paperwork and vendors didn't appeal to her at all.

Kerron raised an eyebrow. "You're welcome to stay," he said. "But I'd have to put you to work."

Darcy laughed. "I have plenty of work waiting back at my flat," she replied. "I have at least a dozen vendors to sort out, publicity to organise and I need to start scheduling site access for the guys who are building the structures."

"I hope no one is in a hurry to get access. I haven't harvested that field yet," Kerron replied.

"But it will be ready in another month, right?" Darcy checked. "I need to come out and go over the whole thing before the vendors and construction guys come in. They're scheduled to start working on the site at the end of October."

"Ring me and let me know when you want to visit," Kerron suggested. "The fields should all be ready for you some time in the middle of October."

Darcy nodded, wondering what possible excuse she could find for seeing Kerron again sooner.

A ringing telephone interrupted her thoughts.

"Hello?" Kerron spoke into the kitchen receiver. After a few minutes, where Darcy heard nothing more than a few muttered words, he hung up.

"Don needs me, I'm afraid," he told Darcy. "We have fencing down, crop damage and a shed that has a tree through its roof. I have to go."

Darcy swallowed the last of her tea and jumped up. "I'd better get going as well," she said. "You'll want to lock up the house."

Kerron shrugged. "Marion is on her way. You're welcome to wait for her. Besides, we don't lock the front door that often."

"I'd still better go," Darcy insisted. She was feeling far too comfortable and at home in Kerron's house.

He walked her out to her car and checked it over. "There doesn't seem to be a scratch on it," he told her. "But if you do find any damage, let me know."

"I'm sure it's fine," Darcy said, having glanced at the bonnet herself.

"I'm glad you're okay, anyway," he said, giving her a quick hug.

Darcy resisted the urge to tip her head back and kiss the man. Instead, she patted him awkwardly on the back and then pulled away.

"You have fences to mend," she reminded him with a laugh.

"I do, indeed," he replied.

Darcy slid behind the wheel and started her engine. She drove slowly and carefully away from the farmhouse, unable to remember exactly where she'd been when the tree fell. She was nearly back to the main road before she came across the crew of men who were still busily cutting the large tree into pieces. They had cleared enough of the driveway for Darcy to get through, and she waved to Don Kelly as she did so. He waved back, but didn't stop working.

10

Back at her flat, Darcy took a long, hot shower and then took an even longer nap. She woke up when her phone rang.

"Hello?" she said, struggling to sound wide awake.

"Having a lie-in?" Lisa asked.

"Having a nap," Darcy answered. "I was stuck out at the Kewley farm overnight and I didn't get a lot of sleep."

"Stuck?" Lisa repeated. "Is that a euphemism for something?"

Darcy laughed. "Not at all. The strong winds brought a tree down right in front of me. It blocked the driveway and I couldn't get out."

"Are you okay? And the car?" Lisa asked.

"I'm fine and so is the car," Darcy assured her. "But I ended up staying in Kerron's guest room for the night."

"And how was that?"

"It was lonely," Darcy told her. "And strange and awkward and a whole bunch of other things that I haven't quite figured out yet."

"We need to get together," Lisa replied. "I feel like I haven't seen you in years. Let's have dinner tonight."

"What about your wonderful husband?"

"He can survive for a night without me," Lisa said firmly. "We've been together rather a lot since the wedding. It will be good for him to miss me for a few hours."

Darcy felt as if she ought to refuse, to allow Lisa time with her new husband, but she missed her friend too much to do it. "If you're sure," she said.

"I'm sure. Let's go somewhere fancy and have too much wine and just get starters and puddings," Lisa suggested.

Darcy laughed. While they'd talked on the phone once in a while, she really missed her friend. With a time and place settled, Darcy spent her afternoon tidying her flat. Before she took another shower, she sent a quick email to Alastair and Michael, letting them know that Kerron had signed the car park contract. With that out of the way, she got ready for her evening out.

Her taxi arrived right on time and she was in Douglas with a few minutes to spare. She took a seat at the bar while she waited for Lisa. The bartender gave her a wave and a smile as he finished filling an order at the other end of the bar. Before he reached her, Darcy felt an arm go around her waist.

"You look incredible," a silky smooth voice whispered in her ear.

"Leave me alone, Finlo," Darcy said without turning her head.

He chuckled softly. "You don't mean that," he told her. "You miss me."

"Actually," Darcy replied. "I really don't." She was surprised to find that she was being honest. Her new job was keeping her so busy that she hadn't even given Finlo a thought in some time.

Finlo just laughed. "Ouch, my poor ego," he complained. "I thought we had something special."

"Maybe," Darcy said with a shrug. "But it was over a long time ago."

"I miss you," he told her.

Now Darcy turned her head and met his eyes. He looked completely sincere.

"I'm sorry," she told him softly.

He frowned and straightened away from her. "You know where I am if you change your mind," he said.

Darcy bit her tongue on the flippant reply that sprang to mind.

Lisa's arrival saved her from finding a kinder response.

"There you are, Darcy," Lisa called from the bar's doorway.

Darcy spun around in her seat and then jumped up and crossed to her friend. They hugged tightly and Darcy felt tears forming in her eyes. It was so good to see Lisa again. Finlo was completely forgotten.

They moved to their table and ordered a bottle of wine and some starters before Darcy asked Lisa all about her honeymoon and how married life was treating her. They were well into the second bottle of wine before Lisa finished telling Darcy all about the last several months of her life.

"We need to do this at least once a month," Lisa said after the waiter had taken their pudding order. "It's crazy that we haven't seen each other since June."

"I don't want to annoy your hubby," Darcy protested.

"One night a month isn't a big deal," Lisa said. "In fact, we should try one night a week. He won't mind, really."

Darcy wasn't so sure. "It might have to wait until after Christmas," she said. "I'm only going to get busier as we get closer to opening day."

"I think I saw more of you when you were travelling all the time," Lisa replied. "Anyway, now it's your turn. Tell me all about the new job, the gorgeous Alastair and the sexy Kerron. I want to hear all about your fabulous life."

"I don't even know where to begin," Darcy said with a sigh.

"Start with Alastair," Lisa suggested. "I've heard he's one of London's most eligible bachelors. I've also heard that h's gorgeous and filthy rich."

"He is gorgeous," Darcy admitted. "He has long hair, which I don't normally like, but it suits him. His eyes are bright green and he has a way of looking at you that makes you feel like the only person in the world that matters to him. "

"So are you two dating?" Lisa asked.

Darcy shook her head. "I'm trying to keep things strictly business between us," she told Lisa. "While I'm attracted to him on a physical level, I don't quite trust him."

"That's a problem," Lisa said. "I assume he's interested in being more than friends."

"Yes. He's made that very clear," Darcy said with another sigh.

"When we talked the other day you said he took you to some big deal event in London the last time you were there. Was that fun?"

"I had a bad headache," Darcy told her. "So it wasn't as much fun as it might have been. And then Alastair insisted on bidding on a holiday to Lanzarote. He said he wants me to go with him, but I'm hoping he'll forget about that before January."

"You won't be working for him anymore by January, will you?"

"I don't know for sure. He said, when he first offered me the job, that there might be a way for me to continue working with him after Manx Christmas World is over, but I'm not sure I want to. I think I might be glad to end my association with Alastair Breckenridge."

"Manx Christmas World is a terrible name," Lisa said, frowning.

"I know. I'm hoping to come up with something better, but I haven't had time to think about it."

"Let me text hubby. I'm sure he can come up with something less clunky and awful," Lisa suggested.

"And it gives you an excuse to text your husband," Darcy added with a laugh.

"I don't need an excuse," Lisa told her. "I text him all the time."

The waiter delivered the four puddings that they'd ordered while Lisa was on her phone. Darcy grabbed a spoon and dug into the crème brulee that was closest to her. Lisa was quick to try the jam roly poly. For several minutes the friends concentrated on eating. As Lisa was scrapping up the last of the chocolate lava cake, she restarted the conversation.

"So, what about Kerron Kewley?" she demanded. "What's he like?"

Darcy took a sip of wine as she thought about her answer. "He's different," she said eventually. "He's gorgeous too, in a different way. His hair is short and dark and his eyes are blue."

"Which is your favourite combination for men," Lisa pointed out.

"It is, rather," Darcy replied, thinking about Finlo, Andy, and a few of the other men she'd dated over the years.

"But what's he like?"

"Nothing like the sort of men I usually date," Darcy said. "He's really muscular, for one thing, with broad shoulders. The guys I date tend to be the sort that work out at the gym three times a week. Kerron's muscles have been earned through hard work, and there's a real difference."

"Sounds sexy," Lisa commented.

"It is," Darcy admitted. "He seems like a truly nice person as well, even while he's arguing with me about everything I want to do on the site. His father signed all the paperwork and then moved to the Algarve and left Kerron to deal with Alastair and now me."

"But from everything you've told me so far, you're doing a great job getting his agreement for things."

"It's working out, at least for now."

"And is that relationship strictly business, too?" Lisa asked.

"I'm trying to keep it that way," Darcy said. "But I'm finding it harder with him than I do with Alastair. There's something very attractive about him, and I don't just mean physically."

"So what happens next?"

"I have a lot of organising to do," Darcy said. "I have builders working on the various buildings that will go in place, hopefully starting late next month. I have tents and marquees hired, and those should start going up on the site in the first week of November. I need to hire a bunch of people, from Santa and his elves to ticket sellers and ride operators." She shook her head. "It almost feels overwhelming when I think about it."

"And when will you see Kerron again?"

Darcy shrugged. "I don't have any plans to see him again at the moment. Not until we start working on the site in October, anyway."

"What about Alastair?"

"Again, I'm not planning on seeing him again. I don't have any reason to see him and I'm not about to start trying to find one."

The pair debated ordering a third bottle of wine, but they both knew that wasn't a good idea. They were just walking out of the restaurant when Lisa received a text.

"What about calling it 'Nollick Balley,' which is Manx for Christmas Town," she said after she'd read the message. "That's my favourite from hubby's ideas, anyway."

"Nollick Balley," Darcy repeated. "I like it."

"Glad I could help," Lisa said.

"I'll have to clear it with Alastair and Kerron," Darcy muttered, mostly to herself.

She repeated the words to herself on the taxi ride home. By the time she was back in her flat, she was convinced it was the perfect name. Selling it to the other concerned parties was a job for morning.

The rest of September flew past for Darcy. She was the only one who seemed to care what they called the event, so she moved forward with the new Manx name, satisfied that it was much better than the original. She'd found a large empty car park just outside of Douglas that was willing to let her store things for the event as they arrived from across, and she drove past it nearly every day, smiling to herself as the space got increasingly full. By the first of October, she was ready to start advertising the event and looking for staff.

At Michael's insistence, Darcy made arrangements to fly across to London to go over the plans for promotion, ticket sales and hiring procedures. As there was a lot to cover, she arranged to stay for two nights, ringing Kerron before she left.

"I was sure you'd forgotten all about me," he told her when she reached him. "You haven't rung since the night you stayed here."

"Sorry," Darcy muttered, feeling flustered immediately by his mentioning her overnight stay. "I've been busy getting things arranged. We're just about to announce the event and start selling tickets. I'm going to London to meet with Michael in Alastair's office, to go over everything."

"So it's too late for me to cancel now, is it?" Kerron asked.

"I do hope you're kidding," Darcy replied after a moment.

Kerron laughed. "Of course I'm kidding," he told her. "But you still haven't actually seen the site. I thought you wanted to do that as soon as possible."

"You were going to let me know when it was cleared and ready for me to visit," Darcy reminded him.

"Well, it should be cleared by the end of the day tomorrow," Kerron replied.

"I'm in London tomorrow and Friday," Darcy told him. "How about early next week?"

"Let's make it the ninth," Kerron suggested. "I should have most of the other harvesting done by then and have time to take you around the site myself."

"That's fine," Darcy agreed, mentally adding the appointment to her already busy schedule. "I'll be there around two, if that works for you."

"That's fine. We'll drive over and have a look at the site and then have some dinner."

Darcy frowned as she pencilled it into her diary. The ninth was another Friday, which meant Marion would probably be away again. "Terrific," she said in spite of her misgivings.

Her flight into London was uneventful. The pilot was a new one, flying under Jack's watchful eye, and Darcy was alone in the cabin. She was met at the airport by one of Alistair's staff and driven efficiently to his office. Michael was waiting for her when she arrived.

"Everything seems to be coming together nicely," he said once she'd brought him completely up-to-date.

"I'm going out to the site on Friday next week to go over everything with Mr. Kewley. Once I've done that, I'll feel like we're getting somewhere," Darcy replied.

They spent the day going over the promotional plans and then Michael gave her a crash course in hiring and supervising staff, something she'd never done before.

"As we're only looking for temporary staff, it shouldn't be too bad," he assured her. "The most important thing to get right is Santa. If the elves are a bit surly or the sales assistants are lazy, you can cope. But you really need to get Santa right."

"I actually have someone in mind," Darcy told him. "My next-door neighbour when I was a child is retired now and he often plays Santa for church groups or schools. I've been waiting to get in touch with him until after the official announcement, but I think he'd probably really enjoy doing it."

"Excellent," Michael said.

They finished around five, arranging to meet again in the morning.

"We can go over more about staffing issues. We haven't even touched on scheduling or how to get rid of staff that isn't working out."

"I'll look forward to it," Darcy said with a chuckle.

A car took her back to her hotel, where she ordered dinner from room service and then watched telly until she was tired enough to sleep. Michael had told her that Alastair was in Scotland at the moment, but he was due back sometime the next day. Darcy wasn't looking forward to seeing him.

Friday was spent with Michael again, and aside from a short lunch break, they talked their way through more staffing issues than Darcy had ever realised even existed. She took pages and pages of notes, feeling only slightly overwhelmed by the whole thing.

"That's all for today, I think," Michael said eventually. "I'm only a phone call or an email away if you have any issues once you get home, of course."

"For which I'm hugely grateful," Darcy said. "I'm really excited to get things moving along. It seems as if I've been working on it forever without anyone knowing what's happening."

"Excellent," Michael said with a smile. "I'm more than happy to leave everything in your capable hands."

"I bet you never thought you'd be saying that when I hired her," a voice said from the doorway.

Darcy felt her smile falter as she turned to face Alastair. "That sounds like an insult," she said, trying to keep her tone light.

"We were desperate," Alastair said, waving his hand. "I was just happy to find someone to take the job. When I hired you, I did think that Michael was going to have to do a lot more of the work than he has, though. You've been really excellent."

Darcy nodded, determined not to get upset with the man. "I'm glad you're pleased," she muttered.

"Did you bring something formal for tonight?" the man asked her.

"I brought something formal, just in case I needed it," Darcy replied. "What's happening tonight?"

"The official launch of Manx Christmas World," Alastair said in a dramatic voice. "Don't tell me that Michael didn't mention it?"

"He didn't," Darcy said, frowning. "And I thought we were going to call it Nollick Balley."

"Whatever," Alastair shrugged. "The press launch is at seven and you need to be at your most gorgeous."

He didn't wait for her reply, just turned and left the room. Darcy stared after him, open-mouthed. When the door shut behind him, she turned to Michael.

"Did you know about this?" she demanded.

Michael sighed and shook his head. "Alastair said something yesterday about arranging a press launch, but I suggested we wait until you were here to discuss the issue. Obviously, he didn't listen."

"Why would we have a press launch in London for an event being held on the Isle of Man?" Darcy asked.

"Because that's Alastair," Michael said dryly. "I'm sure it will be an excellent party."

Darcy shook her head. "I don't want to go," she said crossly.

Michael laughed. "I'm afraid you have to," he told her. "I'm just wondering if I'm even invited."

"Of course you are," Darcy said. "You've done most of the work."

Michael smiled. "Happily for me, that isn't true. You've done more than your job description dictates. However, I have been involved since the very beginning and I'd really like to be there tonight for the launch."

"Let's go together," Darcy suggested.

"I wish we could," Michael replied. "But I've no doubt Alastair intends for you to walk in on his arm."

"And what Alastair wants..." Darcy said grumpily.

Michael shrugged. "He's the boss," he said.

Back at the hotel, Darcy took a shower and then shimmied her way into the long silver gown she'd brought. She did her hair and makeup and then fastened on a pair of matching silver stilettos. For a brief moment she let herself think about Kerron, at home in his cosy kitchen where she'd wandered around in warm fuzzy socks. As she waited for Alastair her feet began to ache, her lipstick felt sticky and all of the grips in her hair seemed to be sticking straight into her skull. She walked over to the mirror and frowned at herself.

"You love this sort of thing," she reminded her reflection. "You get to dress up and look your best and hang off the arm of a very rich man."

Her face in the mirror didn't look convinced, so she turned away and paced slowly around the room. Maybe she was getting old, she thought. What she really wanted to do was wash her face, put her hair in a ponytail and then curl up in front of the telly in her pyjamas. A knock on the door had her hurrying across, a forced smile on her lips.

"That is a terrific dress," Alastair said, taking her hands and kissing her cheek.

Darcy waited for the rush of chemistry between them, but didn't feel it. She frowned and then quickly turned it to an artificially bright smile.

"Why aren't we having the press launch on the island?" she asked as Alastair escorted her towards the lifts.

"London's more fun," he answered.

Darcy opened her mouth to object, but changed her mind. Alastair didn't really appreciate the island; it was just a place to make some money to him. There was no real point in arguing about it.

In the limousine, Alastair pulled out his mobile and sent a bunch of text messages. Darcy watched the busy street life of London, happy to be ignored.

"Sorry about that," he said as the car came to a stop in front of a luxury hotel near the city centre. "I have lots going on right now."

Darcy didn't bother to reply. The driver opened the door and helped her from the car. There was no red carpet tonight and no press snapping photos, either.

"Here we go," Alastair said, offering her his arm.

Darcy took it and tossed her head, plastering a smile on her face. They walked into the hotel lobby and crossed to the ballroom. Inside, the room was already crowded and Darcy didn't recognise anyone as she scanned the room.

Alastair took two glasses of champagne from a passing waiter and handed one to Darcy. "Here we go," he muttered before pulling her into the crowd. An hour later, Darcy's cheeks hurt from smiling constantly and she was starving. She'd managed to grab a couple of tiny starters from the various passing waiters, but they'd done little more than remind her of how hungry she was. Lunch felt as if it had been a very long time ago.

"Show time," Alastair told her, leading her to the front of the room. The large table there was covered with a sheet that was hiding what Darcy could only assume was a model of Nollick Balley. Alastair cleared his throat and conversations around the room slowly stopped.

"Ladies and gentlemen, family, friends and members of the press, I present to you 'Manx Christmas World,' or, as my lovely companion insists on calling it, 'Nollick Balley.'"

He pulled the sheet away and revealed a larger version of the model he'd shown her when he'd first offered her the job. Darcy was relieved, as she looked over it quickly, to see that it more or less matched the one she'd been working from. She wouldn't have been surprised or happy to find that Alastair had added a dozen new things before showing the world.

There was polite applause and then a few people began to ask questions. Alastair held up a hand. "There's no point asking me anything," he said with a chuckle. "Darcy Robinson is site manager for the event. She'll be able to provide much better answers than I will."

Darcy blinked and then took a deep breath before turning to face the crowd. She smiled brightly and silently cursed Alastair before taking the first question.

It seemed hours before the questioning stopped, but when Darcy checked the time, it was only half eight. Alastair had wandered off to the bar while she'd been talking to everyone; now she found him.

"That was interesting," she said tightly.

"I was afraid if I warned you, you wouldn't want to do it," Alastair told her. "Anyway, you were brilliant."

"I'm tired and hungry, so if you don't mind, I'll head back to my hotel and get some dinner sent up to my room," she told him.

"Oh, no, give me five minutes to wrap up a few things and we'll go somewhere for dinner," he replied. Before she could object, he took her arm and began to make a circuit of the room.

"She's lovely, and much smarter than your usual girlfriends," one man said, slapping Alastair on the back.

Darcy frowned, but bit her tongue. Making a scene wouldn't do Nollick Balley any good and that was her chief concern tonight. Alastair's 'five minutes' took over half an hour, but eventually they made their way back out of the hotel.

"Where would you like to go?" he asked as they settled back in the car.

"Somewhere fast," Darcy said. Not only was she ravenous, she really didn't want to spend more time with the man than she had to.

Alastair laughed. "We aren't exactly dressed for fast food," he pointed out. He leaned forward and said something to the driver and then slid back into his seat. "Champagne?" he offered.

"Not on an empty stomach," Darcy declined. The man shrugged and put the bottle back in the car's refrigerator. Just then his phone buzzed. While Darcy watched traffic again, Alastair dealt with whatever he needed to sort out.

"Sorry," he said when the car stopped in the middle of a row of trendy shops and restaurants. "I'll try to ignore it if it goes off again while we're together."

"It's fine," Darcy assured him. "You do what you need to do."

They ended up in a tiny Italian restaurant that was only about half full. Darcy worried that the lack of customers meant the food wasn't good, but she was pleasantly surprised by everything she'd ordered. The pair chatted about nothing much, the conversation continually interrupted by Alastair's phone.

Back at Darcy's hotel, Alastair insisted on escorting her to her room.

"I'm sorry I've been so distracted tonight," he told her at the door. He leaned in to kiss her, but his phone buzzed right before their lips met. Darcy couldn't help but laugh.

Alastair glanced at his phone and then shook his head. "I have to deal with this," he told her. He walked a few steps away and then turned back. "I promise I'll leave my phone off when we're in Lanzarote," he said, blowing her a kiss and then disappearing down the corridor.

"But I'm not going to Lanzarote," Darcy said to the empty air. She shook her head and then went into her room, unable to remember another time when she had been so looking forward to getting back to the Isle of Man.

❧ 11 ❧

The days began to fly past for Darcy as she dealt with the press and started sending out promotional materials. She also began her efforts to recruit the large number of staff that she was going to need to make the event happen. By the time Friday rolled around, she was looking forward to visiting the site so that she could spend some time away from her desk. At least that's what she told herself. Seeing Kerron Kewley again had nothing to do with her eager anticipation.

After a busy morning, she ate a quick lunch and then showered again. She got dressed with care, in black trousers with a matching jacket. It was a typically cool autumn day and she anticipated being outdoors for some time. A skirt simply wouldn't do. The bright blue silk blouse she put on under her jacket was one of her favourites. With her hair pulled up and firmly pinned into place, she redid her makeup, using waterproof mascara and hoping for the best. The day had been dry thus far, but at this time of year rain was seldom far off.

The drive felt familiar and Darcy found herself speeding faster and faster as she neared her goal. "I really needed to get out from behind my computer," she reminded herself. As she turned up the drive to the Kewley farm, she couldn't help but look to see if she could spot where the tree that had fallen in her path had once stood. She spotted the large stump that remained as she drove towards the farm.

It was a few minutes before two when she arrived at the farm. The parking area was empty and she wondered if Kerron was at home. "Only one way to find out," she muttered to herself as she climbed out of the car. She'd worn her Wellington boots and now she was glad she had, as they sunk into the mud that seemed to be everywhere.

She made her way to the farmhouse and knocked loudly. After a few minutes she knocked again. Kerron had told her that they rarely locked the front door to the house. She was tempted to try the door, but that felt wrong. Instead, she turned and headed back to her car. She pulled out some paperwork and her phone and spent several minutes going over various figures while she waited. Eventually she heard the sound of a farm vehicle coming down the road.

"I'm sorry I'm late," Kerron announced as he jumped down from the large tractor he was driving. "Harvest time is always interesting."

"I had plenty to keep me busy," Darcy replied easily.

"Excellent," Kerron said, giving her a dazzling smile. "Are you ready to see your site, then?"

"More than," Darcy exclaimed. "We open in less than two months and that means construction has to start soon."

"I thought we'd agreed that construction would start on the first of November," Kerron countered.

"That's only a few weeks away," Darcy replied.

"I suppose so," Kerron said with a shrug. "Of course, I might be able to be persuaded to let you start earlier. We're done with the field until spring, anyway."

Darcy smiled brightly. "That would be great," she said happily. "But first I need to see the site."

"Your chariot awaits," Kerron told her, gesturing towards the tractor. Darcy wrinkled her nose but walked over to the large machine. Kerron opened the door for her and then helped her climb inside. When she was seated, he shut the door behind her and then went around to the driver's side. Once he started the engine, conversation became impossible. Darcy sat back and watched as they drove past the various barns and livestock buildings on their way towards the huge fields that surrounded them. After several minutes, Kerron stopped in the middle of the road.

"There's your car park," he told Darcy, pointing to a large empty field. "According to the plans that you sent to Don, there will be a fence built around the entire perimeter, with an entrance and exit gate and staff on hand to direct the cars in and out."

"Yep," Darcy replied. "I've actually hired a car park manager this week and he'll be making arrangements with Don to get the site set up as soon as possible."

Kerron nodded and looked as if he wanted to add something, but then he shook his head and turned the engine back on. They moved slowly along the road for a short time before he stopped again.

"There you are," he said, waving his arm. "Manx Christmas World."

"Nollick Balley," Darcy corrected him. She looked over at the huge field and felt a rush of excitement. In her mind, she could see the various tents popping up around the site. In the very centre, Santa's Castle rose up, ready to welcome the island's children who were eager to share their Christmas wishes with the mythical man.

"You're really excited, aren't you?" Kerron asked.

Darcy flushed as she realised how closely he was watching her. "It's all starting to come together," she told him. "Anyway, I absolutely love Christmas and I think Nollick Balley is going to be amazing."

"It's a big muddy field," Kerron pointed out.

Darcy shook her head. "Close your eyes," she instructed him. "Picture your big muddy field covered in a layer of fluffy white snow. There are tents with food vendors scattered around the site. There are rides and games. A large pen houses reindeer and a larger building showcases the hard-working elves. And at the centre of it all, a huge castle houses the star of the show. Santa sits on his throne, ready to receive visitors."

"Good luck with the snow," Kerron commented. "I don't think we've had any up here more than once or twice in the last ten years."

"Oh, it's fine," Darcy assured him. "We're bringing our own."

"I'll need to see the specifications for that," Kerron said sharply. "I don't want anything spread all over my fields that might be harmful to either the crops or the livestock."

"I'll have Michael send you all of the details," Darcy replied. "I'm sure he knows what he's doing."

"Your faith in the man is touching," Kerron said lightly. "I don't share it."

"I want to walk around the site," Darcy said, ignoring the tension that was developing between them.

"Go ahead," Kerron drawled. "I'll wait here."

Darcy opened her mouth to object, and then pressed her lips together and opened the tractor door. She took a deep breath and then jumped down, hoping she wouldn't slip and fall in the mud and embarrass herself. She did slip slightly, but recovered quickly and then stomped away from the tractor. Within minutes, Kerron was forgotten as she walked around, imagining how the site was going to look in just a few short weeks.

There was no doubt she was going to have to spend a great deal more time there as opening day drew nearer. For just a moment the whole project felt unbelievably daunting, but Darcy refused to let herself think about just how much needed to be completed and focussed on what she hoped to accomplish.

She walked all the way to the farthest edge of the field and then slowly made her way back, pacing out approximations of where the different structures would go. They'd had to scrap the idea of a train around the site as impractical with the time constraints, but otherwise everything Alastair originally wanted was still in the plans.

After a while a light rain began to fall, but she ignored it, carrying on with her mental calculations. She was surprised when she heard the tractor door slam. When she looked up, Kerron was crossing the field towards her, his face stormy.

"You've been stomping around in the mud for over an hour," he said grumpily. "Surely you've seen enough."

Darcy looked at him in surprise. "I didn't realise it had been that long," she said in an apologetic voice. "I'm just trying to take it all in. I didn't realise how different it would feel on the ground to what I've been imagining on paper."

"It's raining," Kerron pointed out.

"Only a little bit," Darcy countered as the wind picked up and the rain turned heavier.

"I'm going home," Kerron told her. "If you want to stay here and wander around more, you go ahead. I'll tell Don to come and get you in another hour."

Darcy flushed and shook her head. "I'm sorry. We can go now," she said quickly. "I didn't mean to inconvenience you," she added.

Kerron frowned and then, without a word, strode back to the tractor. Darcy followed as quickly as she could on the slippery surface. Kerron was behind the wheel before she'd managed to get her door open. She pulled herself up and slipped into the seat as Kerron started the engine.

The noise that filled the cabin meant they couldn't speak and left Darcy with time to try to figure out why Kerron was in such a miserable mood. Perhaps she was keeping him for some other work that he felt was more important, she thought. Or maybe he has a date and needs to get ready, a little voice in her head suggested. She sternly told the little voice to shut up and tried to turn her thoughts to other things, but Kerron's mood appeared to be contagious, and by the time they'd reached the farmhouse Darcy was feeling cross with the world.

"Marion left a chicken in the oven," Kerron told her once he'd turned off the engine. "With roast potatoes and stuffing and all the trimmings."

Darcy shrugged. "How very nice for you," she commented mildly.

Kerron stared at her for a moment and then laughed. "Sorry, that was meant as in invitation," he told her. "I'm in a terrible mood and I'm taking it out on you, and for that I'm sorry. Today hasn't been the best day."

"I'm sorry things aren't going well," Darcy said softly. "If you'd like to talk about anything, I'm happy to listen."

Kerron looked at her for a long time and then sighed. "Let's get some food," he said. "I'm sure I'll feel better with a full stomach. I didn't get any lunch."

Darcy nodded. She'd never met a man whose mood didn't improve when he was fed. This time, when Darcy opened her door, Kerron dashed around to help her down. For just a moment, he held her close and Darcy felt her heart race. Then he released her and led her into the house.

At the door, she pulled off her Wellies and took off her rather wet jacket, hanging it on the nearest hook.

"Do you need dry clothes?" Kerron asked, looking her over.

"I'm fine," Darcy said, blushing. "My coat kept me pretty dry."

"I'm going to grab a quick shower," he told her. "I've been out in the fields all day. I promise it will be quick, though. I'm starving. Make yourself at home while I'm gone."

Darcy nodded and then made her way into the kitchen. She filled the kettle and switched it on before peeking into the oven and the refrigerator. Marion had left enough food to feed an army. What wasn't in the oven staying warm was in containers in the refrigerator ready to be heated. Darcy began to pull out the containers, chuckling when she saw the carefully printed note that was attached to each one.

Microwave this first for four minutes, then set aside for the next thing.

Darcy peeked inside the wrapping and found sprouts. Each container, from the broccoli to the peas, had similar instructions. Darcy lined them up on the counter and popped the spouts in the microwave. She set them going for their initial minutes while she checked the oven.

The chicken was beautifully browned, and when Darcy pulled it out of the oven she found that it was surrounded by carrots, pearl onions and baby potatoes. Small foil packages on the other oven shelf held stuffing, mashed potatoes and the promised roast potatoes as well. Darcy rotated each thing through the microwave in turn, following Marion's instructions. She was just putting the peas in for their final two minutes when Kerron walked into the room.

"Everything smells great," he said, giving her a warm smile.

Darcy nodded her agreement, inhaling the soapy and spicy scent that was coming from the man.

Kerron got out plates and serving spoons, and he and Darcy dug into the many containers, filing plates full of the delicious feast.

"Let's just eat in here," he suggested.

"Sure," Darcy was quick to agree. The bright kitchen was warm and homey and Darcy could see no point in moving into the larger and less welcoming dining room.

Kerron put his plate down and then pulled out a bottle of wine. He opened it and poured them each a glass.

"I'm driving," Darcy said, looking doubtfully at the drink.

"I won't let you have any more, then," Kerron said. "But you'll be here for at least another hour. There's apple pie in the oven as well."

Darcy grinned. She'd spotted the pie and left it in to stay warm. Kerron was right; she wasn't going to be rushing off anywhere in a hurry.

Over dinner they chatted lightly about the weather and island politics, disagreeing good-naturedly about a few little things. It wasn't until they both had large slices of pie with cream in front of them that Kerron brought up his earlier mood.

"I'm sorry I was a bit out of sorts earlier," he said. "My father rang this morning. He's coming home in a few days and he seems to think he'll be taking back over the running of the farm."

Darcy thought about things for a moment before she spoke. "Isn't he enjoying the Algarve?" she asked.

"Apparently, he's bored," Kerron said dryly. "Although it hasn't escaped my notice that he didn't get bored until after our busiest time of year. Now that the fields have been harvested, he can come home and entertain himself with the livestock until spring. Once it's time to plant, no doubt he'll decide to give the Algarve another try."

Darcy shook her head. "I'm sorry," she said.

"You'll be even sorrier when I tell you how unhappy he is about Nollick Balley," Kerron remarked.

"But he signed the original agreement," Darcy said in surprise.

"I gather he thought I would be able to get out of the agreement," Kerron replied. "Anyway, he saw a photo of you with Alastair and he seems to think that you've seduced me into renting you that extra field and letting you have free reign to ruin the farm."

"I'm not going to ruin the farm," Darcy exclaimed angrily. "And I haven't seduced anyone."

"From the photos I saw most recently, it seems as if Alastair is the one seducing you," Kerron said quietly.

Darcy sighed. She'd seen the photos that the tabloids had run after the promotional event. It seemed as if Alastair had his arm around her in every single picture, and more than one showed him whispering in her ear. She'd been hoping that Kerron hadn't seen them.

"He isn't," she said sharply.

Kerron shrugged. "Anyway, I suspect my father will have a lot to say to you about the whole extravaganza once he arrives. You should plan on meeting with him late next week."

"I'll look forward to it," Darcy replied sarcastically.

"I think it's fair to say I'm not looking forward to the man coming home and changing everything that I've been working on for the last six months, but that's my problem. You'll soon have enough problems of your own with him, I reckon."

Darcy sighed. "Just what I don't want to hear, now that things are starting to come together."

"He'll be here on Wednesday. If you want to start getting things set up and built before he gets here, that's fine with me. The fields are yours as of right now. Just make sure you remember that our agreement says you'll return them to me in the same condition you got them."

"That won't be a problem," Darcy said airily.

"It might be with your fake snow," Kerron replied. "It seems like it will be a difficult thing to get rid of."

"I'll have Michael get in touch. I'm sure it will be fine," she said with far more confidence than she felt.

"It's cold and wet outside," Kerron pointed out as she helped him load the dishwasher. "You're welcome to stay the night."

Darcy shook her head. "It's a tempting thought, but I need to get home so that I can start mobilising the troops first thing tomorrow."

Kerron looked as if he was going to argue, but then he shook his head. "I've too much on my mind to be good company anyway," he told her.

With the kitchen tidy, he walked Darcy back out to her car. "Drive carefully," he told her as he held her door open for her. Darcy climbed into the car.

"Good luck with your father," she said.

"Thanks," Kerron replied. He stood holding her door for a long minute and then leaned down and gave her a soft kiss. When he lifted his head, Darcy held her breath, hoping he'd do it again. Instead, he took a step back and shut her car door. He gave her a quick wave and then stepped further back to allow her to drive away. Feeling miserable, Darcy did just that.

Back in her flat, Darcy filled her bathtub and then climbed in for a long soak. She lay back in the tub and tried to remember the last time she'd been out on a date. If she didn't count the evenings with Alastair, which Darcy didn't want to think of as dates, and she didn't include the evenings with Kerron as they weren't dates, either, Darcy realised she hadn't been on a date since Lisa's wedding. She'd been so busy with her new job, that she hadn't really given it any thought. Now the idea upset her.

When she'd worked for Finlo, barely a day went by when she wasn't asked out by a passenger or someone she encountered on her travels. Working from home had destroyed her social life. She thought about Lisa's offer to fix her up on a few blind dates and shuddered in spite of the warm water. Surely she hadn't sunk to that level, at least not yet.

Dried off and in her pyjamas, Darcy flipped through her address book. There were quite a few names and numbers in the book for former boyfriends. Darcy was pretty sure she could ring one or two of them and find a date for any night she chose. She frowned and shut the book. There was a reason they were all former boyfriends. What she really needed was to meet someone new. She dialled Lisa's mobile number.

"I haven't had a date since your wedding," she said when Lisa answered.

"Really?" Lisa replied in a shocked tone. "You'll be looking at cats next."

"It isn't funny," Darcy wailed. "I've been so busy with work that I didn't even notice that I haven't been dating. I haven't been without a boyfriend this long since I was twelve."

"But your work is keeping you busy and you haven't missed it," Lisa said calmly. "I'm sure once Nollick Balley is over you'll find a new guy right away."

"But it's only the middle of October," Darcy replied. "Christmas is a long way off."

"I thought you were supposed to going to Lanzarote in January with Alastair?" Lisa asked.

"That is so not happening," Darcy replied. "I'm not getting involved with another rich man who won't commit."

"Are you sure he won't commit?"

"Oh, absolutely," Darcy replied. "He spent most of his evening on his phone the last time I saw him. He's already stopped caring what I really think and assuming I'll just fall into bed with him once Nollick Balley is over."

"What about Kerron?"

Darcy sighed deeply. "I went out and saw the site today," she told Lisa.

"And?"

"And it's perfect for Nollick Balley, but Kerron was, well, distracted, I guess."

"He isn't still objecting to you having Nollick Balley there, is he?"

"No, he isn't, but apparently his father might be."

"I thought his father was in Portugal?"

"He was, but he's coming home in a few days. Kerron said his father thinks I've seduced him into agreeing to let us use the farm."

"But he signed the original agreement," Lisa pointed out.

"Yeah, I guess dear old dad reckoned Kerron would be able to get the agreement cancelled or something."

"So what are you going to do?"

"Meet with dad and make sure he understands that we have signed contracts and he's stuck with Nollick Balley, whether he likes it or not."

"Well, that sounds like fun," Lisa said, her voice dripping with sarcasm.

"Yeah, I'm looking forward to it," Darcy laughed. "But the good news is that Kerron has given us permission to start building now, a little early. I'm hoping we'll have enough done by the time dad gets here to change the man's mind."

The pair talked for a while longer, but weren't able to solve any of Darcy's problems.

"Oh, goodness, I need to let you go," Darcy said when she looked at her bedside clock. "Your husband must be furious with me."

"Not at all," Lisa assured her. "Anyway, before I forget, I'm putting two tickets in the post to you for Christmas at the Castle. It's a big fundraiser for Manx National Heritage, as well as a really nice evening."

"When is it?" Darcy asked.

"I've sent you tickets for the preview, which is the first Friday in December. Nollick Balley opens on the seventh, right?"

"Yep, assuming all goes to plan."

"I thought so, so I figured the dates later in December wouldn't work for you."

"You're right, they wouldn't," Darcy agreed. "But I should be able to manage the preview. I'll put it on my calendar now."

"I've sent two tickets," Lisa repeated herself. "You can bring a date if you want."

Darcy laughed. "And now we're back to my first problem," she said. "I wouldn't know who to invite."

"If I were you, I'd invite Kerron. He sounds gorgeous and incredibly nice, as well."

"But if I bring Alastair, he'll probably donate lots of lovely money to MNH," Darcy pointed out.

"Your happiness is just a tiny bit more important to me than MNH," Lisa told her. "But if you want, I can send you another ticket and you can bring them both."

Darcy laughed and hung up feeling slightly better. She knew she needed to embrace the new, self-sufficient Darcy and remember that she didn't need a man in her life to be happy. She spent most of Saturday ringing her various builders and suppliers to see who could start earlier than originally planned. Most of them were happy to accommodate the new arrangements.

"I didn't really fancy trying to get everything done in less than a month," the man building Santa's castle told her. "I'll be up at the

Kewley farm first thing Monday morning to get started on assembling our finished panels."

On Saturday night Darcy was tempted to go out for a drink. There was no doubt she could have found a friend or two to join her, but in the end she decided it was more trouble than it was worth. Instead, she curled up with a magazine and flipped through it while watching a bit of telly. Sunday she caught up on her grocery shopping and cleaned her flat, ready for a busy week ahead. When her phone rang, she was surprised.

"Hey, gorgeous, I was just sitting here thinking about you." Alastair's voice was low and sexy.

"Really? Why?"

Alastair chuckled. "I miss you," he said softly. "Why don't you come and visit me this week?"

"I'm rather busy," Darcy told him. "We've been given permission to start building at the farm a little early, so I'm going to be driving up and down all week keeping an eye on things."

"Surely you can delegate that to someone and come to London instead?"

"There isn't room in my budget to hire a site manager," Darcy countered sweetly.

Alastair laughed. "I'll tell Michael to approve it," he said. "I'm bored and I want to see you."

Darcy took a deep breath. "I've been working too hard to stay on budget to agree to such a thing," she said. "You'll just have to find someone else to entertain you."

"Oh, come on. I hired you because Finlo said you were fun. Let someone else worry about Manx Christmas World."

"It's Nollick Balley, actually," Darcy said in a cool voice. "And I've spent the last four months working with ideas and concepts and drawings. The last thing I want to do, now that it's finally starting to be built, is go away."

Alastair sighed deeply. "I'm deeply disappointed in you," he said. "After this week I'm going to New York for most of November. I won't have a chance to see you until just before Christmas World opens."

"If you're back by the first weekend in December, there's a

fundraiser at Castle Rushen called Christmas at the Castle. I can have my friend send you a ticket."

"Will you be there?"

"I will."

"Send me a ticket. I can't promise to be there, but I'll try. I'm planning to come over for the grand opening of Christmas World, anyway. I can probably come over a few days earlier."

"Well, have fun in New York," Darcy said, hoping to wrap up the conversation. "I'll keep Michael informed as to how things are going here."

"Excellent. Don't be surprised if I ring you from New York. I'm sure I'll miss you when I'm there as well."

Darcy didn't reply she just hung up the phone feeling frustrated and annoyed with Alastair. How could he suggest that she simply turn Nollick Balley over to someone else? He was far too used to getting his own way.

Monday morning was cold and rainy, and after giving it a lot of thought, Darcy got dressed in an older pair of trousers and a warm jumper. She expected to spend much of the day outdoors and she'd clearly need a raincoat and her Wellington boots.

At the Kewley farm, she followed the road that Kerron had taken when he's shown her the site. When she arrived at the field, she found several people already hard at work. She parked her car along the road and then headed for the nearest person. That turned out to be Don, Kerron's manager.

"Good morning," he said brightly.

"It's a bit damp," Darcy replied, casting an anxious eye at the sky.

"When you farm for a living, you stop noticing the rain unless it's torrential," the man replied cheerfully.

"I'll have to take your word for that," Darcy said with a grin.

"Everything seems to going well over here," he told her. "There are four different groups working, and so far they're all following your plans exactly."

"They'd better be," Darcy replied. "I worked hard on those plans."

"I'm just going to head over to the car park field and make sure things are going as smoothly there as they are here. Are you planning on being here for long?"

"Probably most of the day," Darcy told him. "I'll have to check my phone periodically for emails and messages, but otherwise I want to be here making sure everything goes to plan."

"I'll let the boss know," Don said. "And I'll probably stop back a couple of times myself. I expect they'll make good progress today."

"I certainly hope so," Darcy told him.

The day flew past for Darcy. Don visited a few more times, but Kerron never made an appearance. Darcy told herself she wasn't the least bit disappointed, but she didn't really believe herself. The various groups on the site made a huge amount of progress and Darcy drove home with visions in her head of happy reindeer prancing about in their new pen. The rest of the week continued in the same way, with Don checking in with Darcy several times a day.

"William should be here tonight," he told Darcy on Wednesday evening. "I understand you're meeting with him on Friday. I suspect he might drop by the site tomorrow for a visit, though."

"I hope not," Darcy muttered before she forced herself to smile. "He's more than welcome, obviously. It is his farm, after all."

"Actually, it's Kerron's farm now. He bought his father out a few years ago."

"If Kerron owns the farm, how could his father sign the agreement for our event?" Darcy asked.

"Legally, he probably couldn't," Don told her.

Darcy had a dozen more questions, but she was interrupted by one of the men building the workshop for the elves. By the time she'd sorted him out, Don had disappeared.

In spite of Don's warning, William didn't appear on-site on Thursday. She was standing in the middle of Santa's Castle on Friday afternoon when Kerron suddenly walked in.

"Wow, it's actually starting to look like something," he said.

"It's starting to look magical," Darcy countered. "I'm so pleased with everything so far."

"I've been unbelievably busy all week, so I haven't been out here at all," he told her. "But Don's been updating me. It looks like everything is going to plan."

"So far, so good," Darcy replied.

"Yes, well, I just stopped by to ask you what time we should expect you at the house tonight. Dad is quite eager to meet you."

Darcy glanced at her watch and the looked around. "How about four?" she suggested. "I think we'll probably wrap up early here tonight as we're so far ahead of things. That way I can meet with your father and then be out of the way in time for you to have dinner."

"I was hoping you'd join us for dinner," Kerron told her. "But you might not want to after you've met my father. He isn't exactly the friendliest man around."

"I'm sure we'll find common ground," Darcy replied. "I'm looking forward to meeting him."

"We'll see you at four," Kerron said. "And good luck."

The afternoon suddenly seemed to speed up and Darcy found herself in her car, heading for the farmhouse, long before she felt ready to meet Kerron's father.

🌿 I 2 🌿

In the parking area outside the farmhouse, before she got out of her car, Darcy took a moment to take down her hair and comb it out. She touched up her makeup and changed out of her Wellies and into a pair of black pumps. After the heavy rain on Monday, it had been dry the rest of the week, so the parking area outside the farmhouse wasn't as muddy as normal. She figured she could risk the pumps in an effort to make a good first impression on the man everyone seemed to think was going to dislike her.

She knocked on the door with more enthusiasm than she felt. When she heard movement behind it, she straightened her shoulders and forced a smile onto her face. The door swung open slowly and Darcy gasped.

"But you're perfect," she exclaimed as she studied the man who'd opened the door. He was right around six feet tall, with grey hair and a bushy grey beard. While he still looked fairly fit, he had a rounded tummy.

"Perfect?" he said, sounding confused.

"I haven't found the right Santa yet," Darcy told him as he took a step backwards and waved her into the house. "You're exactly what I need."

The man laughed and shook his head. "I'm not having anything to do with your Christmas World fiasco," he said firmly. "If I can find a way, I'll get the whole thing cancelled yet."

"But it's your signature on the contracts," Darcy reminded him.

"Yeah, but I didn't think I was going to be here when I signed," he told her. "I thought I'd be in Portugal, enjoying the sunshine. How was I to know that the Algarve was full of miserable British expats who do nothing but complain about how different everything is from home?"

Darcy laughed. "Well, welcome home," she told him brightly. "Here we all complain about the weather and how much better life would be in sunny Portugal."

The man shook his head. "Take it from someone who knows, it isn't better anywhere. Anyway, I missed my boy," he said in a confiding tone. "I brought him up by myself, you know, and I felt bad about leaving him to manage everything on his own."

"He seems to be doing quite well with it," Darcy replied.

"He's doing okay, except for going along with this crazy Christmas thing."

"Again, you signed the contracts. He was rather stuck," Darcy said.

The man shrugged. "There are always ways around such things," he said. "Our advocate could have sorted it out if Kerron had really wanted to fight it. I guess he took one look at your big green eyes and agreed to everything you wanted."

Darcy laughed again. "I wish it had been that easy," she told him.

"Bah, I know my son. He has a weakness for beautiful women. He was putty in your hands."

"Not exactly," Kerron said from the corridor doorway. He walked into the room. "I see you've met my father, then," he said to Darcy.

"I have, although we've not been formally introduced," Darcy replied.

"Darcy Robinson, meet William Kewley, my father and the man to blame for Manx Christmas World," Kerron said.

"Nollick Balley," Darcy said.

"Whatever," Kerron said with a shrug.

"You've given it a Manx name?" William asked.

"We have. It seemed fitting and sounds much better than Manx Christmas World," Darcy told him.

"You're not wrong," he admitted.

"Kerron, I've been trying to persuade your father to play Santa for me," Darcy said. "You have to admit he'd be perfect."

The younger man chuckled. "I've never thought of my father as Santa," he said slowly. "But I can see the resemblance now that you've mentioned it."

"I'm not interested," William said firmly.

"I don't know, you were just complaining that you didn't have any money of your own now that the farm is in my name. I bet Darcy would pay you a pretty good wage," Kerron said.

"Are you going to start charging me rent, then, son?" the man demanded.

"Of course not," Kerron replied. "But I have to say I can't see you being happy asking me for petrol money."

The man flushed. "I can't imagine spending all day listening to children whining about what they want for Christmas," he said.

"It would only be for a few hours each day," Darcy told him. "Santa only appears for an hour at a time, three or four times a day. He's too busy with making toys the rest of the time."

The man opened his mouth to object further, but Kerron interrupted. "We should eat," he said. "Marion said not to leave everything in the oven for too long."

Darcy quickly followed Kerron to the kitchen, hoping that William might give her idea some thought while they ate. Over dinner, Darcy kept the men entertained with stories about her travels. When she ran out of tales, William shared some of his adventures from the Algarve.

"Well, I'm feeling quite left out," Kerron said after a while. "I haven't any fascinating stories from around the world. I've never been anywhere interesting."

"I never travelled until I retired," William told him. "You have another thirty years or so to go."

Kerron groaned. "I was hoping, with you back, that I might be able to take some time off," he told his father.

"No way," William replied. "I'm not back to look after the farm.

I'm just home because I hated Portugal. I haven't sold the house there, though. I reckon I'll be ready to give it another go in the spring."

Kerron nodded, and Darcy remembered him telling her that he suspected his father would do just that.

"Have you been out to the site yet?" Darcy asked William as they ate their pudding.

"Nope, and I'm not interested in going," the man replied.

"You should come and see it on Monday," Darcy suggested. "Santa's Castle is just about finished. They'll be working on his throne on Monday."

"Throne?"

"Oh yes, Santa gets a huge padded throne to sit on," Darcy told him. "We want to take good care of the most important resident of Nollick Balley."

"Hmm," was William's only reply.

"It's getting late," Kerron said as he and Darcy loaded the dishwasher. "I'm sure you're ready to head to bed, dad."

William shook his head. "I'm wide awake," he said. "I think I'll watch a movie. You two coming?"

"Thanks, but I need to get home," Darcy replied. "I have a lot of phone calls and emails to get through tomorrow."

"I'll walk you out," Kerron said.

"Do give my idea some thought," Darcy told William. "I know you don't much like me, but I'm sure you like Alastair Breckenridge less. Every penny I pay you comes right out of his profits from the event."

William chuckled. "You know what, young lady? That was just about the only thing you could have said to me to make me seriously consider the idea."

Darcy grinned and then followed Kerron back through the house. At the front door, she pulled her jacket back on and then the pair walked out to her car.

"I think he likes you," Kerron said, sounding surprised.

"I'm very likeable," Darcy replied.

"You are, rather," Kerron agreed. She unlocked her car and he pulled open her door for her. Before she could climb in, he put an arm around her. "I've had a long day," he said softly. "I can only think of one thing that might make it a little bit better."

Before Darcy could reply, he lowered his lips to hers. In spite of her misgivings, she let herself get lost in the kiss. She was confused when Kerron pulled away, but then she heard the voice coming from the house.

"Come on, son. I've popped some popcorn and found an old action movie we haven't watched in years. Send the young lady on her way and get in here."

Darcy sighed and leaned against Kerron for a moment. "You have to go," she said.

"I do, really," he replied, removing his arms from around her waist.

Darcy sank slowly into her car, trying not to let the man see how disappointed she was to be leaving.

"I'll be back on Monday morning," she told Kerron. "Maybe you can persuade your father to come to work for me by then."

"I can try," Kerron said. "But be careful what you wish for. He'll be a handful for you."

"I can handle him," Darcy said with more confidence than she felt.

"No doubt," Kerron said with a laugh. He shut her door and then stepped back so that she could drive away. She started the engine and then drove slowly down the long drive. When she was nearly at the road, she stopped and burst into tears. The emotional upheaval was short-lived, but it felt cathartic to Darcy. She dried her eyes and drove back to Castletown feeling better in an odd way.

The weekend was a quiet one for Darcy. She met Lisa for some shopping on Saturday and then cooked herself an elaborate three-course feast for dinner. Sunday was all about cleaning her flat and food shopping for the week ahead. On Monday she headed back to the Kewley farm, hoping to find everyone hard at work.

With the basic construction already done, Santa's Castle was now being painted and decorated, and Darcy was thrilled to see her ideas coming to life. Nearly all of the tents were in place and the pens for the deer were built and readied for their temporary residents. Just after midday, as Darcy washed down a sandwich with coffee thoughtfully provided by the crew working on the castle, Kerron and his father arrived to have a look around.

Darcy proudly showed them around the site, explaining what was going where.

"And this is Santa's Castle," she said as she finished the tour at the centre of the site. "This is where you would be spending your time, if you choose to take the job."

She ushered the men inside the building. The outside of the building was being painted to look like it was made up of huge ice blocks. Inside was a bright mix of red and green walls and floors. There was a small waiting area. Darcy now led William and Kerron through it into the throne room behind. The room had several posts where ropes could be attached to provide a lengthy queuing system. Beyond that, a raised platform held a plain wooden chair.

"Obviously, we'll be replacing that chair with a proper and fitting throne for our star," Darcy said.

"I certainly hope so," William said.

"Does that mean you'll be sitting on it?" Darcy asked hopefully.

William shrugged. "I may as well," he said. "I'm going to be here anyway. This way I can take some money away from that pompous windbag you work for and keep myself busy and out of Kerron's way."

"Excellent," Darcy said. She introduced the man to George, her newly hired assistant, and the pair fell into a discussion of exactly what Santa's throne should look like. After a moment, Kerron touched Darcy's arm.

"Can we talk outside?" he asked.

"Of course," Darcy agreed, happy to leave the throne discussion behind. She would have final say in whatever they agreed on, and as long as they stayed on budget, she didn't really care what they did, anyway.

Outside the wind was picking up and it was starting to spit with rain. Darcy led Kerron into one of the small tents so they could avoid the worst of the weather.

"What's wrong?" she asked.

"I'm concerned about the artificial snow," he told her. "I've been doing some research and there are several different products that can be used. Some of them are much safer than others. You know as well as I do that the wind will have the stuff all over my farm. Whatever you use has to be safe for livestock and also for my crops."

"Michael is meant to be handling the snow," Darcy told him. "I'll get in touch with him and have him send you the specifications for what he's chosen. If you aren't happy about it, please let me know."

Kerron nodded. "I'd appreciate getting the information as soon as possible," he said. "Just in case we have to make any changes."

"I'll email him right now," Darcy said. She took a few steps away and fired up her phone. "What's your email address?" she asked after a moment. Kerron replied and she quickly finished the note.

"I can't promise when he'll reply, but if you haven't heard by the end of the day tomorrow, let me know and I'll chase him up, okay?"

"Fine," Kerron said, frowning.

"What else is wrong?" Darcy asked.

"Nothing, really," Kerron replied. "I guess it's all just starting to feel more real and I'm less and less happy about the whole event."

"It will be wonderful," Darcy told him, crossing back to his side and taking his arm. She led him to the opening in the tent and gestured outside.

"Just imagine the place teeming with families with small children," she said excitedly. "The rides will be along the back fence on the path we're calling Sugarplum Way. The food vendors will be down Candy Lane and the elf workshop will be at the corner of that and Santa Claus Road, where the reindeer pens and the castle will be."

Kerron sighed. "You told me all of this when you showed us around," he reminded her. "I guess I just don't share your enthusiasm."

"It's going to be fabulous," Darcy said firmly. "You'll see."

"I think you're doing a great job," Kerron said. "It just isn't really what I want on my farm."

"Well, you only have to get through the next couple of months and then it will be all over. I've already heard from two other farmers around the island who are interested in having Nollick Balley on their property next year. I guess word has gone around that Alastair paid you quite a lot to have it this year."

"Who wants to have it next year?" Kerron demanded.

"I'm sorry, but I can't tell you that," Darcy replied. "All I can tell you is that a few people have realised that their empty fields might have some value between harvest and planting seasons."

Kerron nodded. "I suspect their willingness to host next time will depend on how things go this year," he said. "If there are any big problems, you might find them less willing to talk."

"There aren't going to be any big problems," Darcy said confidently. "I've worked too hard to this point to let anything go wrong."

"I suppose it helps that there isn't anything else quite like it on the island," Kerron said thoughtfully. "I wonder if anyone else might try a similar event next year if this one goes well."

"I hope not," Darcy said. "I don't think the island can support two such events. Hopefully, because Alastair did it first, no one will try to compete."

"Aside from visiting Father Christmas at various shops or craft shows, what else is there on the island for families at Christmas?" Kerron asked.

"The Wildlife Park hosts a Santa as well," Darcy replied. "That's where my first choice for Santa here is going to be working."

"Don't tell my dad he wasn't your first choice," Kerron cautioned her.

"He would have been my first choice if I'd met him before I asked the other guy," Darcy replied. "Your father is just about perfect."

"There's Christmas at the Castle, too, but I've always thought of that as being mostly for adults."

"It is," Darcy agreed. "Have you ever been?"

"No. I've heard good things about it, but I've never bothered."

"I have two tickets to the preview evening. Would you like to come with me?"

Kerron stared at her for a moment. "Is this a date?" he asked eventually.

Darcy flushed. "I just thought, that is, I mean, I wasn't thinking of it that way."

"Just checking," Kerron replied. "Whatever, when is it?"

Darcy gave him the date and he checked his phone. "I guess I'm free that night," he said. "Really, I'm free every night. Sure, why not? As I said, I've never been. It supposed to be really nice."

"It's one of Manx National Heritage's most popular fundraisers," Darcy replied. "Alastair might be there."

"Did you invite him as well?"

"Sort of," Darcy replied. "I thought he'd be good for a big donation."

"So I guess it's definitely not a date, although maybe it is for you and Alastair," Kerron said, sounding annoyed.

"It isn't," Darcy replied coolly.

Kerron nodded, but he didn't look convinced. Darcy thought about arguing further, but decided it wasn't worth the effort.

They chatted a bit longer about the site and how well it was coming together before Darcy's mobile rang and she had to excuse herself to deal with a supplier. When she was done with the call, Kerron and his father were both gone.

Darcy spent the rest of the day on the site and then, when she got home, she sent an email to Michael, asking about the artificial snow. She ate a ready meal in front of her laptop, while she tried to find out as much as she could about the different types of artificial snow that were available. The ringing of her phone was a welcome interruption.

"So, how are you?" Lisa asked.

Darcy sighed. "I'm getting a headache from trying to understand the chemical formulas for different types of manufactured snow," she told her friend.

"You never were any good at chemistry, except for the type between men and women," Lisa replied with a laugh.

"I'm struggling with that sort now, too," Darcy said grumpily.

"Oh, dear," Lisa said. "You are feeling sorry for yourself, aren't you?"

Darcy forced herself to laugh lightly. "I don't suppose you know anything about chemical polymers?" she asked.

"I'm a computer geek, not a science geek," Lisa replied. "I don't even know what a chemical polymer is."

"Yeah, I'm not sure I do, either, but I've been trying to figure it out."

"Should I ask why?"

"Kerron is concerned about the artificial snow that we're going to be using at Nollick Balley," Darcy explained. "He doesn't want us to use anything that might be dangerous for his animals or crops."

"That makes sense," Lisa replied.

"I know it does, but I don't know enough about the various products out there to be sure what's best to use."

"Surely Alastair has someone on his staff that understands such things," Lisa suggested.

"I'm sure he does. Michael is meant to be handling the whole issue," Darcy told her. "But I'm not entirely sure I trust Alastair to have Kerron's best interests in mind. I feel like I need to know what's happening, to protect the farm."

"You've really fallen for the man, haven't you?" Lisa asked in a teasing voice.

"Not at all," Darcy said quickly. "I'm just trying to do my job."

"But you work for Alastair. Surely your job is to protect his interests, not Kerron Kewley's?"

"Maybe, technically," Darcy said after a moment. "But Kerron trusts me and I can't let him down."

"So aside from studying chemistry, what else is going on with Nollick Balley?" Lisa asked.

"Well, Kerron's father is back from the Algarve and he's going to play Santa for me," Darcy told her.

"Really? What's he like?"

"He seems like a really sweet guy who pretends to be grumpy. I wouldn't want to cross him, for sure, though," Darcy replied. "He's only playing Santa in order to get more money from Alastair. He'd really like to cancel the whole thing, just like Kerron."

"But he already spent the money, right?"

"He did, but from what I've heard, Alastair would struggle to get the money back. It's all very confusing, but I don't think William had the legal right to sign the contract for the event anyway. It looks like Alastair's legal team missed something critical. I'm just glad Kerron is honouring the contract anyway."

"That doesn't sound like the Kerron you've described to me in the past."

"No, it sort of doesn't. He fought everyone so hard about the car park that I was sure he really didn't want the event held at his farm. I can't quite figure out why he's letting it go ahead now."

"Maybe he'll tell you one day," Lisa speculated.

"I'm not sure I want to know," Darcy said with a laugh.

"So when are we going to get together?" Lisa demanded. "I haven't seen you in ages."

"I'm so crazy busy right now, I just don't know," Darcy replied. "Unless you want to come and visit me on-site, it might be a while. I might be able to squeeze in lunch or something one weekend."

"You are coming to Christmas at the Castle, right?"

"I am. I've invited Kerron to come with me, and I sent a ticket to Alastair as well."

"Yikes, that sounds dangerous."

"Not at all. I'm not involved with either of them."

"Do they both know that?"

"I don't know," Darcy said, trying to sound unconcerned.

"Just so you know, Finlo and Andy are both going to be at the preview evening as well," Lisa told her. "The planning committee is inviting everyone who might be willing to donate generously."

"It should be an interesting evening, then, shouldn't it?"

"I'm not sure that interesting is the right word," Lisa replied. "The four of them might get into a huge fight over you."

"Not going to happen," Darcy said airily. "I'm not involved with any of them."

"Maybe Manx National Heritage should auction off a date with you," Lisa said, thoughtfully. "They could make a fortune."

Darcy laughed. "Andy and Alastair might get into a bidding war just because they can. Finlo and I dated for too long for him to waste money on going out with me again, and I don't think Kerron's farm makes much money. He couldn't afford to bid against the others. Anyway, I thought the auction was all about selling the decorated rooms?"

"This year there are going to be two auctions," Lisa told her. "One will be a silent one, where everyone just submits bids, and the other will be the standard one. There will be all sorts of wonderful Christmas-themed prizes in both auctions."

"Well, I'm not prepared to be a prize, but I am willing to donate a few," Darcy said. "How about some family packs of tickets to Nollick Balley for the silent auction?"

"Why didn't I think of that?" Lisa asked. "I'm sure they'd love to have those to offer."

"I can drop them off to you over the weekend," Darcy suggested. "Maybe we could have lunch on Saturday?"

"That sounds good," Lisa replied. "Hubby is going away for the weekend, so if you have the time, we could spend the day together. If you have the time, you could even stay here Saturday night, if you want to."

"Really?" Darcy asked happily. "I'd love that! And I'll find a way to make time."

Lisa laughed. "I miss you as well," she told her friend. "Hubby leaves at nine on Saturday morning and you're welcome to stay at my house from any time after that until Sunday afternoon at five."

"I'll be there some time Saturday morning," Darcy told her. "I won't promise how early, as I've been having a lot of late nights, and I might lie in a bit."

"Saturday night will be a late one," Lisa said. "We'll be up giggling and talking all night, won't we?"

"I certainly hope so."

Looking forward to her weekend made the week seem to drag for Darcy, but she had so much to get done at the farm that in some ways that was a good thing. The site was coming together beautifully, and by Friday she was happy to let herself have the weekend off.

Michael had sent a brief note about the snow midweek, simply saying he was looking at the options, so that was all she could tell Kerron. He didn't appear on-site all week, so she sent him an email on Friday to keep him up to date.

That night she took a long hot bath and then painted her nails and gave herself a facial. She woke up early on Saturday, feeling as excited as she had when she was ten and she was going to sleep over at her best friend's house. It didn't take her nearly long enough to pack up an overnight bag, so after breakfast she drove into Douglas and walked along the promenade until it was late enough to head to Lisa's little house. It was a lovely November day, cool and dry.

When Lisa opened her door, the two friends hugged for a long time.

"I can't wait for January," Lisa said as she ushered Darcy into the house. "I was worried that my marriage might change things between us, but really, your job is keeping us apart more than my husband is."

"I know," Darcy said apologetically. "I love what I'm doing, but I do miss you awfully."

"It isn't forever," Lisa replied. "I just hope your next job won't take up as much of your time as this one does."

"When I worked for Finlo, I travelled all the time," Darcy reminded her friend. "At least now I'm on the island."

"I suppose," Lisa said, shrugging. "But enough about that stuff, tell me all about everything that you've done since the last time we talked."

Darcy laughed and then the pair curled up on Lisa's couch and talked for hours. When their stomachs were growling too much to ignore, they headed out to the closest coffee shop and had a quick lunch.

"I want to go out for a really nice dinner," Lisa said. "Some place really fancy."

"I haven't been out to eat in a long time," Darcy was quick to agree. "I don't know if I brought the right outfit, though."

"You still have a bunch of things in my spare room," Lisa reminded her.

After lunch they walked into Douglas and did a lot of window shopping and a little bit of actual purchasing. Back at Lisa's, Darcy found an ice blue dress she'd forgotten she owned in the wardrobe in Lisa's second bedroom. There was a jacket there as well that went with the dress perfectly, and several different pairs of shoes for her to chose from.

"You're going to want me to clear out that wardrobe one day, aren't you?" she asked her friend when she joined her in Lisa's sitting room.

"One day," Lisa agreed. "But not yet."

Lisa was wearing a little black dress that Darcy immediately loved.

"I've never seen that dress before," she exclaimed. "It's perfect for you."

"I bought it when we were on our honeymoon," Lisa explained. "It turns out hubby doesn't mind a little bit of shopping. He likes to feel as if he's spoiling me."

"Well, whichever of you picked it out, it was a great choice."

"He did, actually," Lisa admitted.

The pair walked back down to the promenade to Lisa's favourite Italian restaurant. They got a quiet table in the back and ordered a feast. They ate slowly, laughing and talking until nearly midnight.

"We should get a taxi," Darcy suggested, only half teasing. "I feel as I'm going to have to waddle home. I ate too much."

"That's why we're going to walk," Lisa told her firmly. "We both need to burn off a few calories."

"I can't imagine that the walk back to your house will burn many," Darcy argued.

"It's all uphill," Lisa pointed out.

"Yeah, that's why we should take a taxi," Darcy muttered in reply.

The walk was a short one and Darcy only grumbled about half the way. Back at Lisa's, both women changed into their pyjamas, and then they snuggled up on the couch together and continued their conversation. It was only when Lisa fell asleep in the middle of a sentence that they reluctantly headed to bed. They both slept late the next day and then Darcy insisted on treating Lisa to brunch before she headed for home.

"I'm hoping to have an answer for Kerron about the snow," she told Darcy. "Although I doubt Michael is working over the weekend."

"Well, good luck," Lisa told her. "If I don't see you before, I guess I'll see you at the castle."

"Definitely," Darcy replied.

When Darcy fired up her laptop, she found that she did have a message from Michael. What it said made her frown.

Alastair is dealing with the artificial snow himself. Tell Mr. Kewley to contact Alastair directly with any concerns.

❧ 13 ❧

T he rest of the month rushed past as work on the site continued. By the time the preview evening for Christmas at the Castle arrived, Nollick Balley was just about ready to open. Darcy had her staff in place and was working on training everyone to meet her very high standards. The only thing missing was the artificial snow, but Michael assured Darcy that it would be delivered in plenty of time.

"Alastair has ordered it. There's just a small shipping delay," he told Darcy when she rang to ask him about it for the third time. "We have a week," he reminded her as well.

At four o'clock that afternoon Darcy stood in the middle of the site and turned in a slow, full circle. Everything looked just right, almost exactly the way she'd imagined it. They'd had to make a few small changes, here and there, but for the most part she felt as if she'd shrunk down inside Alastair's model, with some very important improvements.

She walked along the row where the food vendors would be setting up, beginning over the weekend. The grand opening was set for midday Monday, the eighth of December. Nollick Balley would be open daily until the 31st of December, except for Christmas Day, and Darcy knew it was going to be a long month as she drove back and forth every day from Castletown.

Now she glanced at her watch. She needed to get to Lisa's to get ready for Christmas at the Castle. Lisa wasn't even going to be there; she was already at Castle Rushen, helping with last-minute issues and with ticket sales. As Lisa had installed the ticketing system, she wanted to make sure everything ran smoothly. Because Darcy lived in Castletown, stopping in Douglas to get ready made little sense, but she was doing it to avoid Alastair. He'd rung her early in the week to check on the arrangements for the night.

"So what time do I pick you up?" he'd asked.

"I don't know when I'll get finished for the day at Nollick Balley," she replied. "It will be much easier if you just meet me at the castle."

"But I won't know anyone."

"Everyone will be very friendly," Darcy told him. "Especially once they find out who you are. Your reputation precedes you."

Alastair's chuckle sounded arrogant to Darcy and had her shaking her head as he wound up the call. "I guess I'll see you there, then."

"Not if I can help it," Darcy had muttered into the dead phone.

Now she was regretting inviting the man at all. She just hoped he would be generous to Manx National Heritage to make up for her having to spend time with him.

She headed towards her car. A quick stop at the Kewley farmhouse to drop off Kerron's ticket and she'd be on her way to Douglas. Just before she reached her car, she heard the sound of a vehicle approaching.

"Now what?" Darcy sighed. She was eager to get away and the last thing she wanted to deal with just then was another problem. When Kerron pulled up in one of his huge farm machines, she forced herself to smile at him.

"Please don't tell me something's wrong," she greeted him.

"I don't think so," Kerron replied with a chuckle. "I just wasn't sure what the arrangements were for tonight, and you aren't answering your texts."

Darcy frowned and pulled out her phone. There were three unread texts from Kerron on it. "I'm so sorry," she said. "It's been crazy here today, but I usually check my phone every half hour or so. I guess I was distracted."

"Everything looks great," Kerron said, his tone surprised. He looked around and Darcy could tell he wasn't missing a thing as he studied the site.

"It does feel rather magical," Darcy told him. "Once the snow arrives, it will be perfect."

"When does that get here?" Kerron asked.

"Any day now," Darcy replied. "Apparently Alastair ordered it and it will be here; it's just taking a bit of extra time."

"I do hope Alastair is going to deliver on what he promised me," Kerron said seriously. "We're hoping to get some sections of the farm certified as organic, and the wrong snow could seriously upset that."

"I'm sure it will be fine," Darcy lied brightly.

"You aren't, are you?" Kerron asked, staring hard at her.

"I don't entirely trust Alastair," Darcy admitted. "But he's not going to risk ruining everything here at this late date."

"Or so you hope," Kerron muttered.

"Yeah, so I hope," Darcy agreed.

"Anyway, what time are we due in Castletown?"

"The event officially starts at six, but no one will be there much before seven," Darcy told him.

"Don't you need to get ready, then?"

"I do. I was just about to head out for that very reason."

"If you have your things with you, you're welcome to get ready at the house," Kerron offered. "Then I can follow you down to your flat and we can go to the castle together. I don't really want to walk in alone. I won't know a soul."

Darcy hesitated for a moment and then smiled. "That sounds like a good plan," she replied. "I do have my things. I was supposed to be getting ready with a friend, but she's actually gone down to the castle early, so I may as well get ready at your place, if you're sure you don't mind."

"Not even a little bit," Kerron said with a wicked grin. "But we'd better hurry. I'd hate for you to run out of time."

"I am a muddy mess," Darcy laughed, looking down at her dirty clothes. "I'm actually quite used to being a mess at the end of every day, though."

"Nothing like being an air hostess, then?" Kerron teased.

"Much more fun and way more satisfying," Darcy replied.

As she drove behind the tractor back to Kerron's house, she thought about what she'd said. It was absolutely true. She loved her new job, and now that everything was coming together it was incredibly satisfying to see what she'd managed to organise. She was really looking forward to opening day and seeing to the excited children enjoying her hard work. She parked at the farm and then pulled out her phone quickly.

A few taps of the keypad told her that forty-seven per cent of the tickets for Nollick Balley had now been sold, an increase of seven per cent over the morning. She only let herself check the numbers twice a day, so now she put her phone away and grabbed her overnight bag from the boot. For the rest of the evening she would try hard not to think about Nollick Balley. Tonight was about having fun at one of the island's most popular Christmas traditions.

Kerron let her into the house and motioned towards the stairs. "You know where the spare room is," he told her. "I'll be ready in half an hour, but I don't expect you to be."

Darcy laughed. "Give me more like an hour," she suggested. "I'll be ready to go by six, give or take a few minutes."

"I'll see you then."

Darcy headed up the stairs and quickly shut herself up in the spare room. Marion was probably at her sister's house, but Darcy couldn't help but wonder where Wiliam Kewley was tonight. She took a shower and washed her hair with her favourite shampoo, and then she smoothed on a layer of body lotion in her favourite scent all over. Her dress was black velvet, with silver sequins in an almost random pattern that seemed to suggest stars or snowflakes but weren't exactly either. She slid on matching silver shoes and then concentrated on her hair and makeup. A coat of quick-drying nail varnish in silver finished her look, and once she was done she stood in front of the mirror on the back of the bathroom door and studied herself. After a full minute, she shrugged.

"You'll just have to do," she told herself firmly. She'd always been supremely confident in her looks, and the odd whisper of worry bothered her. It's just been too long since you went out anywhere, she told herself as she packed her muddy clothes into her overnight bag. Dressing up used to be an every night occurrence, especially when she had been dating Finlo. She was surprised to realise that she didn't really miss it. Now she headed down the stairs, suddenly conscious that her high heels hurt her feet. She'd been spending all of her time at the farm in either trainers or Wellington boots. The high heels felt strange.

"You look amazing," Kerron said as she walked into the kitchen.

"You look pretty good, too," Darcy replied, trying to hide the surprise in her voice. Kerron was wearing a black suit that appeared to have been made for him. It fit perfectly over his muscular build. His shirt was a bright Christmassy red and his black tie had a very slender red stripe that matched it exactly.

"You thought I'd be wearing jeans and a T-shirt?" Kerron asked, his tone teasing.

"I didn't expect you to own anything that fancy," Darcy replied honestly.

"I'm a businessman as well as a farmer," he replied. "I actually go to a lot of meetings with bankers and investors and the like. I like to make a good first impression. Then, if the next time they see me I'm covered in mud, they know I don't always look like that."

Darcy nodded. "If you dress like that, I'm sure it works well," she told him. "That's a gorgeous suit."

"It should be," a voice came from the doorway. "He paid more for that suit than I paid for my first car."

Darcy turned and smiled at Kerron's father. "It was worth every penny," she told the man. "I'm feeling quite intimidated by him."

William chuckled. "In that dress? No one will notice Kerron. He could wear anything or nothing at all."

Darcy laughed. "I think everyone would notice if he turned up naked," she told him. "But I'm glad you like my dress."

"It's very sparkly," William said. "And very Christmassy."

"That was what I was hoping for," Darcy replied.

"And we'd better get going or we'll be late," Kerron interrupted. He came around the table and offered Darcy his arm. She took it and walked slowly out of the kitchen with him. William followed them to the door.

"You go and have a good time, then," he said. "I'm going to watch some old movies that Kerron doesn't like."

"You're welcome to join us," Darcy said. "I'm sure we can get you a ticket."

"Nah, it's too fancy for me," he told her. "I was at the very first one, some fifteen or so years ago. That was enough Christmas at the Castle for me for at least twenty years."

Darcy laughed and then she and Kerron walked out into the crisp evening. He walked her to his car.

"Give me your address and I'll meet you there," he said. "I have to get my car out of the garage and I don't want to hold you up."

Darcy jotted the address on a card for him and then watched as he walked away. He not only looked incredible, he smelled amazing. She'd have to ask him what cologne he wore. It smelled clean and fresh, with a hint of spice and something else that reminded Darcy of pine trees. Darcy wasn't sure exactly what it was, but she absolutely loved it.

She drove away from the farm and headed for home, wondering what sort of car Kerron owned. She'd only ever seen him driving farm machinery. She finally decided that he probably had some sort of estate car that would be useful for hauling small loads and whatnot. She parked at her building and sat in the car, waiting for Kerron.

A few minutes later a sleek black sports car pulled into her car park. It looked a lot like Finlo's car, but Darcy was sure it was a newer model. She couldn't help but watch to see who climbed out of it. Her jaw dropped when Kerron emerged.

"I wasn't expecting that car," Darcy told him as she crossed the car park.

"It's my toy," he told her. "We had a couple of very good years and after I bought my father out I treated myself to this. I don't get to drive it nearly enough, but I still love it."

"It's gorgeous," Darcy said, running a hand along the top.

"Thanks, hop in."

Darcy slid into the passenger seat and sighed. The car smelled of expensive leather and Kerron's cologne. It was a heady combination.

"Did you want to drive?" Kerron asked after he'd slid behind the wheel.

"You'd let me drive your car?" Darcy gasped.

"Sure, why not?"

"Because it's your baby."

Kerron chuckled. "It's a great car and I do love it, but it doesn't make owning it any less special if I let someone else drive it once in a while."

Darcy thought about for a minute and then shook her head. "I'd love to drive it someday," she told him. "But tonight we have to get somewhere. When I take it for a drive, I want to be able to drive for hours."

Kerron laughed. "Remind me," he told her.

"I will," Darcy said.

The drive to the castle was a short one and Kerron found a parking space not far from the castle entrance.

"I thought we'd have to park miles away," he told Darcy as they climbed the steps to the castle entrance.

"It's not quite seven yet," Darcy replied. "We've just beaten the rush."

Darcy found the tickets in her handbag and handed them to the man at the entrance. He gave them each a copy of the programme that explained the evening's events.

"Welcome to Christmas at the Castle," the man said. "I won't take up too much of your time, but I will tell you a few things about the event. Tonight is the preview evening and then the castle will open for the next three weekends for tours. Nearly every room in the castle has been decorated by a different local charity. As you exit the tour, you'll be asked to vote for your favourite rooms, and the top three guest favourites win a portion of the profits from the tickets sold for their charity."

"Wait until you see the rooms," Darcy told Kerron. "You'd think voting would be easy, but every year it gets more difficult as the charities get increasingly creative and competitive."

"They do indeed," the man agreed. "Tonight's event mostly raises funds for Manx National Heritage itself. There is a silent auction as well as a traditional auction. The most popular items up for bid are always the contents of the different rooms. Unlike most of the items being auctioned, for the rooms each charity gets the proceeds from the sale of their room, and some do extremely well."

Darcy laughed. "Last year two very wealthy women both fell in love with one particular room and the bidding got absolutely crazy. The winner ended up paying about ten times what the actual decorations were worth. It was crazy, but wonderful for the charity involved."

"Those two ladies are both here again tonight," the man told her. "We're hoping they'll both like the same room again."

"What else happens tonight?" Kerron asked.

"Food and drink, music and folk dancing, and lots of opportunities to donate to Manx National Heritage," the man said.

Kerron nodded. "I think I'm ready to see for myself," he said.

"Excellent, and Nollick Ghennal to you both," the man said with a bright smile.

"Nollick Ghennal," Darcy replied.

They made their way into the castle's courtyard, where large outdoor heaters had been set up to take the chill from the air. Darcy found Lisa in the small crowd and headed straight for her.

She quickly introduced Lisa to Kerron. "It's nice to meet you," Lisa said. "I've heard so much about you."

Kerron raised an eyebrow and gave Darcy a quizzical look. "I hope at least some of it was good," he replied.

"Oh, at least some of it was," Lisa shot back.

Darcy grabbed a glass of wine from a passing waiter and took a quick sip. A moment later she heard someone calling her name.

"Ah, Darcy, there you are," Finlo Quayle called from across the courtyard. "I knew you'd be here somewhere."

She turned to watch his approach. Just before he reached them, Kerron turned and slid his arm around Darcy. She felt herself blushing, but she didn't try to step away.

"Darling, you look amazing, as always," Finlo said when he reached her. He ignored Kerron and leaned in to kiss Darcy's cheek. She felt herself stiffen as she waited to see how Kerron was going to react.

"Always nice to see you on the island, Finlo," Kerron said easily. "I know you're usually too busy flying to exotic places to spend time here."

"I try to spend Christmas on the island," Finlo replied. "But I always spend New Year's Eve in Paris. It's truly special, isn't it, Darcy?"

Darcy sighed. She hated when men behaved stupidly over her. "It was fun the year I went," she conceded. "But that's ancient history."

Finlo chuckled. "It doesn't have to be," he told Darcy in a low voice. "Always nice to see you as well," he said to Kerron. Before either of them replied, he turned and disappeared back into the crowd.

"I didn't know you knew Finlo," Darcy said to Kerron as soon as the man was gone.

"We went to school together for a while," Kerron told her. "We weren't friends by any means, but we're friendly."

Darcy spotted Andy Kenyon in the crowd and deliberately turned away. She wasn't interested in talking with him. As she turned, she noticed that he had a beautiful blonde on his arm, and felt a rush of relief. At least he'd moved on, even if Finlo didn't seem to have done so yet.

"You should go around the castle before it gets busy," Lisa said now. "I've been around about ten times already, but I'll go with you if you want."

"Shouldn't you be with your hubby?" Darcy asked.

"I probably should find him," Lisa said with a grin. "I need to make sure he isn't putting in crazy bids for things we don't need."

"Good luck with that," Darcy laughed. "Shall we go and see the decorations, then?" she asked Kerron.

"Sure," he replied with a good-natured shrug.

They made their way to the castle entrance, and Darcy grabbed a sheet that showed who had decorated each room and what the theme of each space was meant to be. The first room had an American theme, and Darcy smiled at trees decorated with American flags and topped with small copies of the Statue of Liberty.

"The woman who runs the charity that decorated this room is American," Darcy told Kerron. "She usually tries to play that down, but I guess this year she decided to embrace it."

"It's different, but I kind of like it," Kerron said. "I wouldn't want it in my house, but it's attractive in its own way."

They wandered through rooms themed to a couple of the most recent children's movies, fairies, unicorns, and one that was a tribute to the traditional Father Christmas. After the throne room, which had been decorated by Manx National Heritage to an "old Manx Christmas" theme, the last few rooms were done by colour schemes. Darcy stopped in the centre of a purple and fuchsia room and shook her head.

"It's just too much," she said, waving a hand at fuchsia feathers that topped dark purple trees.

"I hate it," Kerron said frankly.

Darcy laughed. "I won't be bidding on this one. I wonder if anyone will?"

"So which one was your favourite?" Kerron asked her as they finished their tour.

"Probably the old Manx Christmas, but we can't vote for that one," Darcy replied as she took a voting slip from the girl at the exit.

"Why not?"

"Manx National Heritage isn't eligible to win any of the prizes," the girl replied for Darcy.

"Well, I would have voted for them if I could," Kerron said. "Now I'll have to think about it."

"It's still quiet," the girl said. "You can sneak back through if want a second look at any of the rooms."

"I'll just look through the list," Kerron replied. "I'm sure I'll remember them well enough."

"Well, I want another look at a few," Darcy said. "I won't be long."

She dashed back up the stairs, determined to vote for the very best room in the castle. She found herself retracing her steps almost to the very first room. As she turned around a corner, she heard voices. It seemed as if a large group was on their way in.

"All of the decorations are being auctioned off, Mr. Breckinridge," Darcy heard someone say. Alastair was the last person she wanted to see right now, so Darcy turned back around. The crowd seemed to be moving rather quickly on her heels, so she increased her pace as she reached the throne room.

A strange noise behind her had her stopping in the doorway on her way out of the room. She smiled back at the beautiful woman in the stunning period costume who had just entered the room and taken a seat on one of the thrones. Alastair's voice booming down the corridor had her rushing away without speaking to the new arrival. Back at the exit, Kerron was chatting easily with the young woman at the door.

"Have you figured out your favourite, then?" the girl asked Darcy.

"I have," Darcy replied. She quickly filled in her voting slip and then folded it in half and handed it to the girl. "Thank you."

"Shall we?" she asked Kerron, taking his arm and practically dragging him out of the room.

"Is there a rush?" Kerron asked as Darcy hurried him back into the courtyard.

"There's a huge group behind me, that's all," Darcy replied, glancing back over her shoulder.

"Didn't someone say there was food?" Kerron asked her.

"There's a finger buffet in the outer courtyard," a passing member of staff told him.

"So that's where we need to go next," Kerron told Darcy. "I didn't get any dinner."

"I didn't, either," Darcy told him. The pair headed out to the courtyard and fixed themselves plates of food.

"It looks quiet over there," Kerron said, gesturing towards a corner of the space.

Darcy took a glass of wine from a passing waiter and then followed Kerron across the courtyard. They stood and chatted about nothing much as they watched the crowd and enjoyed their food.

After half an hour and a second serving of the delicious finger foods, Darcy was ready to head for home. Her feet hurt, she was tired of smiling and she didn't want to run into Alastair, either. She was just about to suggest skipping the auction and escaping when she heard her name being called.

"Darcy, there you are," Alastair's voice boomed across the court-yard. "I've been looking all over for you."

"We were just having some food," Darcy replied. "You remember Kerron Kewley?"

"Oh, yes, I've been flooded by emails from you lately," Alastair said to Kerron. "You're very concerned about snow, as I recall."

"I'm very concerned about the chemicals you might be putting into my soil," Kerron replied. "After Nollick Balley is over, I still have a farm to run."

"Yes, yes, well, I'm sure whatever we've ordered will be just fine," Alastair said, waving a hand. "But when does the auction start? All this standing around is getting dull. I want to spend some money."

Darcy glanced at her programme. "You have about ten minutes more to wait," she told the man. "What are you going to bid on?"

Alastair shrugged. "I'll buy a few rooms worth of decorations, just because it's a good cause," he told her. "And I've put in a bunch of silent bids on the various Christmas hampers. Those are excellent to give out this time of year to staff and suppliers and the like."

"We haven't actually been in to look at the auction yet," Darcy said. "We'd better get in and get our bids registered before they close the silent bidding and start the real thing."

She began to lead Kerron away, but stopped when Alastair touched her shoulder.

"Smart plan, playing up to him until after Nollick Balley is over," he whispered in her ear. "Just remember that our flight leaves from London on the first of January. Maybe I should change that. Would you like to spend New Year's Eve in Lanzarote as well?"

Darcy shook her head and opened her mouth to tell him she wasn't going anywhere with him, but just then a voice came over the tannoy.

Ladies and Gentlemen, you have exactly ten more minutes to submit your bids for the silent auction. Once bids are closed, we will be starting our tradi-tional auction, which includes all of the decorated rooms, as well as flights for two to any European destination courtesy of Quayle Airways, a sixty-inch flat screen television and many other wonderful prizes.

"We'd better go," Darcy said to Kerron, ignoring Alastair completely.

The auction was set up in the large gift shop at the back of the site. Darcy bid on a few small items, doubting that her bid would be enough to win anything, but wanting to try. She and Kerron met back up in the back of the room.

"Did you bid for much?" she asked him.

"One or two little things," he said with a shrug. "But I saw a few items from the traditional auction I might like."

"Starting with the huge telly?" Darcy guessed.

"Nah, ours is big enough," Kerron told her with a laugh.

"Darcy, did you see the necklace?" Lisa asked when she suddenly appeared next to them.

"What necklace?"

"It came from someone's estate," Lisa told her. "One of the jewellers in Douglas bought all of the jewellery from the estate and donated this necklace to MNH for tonight's auction. It isn't anything overly special, but there was something about it that I thought you would like."

Darcy quickly followed her friend to the front of the room. The necklace was revolving slowly inside a small display case. Darcy studied it for a moment.

"I see what you mean," she told Lisa. "I love it, but I can't tell you why."

It was basically a very thick, flattened gold wire bent into an irregular circle. At spaces along the wire, small and unusually shaped stones had been set inside irregularly shaped holes.

"It looks like something you'd wear," Kerron told her.

"I'd definitely wear it," Darcy replied. "I wonder how much it will go for."

"Only one way to find out," Lisa said.

She headed off to find her husband while Kerron and Darcy made their way to seats near the back. As they sat down, Kerron's mobile went off. He glanced at the screen and then excused himself for a moment. By the time he got back, the bidding had started on the first item. Darcy felt as if she were sitting on the edge of her seat as the necklace came up for auction.

Kerron glanced at her and then put in a starting bid of a hundred pounds. It seemed as if Finlo was watching and he quickly doubled it. As Darcy sat stunned, Finlo, Kerron, and Alastair began a round robin of bidding that drove the price of the necklace up very quickly.

"Stop," she whispered to Kerron after a short while. "Even if you win, I would never let you buy me anything that expensive."

"Who said I was buying it for you?" Kerron replied.

Darcy blushed. "Oh, of course, I'm sorry," she stammered, feeling foolish.

Kerron laughed. "I was going to buy it for you," he admitted. "But the price has gone a bit higher than I expected."

"Never mind," Darcy said. "Finlo and Alastair are just being stupid. I won't let either of them give me anything like that, either."

After Kerron dropped out, Finlo and Alastair both seemed to lose interest quite quickly. Darcy was just wondering which one of them was going to get stuck with the necklace when the auctioneer announced that they had a phone bid that was higher. When neither Finlo nor Alastair increased their bid, the necklace was sold to the absentee phone bidder.

"Well, that was probably for the best," Darcy said.

"Indeed," Kerron replied, barely paying attention. The next item up for auction was a sightseeing trip to the Calf of Man, and he was focussed on that.

"You want to go to the Calf?" Darcy asked.

"I've never been and neither has my dad. I thought it would be perfect Christmas gift for him. We can go in the spring when they first start the trips back up, before dad goes back to Portugal."

Darcy bit her lip. She didn't see the appeal of the Calf, a tiny and uninhabited island off the southern tip of the island, but if Kerron wanted to go and take his father there, that was his business. After a few exciting minutes, Kerron won the trip and Darcy was amazed at how delighted he seemed.

They sat and watched the rest of the auction quietly. Darcy was pleased to see just how much money was raised for Manx National Heritage and the various charities. Unfortunately, the two women who'd overbid the previous year preferred different rooms this time around, but bidding still went high enough to please the representatives from the various charities who were in attendance. Darcy noticed that Alastair bought several rooms, often bidding against Finlo, who managed to drive up the prices many times but never actually bought anything himself.

When the auction was finished, waiters immediately began circulating with champagne. Darcy took a glass and downed it in a single swallow.

"I think I've had enough excitement for tonight," she told Kerron. "I don't suppose you're ready to go?"

"I was ready as soon as I won my dad's present," he told her with a laugh. "Let me go and pay for it and we can be on our way."

Darcy found Lisa in the crowd and gave her a hug.

"Sorry you didn't win the necklace," Lisa told her.

"A small blip in my otherwise perfect life," Darcy replied, laughing.

"I suppose you're too busy to get together any time soon," Lisa said.

"I really am, but you'll be at the grand opening of Nollick Balley, right?"

"We wouldn't miss it for the world," Lisa assured her.

Darcy skirted the crowd, managing to avoid Finlo, Alastair and Andy as she headed towards the exit. Kerron caught up with her just before she made it to the courtyard. He wordlessly offered his arm and she took it happily. Neither spoke as they drove back to Darcy's flat.

Kerron insisted on walking Darcy to her door. "Thank you for inviting me. It turned out to be an interesting evening."

"I'm glad you enjoyed it," Darcy replied. "And I'm glad you found a present for your father."

Kerron looked as if he were going to speak again, but instead he wrapped his arms around Darcy and pulled her close. She opened her mouth to say something, she wasn't sure what, but he pressed his lips to hers and she got lost in the fireworks. After several minutes, Kerron lifted his head.

"Sleep well," he whispered before he released her and turned away.

Darcy stared after him, unable to speak. By the time she'd recovered from the earth-shattering kiss, Kerron had disappeared into the lift. She shook her head and let herself into her flat.

"No more kissing that man," she told her reflection sternly as she washed her face. The face in the mirror didn't look convinced.

❧ 14 ☙

In spite of the late evening, Darcy was at the Kewley farm early the next morning. The food vendors were starting to arrive and Darcy wanted to make sure that everything went smoothly. Aside from a few small niggles, things went almost exactly to Darcy's plan.

She spent much of the early part of the week handling publicity. She did a few radio interviews for the local stations, spent hours with a reporter from the local newspaper telling him all about the event and supervised a couple of "elves" who passed out flyers and discount coupons in the centre of Douglas. Ticket sales were brisk and Darcy was excited when opening day got close to selling out. Everything seemed to be coming together perfectly.

On Thursday she headed up to the Kewley farm. She hadn't been there since the weekend and she needed to see for herself that everything was still on track at the site. She parked along the road and walked slowly around the entire field. The builders were just putting the finishing touches on the last of the buildings. The reindeer were already in their stalls, and she stopped for a quick chat with their owner.

"I hope they're settling in well," she told the middle-aged man who was spreading hay around the large fenced area for the animals.

"They seem to be," he said with a shrug. "I've brought the friendliest animals I have, but they're still pretty much wild animals. I don't know about letting the little ones pet them."

"We don't have to do that," Darcy told him. "They'll be happy to get to see them. They're Santa's reindeer, after all."

"Well, I hope you're right. I'd hate for some little person to get bit by one of them. Maybe we need another fence between them and the public."

Darcy took a step back and looked at the enclosure. She could see the man's point. The chain-link fence between the deer and the public was just about perfect for little hands to slip inside. She pulled out her mobile and rang George. He was there within minutes.

"Now that the reindeer are actually here, we're a little worried about children getting nibbled on," she told the man. "Can we put another fence around the whole enclosure? It doesn't have to be anything more than a few boards, but it needs to create a buffer zone between the kids and the deer."

George looked at the deer and grinned. "They don't look over-friendly," he commented. "I think an extra fence is a good idea. I can have it done in an hour. We've a lot of fencing left over from the build, anyway. It won't take long to get it set up around the enclosure."

Darcy smiled and moved on, happy to have solved at least one little problem. A couple of food vendors had questions that she answered easily, and then she bought herself a snack as well from the one vendor who was all set up and ready to go.

"You're doing well today," she laughed, as nearly all the other vendors began to queue up behind her at the stand.

"Aye, getting set up is hungry work and no one else wants to have to clean up from just a few customers. I don't mind, though. This time of year, any customers are a blessing."

After lunch she stuck her head into the training session for the elves. It was important that they strike the right balance between giving guests a wonderful and fun experience and keeping a close eye on everyone's safety.

"Our only concern is Santa," George told Darcy. "He hasn't turned up for his training."

Darcy frowned and pulled out her mobile again. When William didn't answer her call, she rang Kerron.

"Your father hasn't come down for his training session," she told him after a quick greeting.

"I'm not sure he's going to want to do that," Kerron replied.

"He's not having second thoughts about playing Santa, is he?" Darcy asked. "I don't know where I'd get another Santa at this late date."

"I'll talk to him," Kerron promised. "Do you want me to send him down there now if I can persuade him to go?"

"Yes, please," Darcy said emphatically.

"And how are you?" Kerron asked just before Darcy disconnected.

"Oh, I'm okay, just really busy," Darcy replied. "And really quite worried about Santa."

"I'll try to get him to come over," Kerron told her. "Hang in there."

As she disconnected, Darcy suddenly thought that she should have asked Kerron how he was doing. It was too late now; she couldn't exactly ring him back to do so. She sighed and dropped the phone into her bag. Work was taking over her entire life. She'd feel much better once opening day had come and gone, assuming the artificial snow ever arrived.

She turned and looked over the entire site. It looked wonderful, but nowhere near as Christmas-like as it would look covered in a blanket of snow. Michael had promised that it was on its way, but time was running out. As much as she wanted to ring him to ask again, she resisted, knowing she was annoying him with the repeated phone calls. They'd worked really well together up to this point, but the snow was causing serious problems. The real problem was that Alastair had insisted on taking charge of that one little thing and Darcy couldn't help but feel that he'd let her down.

The sound of an approaching tractor put all thoughts of artificial snow out of her head. She waved to William Kewley as he approached.

"Kerron said I have to come down and be taught to go 'ho, ho, ho,' and other complicated Santa tasks," he told Darcy when he reached her side. "I told him I'd better be getting paid for my training time."

Darcy laughed. "You're getting paid," she assured him. "But there is a lot to go over. You wouldn't believe the health and safety issues that Alastair's solicitors are insisting all staff members have to be briefed on."

"No way," William groaned. "Maybe you need to find a new Santa."

"Nope," Darcy said, patting his arm and then leading him towards the castle where the elf supervisor was working. "Just sit and listen for a few hours. It won't be that bad and I'll buy you a drink after."

William looked as if he was going to object, but Darcy pulled open the castle door and dragged him inside. She quickly introduced him to George and then dashed out again before William could follow.

A couple of hours later, having dealt with a few other minor issues, Darcy headed back towards the castle. Her mobile rang just before she got there.

"Your snow will be arriving on Saturday," Michael told her without preamble. "It's on the early morning ferry."

"Thank goodness," Darcy exclaimed. "That doesn't give up much time to get it spread out all over the site, but we'll manage."

"Excellent. Alastair and I will be arriving on Sunday evening for Monday's grand opening. We're staying at the Island Plaza Hotel in Douglas."

Of course you are, Darcy thought. The Island Plaza was the most expensive hotel on the island. Alastair would probably find it lacking in some way, however.

"I hope everything is going well there?"

"Everything is great," Darcy assured him. "Santa's just about finished up his training and all of the elves and other staff are ready. We're just putting an extra row of fencing around the reindeer so we don't have to worry about children putting their hands through the fences, and I think we'll be ready, aside from the snow."

"It's a good thing that's on the way, then," Michael said with a laugh. "Before I forget in all the excitement of the next couple of days, you've done a wonderful job with this. Ticket presales are exceeding our expectations and everything seems to have been planned to the tiniest detail. You've surprised me enormously and I hope I have the privilege of working with you again on something else one day."

"Thank you for the kind words. I've really enjoyed working with you as well, but save any additional praise for after opening day," Darcy said. "There's still a lot that could go badly wrong."

"But it won't, because you've planned for every possible contingency," Michael replied. "If you don't need me between now and then, I'll see you on Monday morning."

"Excellent," Darcy replied. She disconnected and dropped her phone in her bag. She turned around and gasped as she nearly tripped over William Kewley.

"There, I did my training, okay?" he asked grumpily.

"Excellent," Darcy said with a bright smile. "I believe I owe you a drink."

"I'm sure I deserve one," he shot back. "Let's take your car and head to the pub down the road."

"What about the tractor you drove over here in?" Darcy asked.

"Ah, Kerron can worry about that later," William said with a shrug. "I'm thirsty."

Darcy laughed and then quickly checked in with George. Everything seemed to be coming together nicely, so Darcy headed off with William to get him the promised drink.

He directed her to a small pub that was on the corner of the nearest main road. When they walked in, the bartender called a greeting to William.

"She's way too good for you," he said, looking Darcy up and down.

Darcy flushed as William chuckled. "She's my boss," he told the man.

"I never thought I'd see you happy working for a woman," the man said.

"I never thought I'd work for a woman that looks like her," William shot back.

Darcy thought briefly about being offended by their words, but they were clearly good-natured and she didn't think they were at all serious. William ordered a pint and then turned to Darcy.

"What would you like?" he asked.

"Just a fizzy drink, I'm afraid," Darcy replied. "I'm driving, after all."

The bartender didn't comment as he got their drinks.

"Put it on my tab," William told the man.

"I said I'd buy you a drink," Darcy reminded him.

"You can get the next round," William said airily.

He walked over to a small corner table and Darcy followed. She was surprised when he held out her chair for her, but she sat down as gracefully as she could.

"So, how do you like working for Alastair Breckinridge?" William asked after he'd taken a big drink.

Darcy sipped her soda while she thought about how she wanted to reply. "I'm loving my job," she said eventually. "Bringing Nollick Balley to life has been amazing. I'm less fond of Alastair, but I've not really worked that much with him. His assistant, Michael, has been good to work with."

"And what's going on with you and my son?" William demanded.

Darcy nearly choked on her drink. By the time she'd stopped coughing, she'd figured out what she wanted to say. "You really should ask Kerron that question," she told him.

William shook his head. "Look, you seem like a really nice girl and you've done much better with this Christmas village thing than I thought you would, but you're all wrong for Kerron."

"Really? What makes you say that?" Darcy tried to keep her voice calm, but she could hear repressed emotion in her words.

"You're gorgeous. I've no doubt you turn heads everywhere you go. Heck, half the men in here are staring at you, and most of them can barely see."

Darcy glanced around and then smiled. There were six men scattered around the dark room and three of them were, indeed, staring at her, or at least in her direction. If she had to guess, she'd have picked William as the youngest one there, aside from the fifty-something bartender who was doing a crossword puzzle behind the bar and ignoring her completely.

"I'm not sure what that has to do with Kerron," Darcy said quietly.

"I married a woman like you," William replied. "She was gorgeous. I can still see her face when I close my eyes. It's burned into my brain. She was a blonde with these enormous blue eyes that seemed to go right through me. I was lost the first time I saw her and she seemed to feel the same about me."

Darcy tried to remember what Kerron had told her about his mother. It hadn't been a happy story, that much she was sure of.

"I'm sorry," she said, feeling as if it wasn't exactly the right thing to say.

William waved a hand. "It was a long time ago," he told her. "But it still hurts," he admitted. "We'd only been married a few years. Kerron was just little and I was hoping for another baby. I may have pushed her a little bit, tried too hard to persuade her. I don't know. She'd really struggled to get her figure back after Kerron and she didn't want to go through it all again. I told her it didn't matter to me if she got fat. I loved her no matter what." He sighed deeply.

"Kerron told me she left you both," Darcy said softly.

"She did," he agreed. "She started going out with her friends more and more and then she met a man. He loved her because she was beautiful and he didn't want her to get fat with his child. His children were already grown up and all he wanted was to take her all around the world and show all of his friends what a beautiful woman he'd found."

"A trophy wife, before they were called that."

"Exactly. I let her go. I didn't have a choice, really. She broke my heart and to this day I don't know how much damage she did to Kerron. I know he has great difficulty in trusting people because of it. And I know he trusts you for some reason. That worries me."

"I'm not her," Darcy said firmly. "Kerron is right to trust me and you can as well. I'm not going to hurt him or you."

"You can't promise that," William said with a sigh. "But I can tell he's falling for you and I want you to let him down gently."

"What if I'm falling for him too?" Darcy demanded.

"You? You don't want to be a farmer's wife any more than my wife did. I'm sure you'd give it a good try, but eventually you'd get bored with all those quiet nights stuck in with sick animals or going to bed early to start planting in the morning, and you'd start going out with your friends again. And then you'd start meeting all those rich men who would start making you feel alive again."

Darcy shook her head, hearing his former wife's words in his ramblings. "I'm not your ex-wife," she said. "And I don't appreciate your automatic condemnation just because I'm pretty."

"He's my only child," William said defensively "I've spent my whole trying to protect him and make up to him for losing his mother."

"I appreciate that, but you should know that you've done a good job. Kerron is a great guy and you should be very proud of him. But you have to let him make his own mistakes from here on. He's old enough to figure out what sort of woman I am for himself, don't you think?"

William shrugged. "I can't figure you out and I have a lot more experience with women than Kerron."

Darcy laughed. "Women aren't really that complicated," she told the man. "It's just that men are so simple."

William chuckled and then swallowed the last of his beer. He got to his feet. "I'd better get back. Kerron will be sending out a search party."

"I was supposed to get the next round," Darcy said as she stood up.

"You can get it next time," William told her.

She drove him back to the farmhouse silently. Her mind was racing and she was trying to figure out exactly what she wanted to say to William when she dropped him off. He obviously had his own ideas about that, though.

"I'd still prefer it if you'd stay well away from my son," he told Darcy. "But I won't threaten to quit my job to get you to agree."

"Thank you for that," Darcy replied, feeling stunned. She hadn't considered that as a possibility. As she slowly drove away, she turned the idea over in her mind. If William had threatened to quit if she didn't stay away from Kerron, what would she have done?

She argued with herself from both sides of the argument all the way home. Too tired to bother with dinner, she ate a bowl of cereal with milk and then fell into bed. Unexpected and unwelcome tears streamed down her face as she tossed and turned until the small hours of the night.

Friday was bright and sunny and Darcy spent another day on publicity. She deliberately stayed away from the Kewely farm, talking with George by phone several times, but leaving him to make all of the final adjustments. The snow would be arriving on Saturday and she'd have to be there to help get that into place.

Saturday morning brought torrential rain and gale force winds. Darcy stood at the window of her flat and watched the seemingly endless downpour. She didn't need to turn on the radio to hear the bad news, but she did so anyway.

Due to the severe weather conditions, all ferry services are cancelled for today.

Darcy sighed and sent an email to Michael, who replied quickly. Apparently the snow would be moved to the Sunday sailing, assuming that happened. Darcy wasn't reassured, but she had no choice. Even if the snow had arrived, they wouldn't have been able to apply it to the outdoor spaces in today's wind and rain, she told herself miserably.

With nothing else to do with herself, Darcy did a load of laundry and cleaned her flat. She thought about ringing Lisa, but she was too grumpy to even make that effort. Then she thought about ringing Kerron, but she quickly squashed that thought as well. After the conversation with his father, she felt somewhat uncomfortable with the idea of talking to Kerron.

She had a light dinner and headed to bed early. Nollick Balley was opening on Monday at midday, whether the snow was there or not.

Sunday was still rainy, but the wind had died down and the ferries were sailing. Darcy was at the Sea Terminal when the first ferry arrived and she watched anxiously for the right lorry to unload. George was there as well, ready to transport the snow to the farm. Darcy was thrilled when he gave her the thumbs up and then headed out to the farm with the huge boxes of powdered snow.

Darcy followed his lorry across the island, mentally prioritising the site. Santa's Castle was most important, she decided. Once the ground outside of that was covered in a layer of snow, she'd move outwards from there until it got too dark to continue or they'd finished, which-ever came first. There was a press preview at ten the next morning, so she had a few hours to finish the job in the morning if she needed it.

She did need it. George, all the elves, and every one else she could find all pitched in to help her, but they didn't get the site completely snow-covered before it was dark. At home Sunday night she slept for about four hours before she got back up and headed back to the farm. As the sun slowly rose, Darcy dumped piles of powdery artificial snow all around the site and then slowly spread it out into what she hoped was a fairly even layer. George and the elves joined her around eight, and just before ten she decided it was as good as it was going to get.

"Let's wrap this up and get rid of all the packaging," she told her crew. "The press will be here in a few minutes and we want everything to look finished."

"Better hope it doesn't get too windy today," George said. "This stuff will just blow away. Not sure what's going to happen to it when it rains."

"It's supposed to be fine in rain," Darcy told him. "And once it's settled in, it isn't meant to blow around too much as long as the winds don't get up too high."

George's look told Darcy that he didn't believe her. She didn't totally believe it herself, but as long as things looked good for today's preview and grand opening, she'd worry about the rest of the month later. They had ordered several extra boxes of the stuff so they could top up the first layer as needed, anyway.

She headed into the loos at Santa's Castle, where she changed clothes and then did her best to brush all of the fake snow from her hair. At ten o'clock she gave up and went out greet the press. She was surprised and a little unhappy to see Alastair and Michael already in the middle of the group of reporters. Michael had told her that they would be arriving around eleven, but clearly they'd changed their plans.

She forced a bright smile onto her lips and joined them. Of course, they were both immaculately dressed in expensive suits that made Darcy even more conscious that she had snowflakes in her hair. The flakes seemed to drift off her as she moved across the room.

"Ah, there she is," Alastair said loudly. "The woman who made all of the magic happen."

As she reached his side, he leaned over and kissed her cheek and then slid an arm around her. A couple of reporters threw out questions, but she held up a hand.

"Let's take a quick tour of the site before I answer any questions," she suggested. "There's a lot to see and not much time."

She quickly moved away from Alastair and began to lead the group around the site. Everything looked gorgeous in the early morning sunshine and the weather even warmed up enough that she wasn't shivering in her favourite black suit. She proudly showed off the various attractions, introducing the reporters to George and just about every other staff member they saw. The little group stopped in the hot chocolate tent for a warm-up and Darcy answered a few questions.

The press preview was scheduled to end at half eleven to give everyone time to get ready for the opening at twelve. The last of the reporters was just leaving when Darcy spotted Kerron walking quickly towards her, a handful of snow in his hand.

"It's the wrong snow," he growled at Darcy when he reached her side.

"Pardon?"

"It's the wrong snow. This stuff isn't what Alastair and I agreed to and now it's all over my largest field, ready to blow all over the entire farm."

"Is there a problem?" Alastair asked smoothly, putting his arm around Darcy.

"This isn't the snow we agreed on," Kerron said angrily.

"No, but it's just as good," Alastair said nonchalantly. "Don't worry."

"Don't worry? You're putting my livelihood at stake here. I'm trying to get certified as organic and this stuff may just ruin years of hard work."

"My supplier assured me it won't be a problem," Alastair said. "You're overreacting."

"Just be prepared to be sued if you're wrong," Kerron said through clenched teeth.

"Darcy and I will be leaving for Lanzarote on the first of January," Alastair told him. "But I'll make sure my solicitors are ready for you."

"Lanzarote? How nice," Kerron said. He turned to Darcy. "I guess trusting you was a mistake after all. I should have listened to my father."

Before Darcy could speak, Kerron turned and stormed off, throwing the handful of snow to one side as he went.

❧ 15 ❧

Darcy forced herself to take a deep breath before she spoke to Alastair. "You promised me you'd make sure the snow was right," she said in the steadiest voice she could manage.

"It's fine," Alastair replied. "I know what I'm doing."

"Even if it is fine, you should have let Kerron know in advance that you'd changed the order," Darcy said, unwilling to drop the subject.

"Please, your job was to keep him happy. Mine is to turn a profit. This stuff was half the price of the stuff he wanted us to use."

"I'm not going to Lanzarote, you know," Darcy said quietly.

"You'll be sorry," he replied. "We could have had a lot of fun together."

"I'm sure," Darcy muttered, and then turned and walked away. Her hands were shaking as she poured herself a cup of coffee. It was nearly twelve and she could see an excited queue of parents and children growing just outside the entrance gate. This was supposed to be her moment, but all she wanted to do was cry.

Her years as cabin crew with Finlo had taught her how to smile no matter what. She'd had drinks spilled on her, been shouted at by drunks, and been thrown up on by small children. Through it all, her smile had never faltered. Now she needed to call on every bit of strength she had to get through the afternoon.

As the clock tower atop Santa's Castle began to play Christmas music at exactly midday, Darcy helped George open the gates. As her staff began to take tickets, Darcy stood back and listened to excited little voices.

"Look at all the snow."

"That's Santa's Castle, isn't it, mummy?"

"Do you think Santa is there?"

"Where are the reindeer? I want to see a reindeer."

Darcy handed out site maps and gave directions to one family after another. She was feeling worn out by the time Lisa found her inside Santa's Castle, where Darcy was watching William laugh and chat with his small visitors.

"It looks incredible," Lisa gushed. "It's so much more spectacular than I was expecting."

"Gee, thanks," Darcy replied.

"You know what I mean," Lisa said with a laugh.

"Everyone seems to be having fun, anyway," Darcy said, looking around.

"Everyone is having a wonderful time, except for you. What's wrong?" Lisa demanded.

"I've barely said ten words to you. What makes you think something's wrong?"

"I've been your best friend forever. I know when you aren't happy, even when you have that bright fake smile on your face."

Darcy sighed and looked around again. There didn't seem to be anything she needed to handle, so she pulled her friend into the small staff room.

"Alastair ordered different artificial snow to what he and Kerron agreed on," she told Lisa.

"Oh, dear," Lisa replied. Darcy had told her about the difficulties the snow had caused all along, so Darcy knew she understood the scale of the problem. "What happens now?"

"I guess Kerron is going to check out what Alastair bought and see if it's okay or not, and then we'll go from there."

"What if it isn't okay? The stuff is everywhere," Lisa gasped.

"I suppose we'll have to try to collect as much of it as we can," Darcy said, with tears in her eyes.

She could see the word "impossible" in her friend's eyes, but Lisa was too good a friend to say it out loud.

"So you just have to wait and see what Kerron finds out?"

"I don't know what else to do. He's absolutely furious with me."

"It wasn't your fault," Lisa said angrily.

"I should have insisted that Alastair order the product that Kerron wanted," Darcy said.

"He's your boss," Lisa pointed out. "You nagged him repeatedly about it, but he told you he'd take care of it. There was nothing else you could do."

"Alastair told Kerron that he was taking me to Lanzarote in January," Darcy added.

"Which made Kerron even more angry," Lisa guessed.

"I don't know that he could have been any more angry," Darcy said with a sigh. "But it certainly didn't improve his mood."

"You need to talk to Kerron," Lisa said.

"I need to get back to work," Darcy countered.

"But you'll talk to him soon," Lisa insisted.

"I guess that depends on how you define soon," Darcy muttered as she walked away. She had a lot to do at Nollick Balley and she had no intention of delegating her responsibilities to anyone. After all her hard work to this point, she deserved to be there, watching everyone enjoy the site. And she wanted to be there to solve all of the little problems that were sure to arise.

The rest of the day dragged as Darcy tried to enjoy the results of all of her hard work. Aside from a few small problems, the day went smoothly and she heard nothing but compliments from the guests she spoke with.

"Santa was perfect," one woman told her. "My little girl loved him."

"My son loved the reindeer," a dad commented. "He was so excited that they were real."

"I want to be an elf," a little boy of about four told Darcy solemnly. "I want to make toys all day."

"All elves must be eighteen or older," she told him. "But wait here a minute." She dashed into the small site office and came back out with an employment application.

"Here you go," she said. "Send this back to me once you've turned eighteen and we'll see about that job."

The little boy's eyes widened as he looked over the form. "I'll have my mummy put this somewhere safe until I can read," he told Darcy. His parents laughed and thanked Darcy for her kindness.

They were scheduled to close at six o'clock each night, but it was past seven when the last of the guests finally made their way out the gate. Darcy pushed it shut and locked it behind them. It took another half hour for her to thank all of the hard-working staff who'd done a great job all day.

"I guess we have to do it all again tomorrow?" George asked as they walked towards the employee parking area.

"Yes, we do," Darcy said tiredly.

She stopped at the farmhouse to try to talk to Kerron, but no one answered her knock. For a moment she was tempted to try the door. Kerron had told her it was rarely locked, but she didn't have the nerve. Instead she drove home with tears streaming down her face. Once there, she went straight to bed and fell into an exhausted sleep that she struggled out of when her alarm went off the next morning.

The rest of the week seemed to follow the same pattern. Darcy got up and drove to Nollick Balley, where she spent her morning checking on things all around the site. At midday the gates opened and the rest of the day was a rush of dealing with guests, handling the odd complaint, and keeping the staff happy. Most evenings she didn't get away from the farm until half seven or eight.

It rained a couple of the days, but the rain wasn't heavy and everyone seemed to simply slog through it with their umbrellas. The winds stayed light, for which Darcy was grateful. When the snow started to look muddy and grey, she reluctantly allowed the site manager to put a fresh layer over the worst spots while hoping that she wasn't making a bad situation worse. She tried stopping at the farmhouse a couple more times, but either no one was ever home or Kerron was deliberately avoiding her.

Darcy was pretty sure it was the latter, as she rang him several times but he never answered her calls. The site was going to be open every day until Christmas, then reopen on Boxing Day for six days with half-price admission. Darcy was already looking forward to the last day of December, when she could lock the gates to the site for the last time. Of course, there would be many days needed to tear down the site, but they had all of January to get that done, and Darcy knew her crew would be quick and efficient. The teardown was scheduled to start on the first Monday in January, the fourth, so that everyone could have a few days off to enjoy the New Year.

As the first week dragged on, Darcy began to feel angry with Kerron for avoiding her. She understood his upset, but ultimately she worked for Alastair and the man had taken the whole snow issue out of her hands. By the weekend, when he still wasn't taking her calls, she decided to give up. He hadn't given her a chance to speak when he'd confronted her and Alastair, and now he was avoiding her. If that was how he wanted to behave, she'd just get on with her life and forget all about him.

The second week ran right into the first. Darcy was thrilled when the weather forecast predicted a week of cold but dry days with virtually no wind. On Monday Darcy found herself working with George on staff scheduling to make sure the elves had enough time off. It wasn't until the Wednesday of the second week that she bumped into William. She hadn't been avoiding him, but she hadn't gone out of her way to talk to him, either.

"So, how am I doing, boss?" he greeted Darcy.

"Everyone I've spoken to has had nothing but good things to say about our Santa," she told him. "I think you're doing wonderfully well."

"That's good to hear," he replied. "As much as I hate to admit it, I'm really enjoying the job. The kids are all so excited to see me, it's incredible."

"I'm glad you're having fun," Darcy said with a grin.

"The whole event seems very successful," William said. "You've done well."

"Except for the snow," Darcy muttered.

"I'm not getting dragged into that battle," William told her. "I wanted to talk to you about tomorrow."

"What about tomorrow?" Darcy asked.

"I'm just a little worried about it, that's all."

"The sensory issues kids, you mean?"

"Yeah, that."

Darcy smiled at him. She'd worked with the schools and children's groups all over the island to try to make sure that Nollick Balley would be enjoyable for every child on the island. That had led her to arranging a special day specifically aimed at children with autism and other sensory issues as well as children with any physical or mental handicaps. The music would be turned down, the staff had had special training in what to expect, boards were going to be laid across the bumpy ground to allow wheelchair access around the site, and even the vendors had been asked to be sensitive to their guests' unique differences.

"You did the training with George, right?" Darcy checked.

"I did, but that was a few days ago. I'm not sure I remember any of it."

"I think the most important thing to remember is to try to lower your voice," Darcy told him. "Every child with special needs is different and will respond differently to you, just like every other child in the world. You may need to talk more slowly and more quietly, but whatever the child's challenges, they're all going to be excited to meet you. Really, as long as you are kind and patient, it will be okay."

"We aren't going to be too busy, are we? I hate when it gets busy and I feel like I have to rush children along."

"We tried to restrict ticket sales to families with special needs children, but we couldn't exactly ask for a note from their schools or doctors to enforce that. Only half as many tickets as normal were made available for the day, although we've sold a few extra due to requests from certain places for some kids who missed out on getting tickets in time. You should be fine, but I'll stick close to the Castle to help handle any issues."

"I'd appreciate that," William told her. "George said there would be a lot of extra elves around as well."

"I've doubled the staff numbers for the day," Darcy confirmed. "Basically, everyone is working tomorrow. We have extra security in case anyone wanders off as well as extra hands available in the craft tents."

"Double staff and half the ticket sales? Did you quadruple the ticket price, then?" William asked.

Darcy shook her head. "Actually, a great many of the tickets were given away by the schools or programmes that help such children. I asked them to identify children who might not be able to afford to attend otherwise and made sure they received tickets for the whole family. We'll be operating at a huge loss tomorrow, but Alastair doesn't know that yet."

William chuckled. "You've just made my day," he told Darcy.

"There should be more than enough profit from the rest of the event to cover tomorrow," Darcy said. "I thought we could give something back to the island."

"Just make sure you stay close to me," William replied.

Thursday was bright and sunny and Darcy drove to the farm feeling happier than she had since opening day. Whatever happened with Kerron and the snow, she felt good about what they were doing that day.

The day turned out to be her favourite day of the event so far. The children were excited to be there and everyone seemed to enjoy themselves enormously. Darcy stood near the door to Santa's Castle and chatted with the parents as the little groups went in and out throughout the day.

"Thank you so much," one mother told Darcy. "I haven't seen my son this happy in a long time."

"My daughter wants to stay here forever," one father said.

Darcy smiled at the little girl. "There aren't any cosy beds here. You're better off at home with your mummy and daddy."

"Okay," the little girl said, shyly burying her face in her father's shoulder.

"She's lovely," Darcy told the girl's mum.

"Thank you. And thank you for arranging a special day like today. Sometimes, when your children have special needs, you get so caught up in the therapy and the treatment plans and the special classes that you forget to let them be kids once in a while."

"We were happy to do it," Darcy replied. "You have the hardest job in the world."

"And the most rewarding," the woman said.

The afternoon was finally winding down and Darcy was just thinking about heading over to get a bite to eat when the sound of bells filled the air. She took off at a run, heading to the front gate. The bells were the site's warning system that a child was missing, and the first priority was shutting the gates to make sure no one left until the child was found.

George was already at the gate, calmly explaining things to a family that was trying to leave.

"If you'll just wait a minute or two, I'm sure the missing child will turn up and we can let you go," he said.

"We won't complain, however long it takes," the husband told George and Darcy. "It could so easily be our child." He looked over at his wife and she smiled and hugged their little boy tightly. The child squirmed and pushed to get away, and after a moment she released him.

The lost child centre had sent a text message to every member of staff. Darcy read that the missing child was a boy called Bobby, aged eight, with brown hair and eyes. With George handling the gate, Darcy headed towards Santa's Castle. Every single staff member was assigned a different area to search if a child went missing, and with double the normal staff on hand it shouldn't take long.

On her way to the lost child centre, Darcy passed Santa's Castle. The castle was supposed to be empty, as Santa had finished for the day. Just to be sure, Darcy unlocked the door and went inside. She did a very quick search of the space, but didn't find anyone.

Back outside, the bells stopped as suddenly as they'd begun, and Darcy hoped that meant what it was supposed to mean. At the lost child centre a mum was sobbing over a small brown-haired boy who was struggling to get away.

"This is our little lost boy, then?" Darcy asked.

"It is," the woman confirmed. "I was waiting to buy some ice cream and he just ran off while I was trying to pay. I wasn't fast enough to catch up with him. Sometimes he just wants to run and he doesn't understand the consequences."

Darcy smiled at the child. "You had us all a little bit worried," she told him. "I'm so glad you're safe."

The boy stared silently at her for a moment and then looked away.

"He doesn't really say much," the boy's mum told Darcy. "But I know he's had a wonderful time today. We both have."

"I'm glad," Darcy told her. "But what happened to your ice cream?"

The woman looked at her for a moment and then shook her head. "I left the counter when I realised Bobby was gone," she said. "I forgot all about it."

Darcy smiled. "Well, let's go see if we can find it, shall we?" she asked as Bobby's eyes filled with tears.

She walked with the pair to the ice cream stand, chatting easily with Bobby's mother about the weather and other inconsequential things. At the stand, Darcy insisted that they both get whatever they wanted.

"It's on me," she told the woman. "Your son helped me check that our lost child procedures work. We owe you a treat."

"But you already gave us free tickets," the woman protested. "You won't make any money on us if you buy our ice cream as well."

Darcy laughed but insisted on paying before she walked the pair to the gate. "I hope you had an enjoyable day, in spite of the scare," she said.

"It was wonderful, aside from that," the woman told her. "I hope you're going to do this every year."

"At this point, I don't know what's going to happen next," Darcy told her honestly. "But I've had at least as much fun organising it as you've had visiting, so I'm hoping we get to do it again."

She watched the pair as they walked back towards their car. It was hard for her to imagine how worried the mother must have been. Having children must be the scariest thing in the world, she thought to herself as she made a slow circuit of the site. It was emptying slowly and Darcy suddenly just wanted to go home.

Her brain flashed up a mental image of the kitchen at Kerron's house. For a moment, Darcy thought how wonderful it would be to be able to drive there now. Marion would make something delicious and then she could curl up with Kerron in front of the telly with a glass of wine and forget all about Nollick Balley for a few hours. Darcy sighed. Thanks to Alastair, that wasn't possible.

The drive home seemed endless and Darcy felt as if she'd run out of energy by the time she reached Douglas. Instead of continuing on to Castletown, she stopped at Lisa's house. She rang the bell and knocked repeatedly, but no one answered. Too tired to worry about being polite, she rang Lisa's mobile.

"I'm at your house. Where are you?"

"We're at hubby's this week," Lisa told her. "We're taking it in turns and hoping eventually we'll be able to chose one place over the other."

"Would you mind terribly if I slept in your spare room?" Darcy asked. She could hear the exhaustion in her own voice.

"Of course not," Lisa said quickly. "Are you okay? Should I come over?"

"I'm fine," Darcy replied. "It was just a long day and a little boy went missing, which was stressful."

"I assume he turned up."

"He did, safe and sound," Darcy assured her. "But I'm just feeling completely done in and Castletown feels like it's a hundred million miles away."

"Stay at my place whenever you like," Lisa suggested. "Hubby and I can stay here."

"I'll think about it," Darcy said. "I might just take you up on it."

"Just text me your plans and I'll make sure we stay here whenever you want to be there," Lisa said. "That will cut a lot off your daily commute."

Darcy thanked her friend and then let herself into the house. She fixed herself a snack and then crawled into bed feeling miserable but not entirely sure why. She slept well in Lisa's comfortable spare room, one of her favourite places in the world. When she got up the next morning, she thought she could smell coffee brewing.

"Hello?" she called out just a little bit nervously as she walked through the house.

"Hello, pet. I thought I'd stop in and make you some coffee."

Darcy greeted Lisa with a hug and then surprised them both by bursting into tears.

"What's the matter?" Lisa asked as she patted Darcy's back.

"Kerron won't speak to me, I still don't know if the snow is okay or not, and then Bobby got lost," Darcy sobbed.

"But Bobby was found safely, right?" Lisa asked.

"He was fine and I bought him ice cream," Darcy said through her tears.

"So that just leaves Kerron and the snow to deal with," Lisa said in a soothing tone. "Have you tried ringing him?"

"I rang him every day last week," Darcy told her as she slowly reined in her emotions. "And twice so far this week. But he never answers and he never returns my calls."

"What about texts or emails?"

"He's not answering those either," Darcy replied. "He's mad at me and he doesn't think he can trust me."

"What does William say about it all?"

"He won't talk about it," Darcy said.

"Have you tried just turning up on his doorstep?"

"Several times. He never answers his door."

Lisa frowned. "It seems like he's trying to avoid you."

"You think?" Darcy sighed. "I've pretty much given up until Christmas is over. I don't have time to keep chasing him right now."

"It isn't like you to chase after a man," Lisa remarked.

"I know, and I don't like it one bit," Darcy said with a rueful smile.

"Christmas is only a week away," Lisa said. "Which reminds me, what are you doing for Christmas?"

"Doing?" Darcy frowned. She'd been so caught up with Nollick Balley that she hadn't given Christmas any thought. For the last several years she'd flown across and spent the holiday with her parents, but she'd already told them she wouldn't make it this year. Now she shrugged at Lisa. "I think I might just sleep all day," she said.

"Come and spend Christmas with me and hubby at my parents'," Lisa told her. "You're practically family to them and I have a very special present for my mum that I'd love for you to watch her open."

"What is it?" Darcy asked.

"I'm not telling," Lisa laughed. "But you'll be glad you're there to see it."

"If I wake up in time," Darcy said. "But I won't promise."

"I'll ring you and make sure you're up," Lisa replied. "If you're going to be on the island, I want you there."

Lisa hadn't just made coffee, she'd brought a box of fancy pastries from the nearby bakery. Darcy was feeling much better after her crying spell and she discovered that she was starving.

"I haven't been eating much on-site," she told Lisa as she took a third pastry.

"You need to take better care of yourself," Lisa chided. "No wonder your emotions are all over the place, you're hungry."

With her tummy full and her system primed with a great deal of caffeine, Darcy drove slowly out to the Kewley farm. She slowed down as she neared the house, thinking that maybe stopping now would take Kerron by surprise. As she pulled past the parking area, she saw the door open and without thinking, she stopped the car. In the rear view mirror she watched Kerron as he walked out of the house.

He was still in pyjamas and he was escorting a stunning blonde woman to her car. Darcy watched as he helped her into the car and then leaned down to speak to her. After a moment he laughed and shut the door for her. She drove slowly away as he watched. Darcy didn't think she had any tears left after her spell with Lisa, but she found tears streaming down her cheeks as she drove the rest of the way to Nollick Balley.

In the loo, she fixed her makeup and then she poured herself another cup of coffee. No wonder Kerron wasn't bothering to ring her back, she thought, he was busy with another woman.

The day seemed to drag on endlessly to Darcy, with one small but frustrating problem after another. By the time the site closed for the day, Darcy was more than ready to get away from the enforced gaiety of the place.

Time ticked on slowly towards Christmas Day. Darcy gave up on talking to Kerron, just hoping that someone would let her know whether the snow was a problem or not. George and his crew applied fresh layers as needed, each one making Darcy more nervous than the last. They'd been very lucky with the weather, as it rained occasionally but the usual winter winds seemed to be taking December off.

Christmas Eve felt special, even in Darcy's tired and miserable state. Every visitor seemed extra excited, from the smallest of children to the oldest of grandparents or even great-grandparents. Darcy made her way around the site at the end of the day, eavesdropping on the excited chatter that seemed to be coming from every group. When they finally closed the gates behind the last guest, Darcy gathered her staff in Santa's Castle.

"I hope everyone has a very wonderful and Merry Christmas tomorrow. Nollick Ghennal to you all. Starting on Boxing Day, we have six more days to run. Tickets for those days were half-price, but we're still going to provide the best possible experience for our guests. Nollick Balley's success has exceeded my wildest expectations and you can all expect a small bonus in your final paycheque to thank you for your hard work and dedication this long and tiring month."

"Can we do it all again next year?" one of the elves called.

Darcy laughed. "Ask me in June, when I've recovered from this one," she told the woman. "Honestly, at this point I have no idea what will happen next year. Mr. Breckenridge will have to go over the figures and decide what he wants to do. If we do go ahead next year, I'd love to have every single one of you back again. You've all been amazing."

Everyone cheered and then there was a flurry of hugs and Christmas wishes all around the Castle. Darcy found herself being handed several small wrapped gifts by various members of the staff.

"You shouldn't have," she tried to tell them.

"I didn't expect," she said.

"You've been the best boss I've ever worked with," George told her. "I haven't had this much fun at work ever."

"You gave me a job with hours to suit my kids' schedules," one elf whispered. "I made enough money this month to give them the magical sort of Christmas I never could afford before."

"You made my son, with all his special needs and behavioural quirks, welcome to just be a kid for one magical day," one of the maintenance crew said gruffly, handing Darcy a wrapped box. "This is just a little something from the wife to say thank you."

Nearly everyone was crying by the time they all made their way to the employee car park. Darcy hugged everyone one last time and then, after everyone else had left, drove slowly home. And we still have a week to go, she thought to herself as she drove. I'm going to miss everyone so much. She'd been invited to spend Christmas with just about everyone on the site, so she was grateful that she could honestly tell them all that she was spending the holiday with her oldest friend.

Back in her flat, she put all of the presents she'd been given under the little tree that Lisa had put up in her flat one day as a surprise. She put on some Christmas music, poured herself a glass of wine, and sat down to think.

She'd made some huge changes this year, but for the most part she figured she'd made the right decisions. Aside from sorting out Kerron's snow, Nollick Balley had been a huge success, and she was impressed with how well she'd done with it all. The regular, congratulatory emails from Michael told her how happy he was with the event as well. Alastair sent one terse note when the event was finally completely sold out, saying "well done" and nothing more.

She'd only drunk about half the glass when she found herself falling asleep on her couch. Crawling into her favourite pyjamas, she slipped into bed and fell asleep almost immediately. A loud ringing noise woke her from a dream. She sat up in bed and shook her head to clear away the image of Kerron's cosy kitchen. Then she grabbed her phone.

"We're expecting you in an hour," Lisa said cheerfully. "Nollick Ghennal, my dear."

"Nollick Ghennal," Darcy replied. "And I'll be there."

She threw back her covers and got out of bed feeling happier with the world than she had in a long time. It was Christmas and there was nothing that Kerron Kewley or Alastair Breckenridge could do to spoil that. Darcy found herself humming Christmas songs as she showered and dressed. She grabbed the bag of presents she'd bought for Lisa's family and dropped it on the passenger seat of her car. The drive to Douglas felt short after all of the long drives north and Darcy arrived at Lisa's parents' house right on time.

The day was filled with love, laughter and fabulous food. Darcy had one glass of wine before switching to fizzy drinks. Lisa's mum and dad had known Darcy since she was a child and they treated her much like a second daughter. After dinner and generous servings of Christmas pudding, it was time to exchange gifts.

Everyone seemed to have made an effort to buy thoughtful and interesting presents for one another, and Darcy enjoyed watching what the others received as much as opening her own gifts. The last gift was Lisa's present for her mother and Darcy found herself sitting forward in her seat as the woman began to unwrap the box. It was a small box that didn't look terribly exciting, but Darcy could see that Lisa was nearly bursting with anticipation as her mother opened the box.

She unfolded piles of tissue paper and then pulled out what was inside with a puzzled look on her face. As she turned the small towelling square in her hands, she read the words on it out loud.

Granny's little angel

Lisa's mum looked up at Lisa and Darcy could see exactly when the meaning of the gift sank in. "You're pregnant?" Lisa's mum gasped.

Lisa nodded and then nearly everyone burst into tears. Darcy hugged Lisa and then Lisa's mum and they all cried together while Lisa's father went out and found a box of tissues. Lisa's husband got his fair share of hugs and congratulations, and Darcy felt as if the day couldn't possibly get any better.

The tears and happiness were interrupted by a loud noise.

"My mobile," Darcy explained as she dug around in her handbag. "It's Kerron," she said, sitting down in surprise.

"Hello?"

"I'm sorry to interrupt your Christmas, but I wanted to let you know that my father has just been rushed to Noble's with a suspected heart attack. You're going to have to find another Santa for the rest of your run."

❧ 16 ❧

Darcy gasped, but before she could speak, Kerron disconnected. She sat back, feeling stunned.

"What's wrong?" Lisa asked.

Darcy looked up to find everyone staring at her. "William Kewley, my Santa, is on his way to hospital with a suspected heart attack," she told them.

"Poor Kerron," Lisa murmured.

"I'm sure his blonde friend will be holding his hand," Darcy said sharply. "I'm more worried about William. I've grown quite fond of the man."

"What will you do for a Santa at Nollick Balley?" Lisa asked.

Darcy shrugged. "I'm sure we can find someone to fill in," she said. "But don't let me interrupt the celebration," she added, trying to lighten the suddenly sombre mood.

After a moment, everyone began speaking again. Lisa shared all the news from her pregnancy so far. As she'd only found out a few weeks earlier, there wasn't much of that. It wasn't long before the conversation petered out. The mood was far more subdued now and the party broke up a short time later.

"You can come over to our house for a little while, if you want," Lisa offered as they were leaving.

"Thanks, but I have a stack of presents from my staff to open and then a matching stack of thank-you notes to write," Darcy told her. "I want to give them out tomorrow. And I have to find another Santa before I go to bed as well."

"Hubby is off work tomorrow," Lisa said. "He can fill in if you can't find anyone else."

Darcy laughed. "Thank you for volunteering your husband, but I'm sure I'll find someone."

Back at her flat, Darcy poured herself a glass of wine and then opened her presents. She very carefully wrote out a thank-you note for each one as she opened it, even through her tears that were brought on by the incredibly kind and thoughtful gifts she'd been given.

In between gifts, she made phone calls, trying to track down a substitute Santa from the list she'd made of original applicants for the position. She was beginning to think she wasn't going to find anyone at home, and that Lisa's husband was about to find himself in a red suit, when she finally found a willing replacement.

"Sure, I'll do it," the man told her. "I've been at the shopping centre all of December, but they don't have Santa after Christmas."

Darcy told him where to go and when to be there and then hung up, feeling relieved. She rang Noble's, but as she wasn't family they wouldn't tell her anything about William's condition. With the last of the gifts opened and the final thank-you note written, Darcy finally fell into bed feeling as if she'd been through every possible emotion that day. Her final thought, as she drifted off to sleep, was that she was going to be an honourary auntie.

Before the site opened the next morning, Darcy had a quick staff meeting. She passed out the thank-you notes and then introduced their new Santa.

"This is Jack Meadows and he's going to be taking over from William. Unfortunately, William is in Noble's. I understand they suspected a heart attack when they took him in, but as I'm not family they won't release any information to me about how he's doing."

Everyone welcomed Jack, but the mood was restrained, as William had been very well liked. The entire day felt gloomy. The skies were dark and it always felt as if it were just about to start pouring with rain, even though it never actually did. The guests were quieter, and while they seemed to enjoy themselves, it was clear that the excitement of Christmas was waning fast.

The remaining days at Nollick Balley ticked by slowly. Darcy rang Kerron once to check on his father, but he didn't answer. She tried ringing the house as well, hoping to speak to Marion, but no one answered there, either. With a few days left in the old year, Darcy was feeling like the new year couldn't come fast enough. On the way home from work one evening, Darcy impulsively stopped at Noble's. Maybe she could persuade someone to tell her something about Wiliam's condition.

"Mr. Kewley is on ward eighteen, our coronary care unit. It's visiting hours just now if you want to go up," the cheerful young woman at the information desk told Darcy.

"He's allowed visitors?" Darcy asked in surprise.

"According to my computer he is," she replied. "I can't promise anything when you get upstairs, though."

Darcy smiled and quickly headed for the lifts. If there was a chance she was going to be able to see William, she wanted to take it.

"Mr. Kewley's family has been here all day, but they've left for the evening now. I'll just walk down with you and we can see if he'd like to see you or not," the nurse at the desk told Darcy.

Darcy was relieved to hear that Kerron wasn't there. She wanted to see William, but she wasn't ready to deal with Kerron just then. The nurse went in, asking Darcy to wait in the hall. A moment later she came out smiling.

"You may have five minutes," she told Darcy. "We don't want to tire Mr. Kewley too much."

Darcy nodded and then smiled her brightest smile. She walked into the room, mentally preparing herself to be shocked by the man's appearance. In a way, she was. The man in the bed looked far too healthy to be hooked up to the many machines that beeped and flashed around him.

"You don't look ill at all," Darcy said in surprise.

"I nearly died, young lady," William told her sternly. "A little more respect for the seriousness of my condition, please."

Darcy laughed. "I was expecting to find you all pale and wan, barely able to open your eyes to see who was here. You look like you're about ready to go home."

"I wish," the man told her. "Apparently I'm recovering nicely, but they still want to observe me for a few more days. I had to have a triple bypass, they tell me."

"I bet you slept right through the whole thing," Darcy teased.

"Yep. It's been a lot easier on me than it has on Kerron, that's for sure."

Darcy felt her smile falter. "I'm not allowed to stay for long," she said, changing the subject. "But I'm really glad to see you doing so well. We've all been so worried about you out at Nollick Balley and they wouldn't tell me anything when I rang."

"I take it you still aren't talking to my son, then?"

Darcy flushed. "He rang to tell me you were here, but we've been missing each other ever since."

William shook his head. "He's gone back to avoiding you, you mean. He's as stubborn as a mule, that man."

"I'd rather talk about you," Darcy said brightly. "I should have brought you something, but I didn't think I was going to get in to see you."

"I don't need anything," William told her. "Except to get out of here."

"I can't help you there," Darcy replied.

"But how are things at Nollick Balley? I feel like I've let you down, not being there for this last week. Were you able to find another Santa?"

"No one else is using Santas now that Christmas is over," Darcy told him. "I had a queue of bearded, jolly men waiting for me on Boxing Day," she joked.

"So that's okay, then," William said quietly.

"Your replacement isn't nearly as good as you were, but he's doing okay. We only have two days to go, anyway."

"Are you going to be doing it again next year?" William asked.

Darcy shrugged. "Alastair will have to crunch the numbers to see if it was worth it, I guess. Would you let us use your farm again?"

William laughed. "That'll be up to Kerron," he told her. "But I know there are a few other farmers around that might be interested in hosting something similar. Word got out that Alastair paid me quite a lot of money and now everyone wants in."

"I just want to get through the next two days," Darcy told him. "Then we can figure things out from there. I don't suppose there's been any word on the safety of the artificial snow Alastair supplied?"

"Kerron hasn't said anything to me about it, but he doesn't talk much. He just sits and looks at me while Marion cries and talks about how she'd never manage without me." He sighed. "It's all very tiring," he told Darcy.

She smiled. "They both love you a lot and you should be grateful for them."

"I am, I just wish they could love me from home and leave me in peace."

Darcy laughed. The door behind her suddenly swung open.

"I'm afraid it's time to let Mr. Kewley rest now," the nurse told Darcy as she entered the room. "I've brought you a small snack," she told William.

He made a face at the tray that held a bowl of jelly and a small packet of crackers. "I'm not hungry," he growled.

"I think I'd better get out of the way," Darcy said, winking at William. "I'll tell everyone at Nollick Balley that you're doing well. They'll all be very pleased."

"Thanks for coming by," he told her. "Stop back any time."

"I'll be back," she promised. "Meanwhile, Happy New Year."

She drove home feeling much happier. There were only two more days to get through and then they could tear the site down and she'd be done with Nollick Balley. She was relieved that William was doing so well. Now she just had to figure out what to do with all the artificial snow that covered the site.

Three days later, on the first of January, she had a plan ready to go. For the first time in many years, Darcy had spent New Year's Eve at home. Lisa was suffering with morning sickness, so she and her devoted husband had decided to have a quiet night in. While they'd invited Darcy to join them, she knew she'd be in the way there. She'd been invited to a few parties as well, but she was so tired from her long December that she decided to stay home and relax. She had a lot planned for the first, anyway, so she ended up going to bed at ten o'clock.

Her alarm woke her at six and for a moment she couldn't remember why. She'd had later starts through December as the site didn't open until midday, but today she wanted to be at Nollick Balley as early as possible. She'd loaded boxes full of rubbish bags into her boot along with several rechargeable mini vacuums. While the rest of her staff had a much-deserved day off, she was going to tackle the artificial snow.

She knew there was no way she'd make more than a small dent in the problem today, but by working hard all day she hoped she'd start to get some idea of the scale of the problem. A crew of twenty was scheduled to arrive on the fourth to start tearing down the site. With an army that large, they should be able to get rid of much of the snow. At least that was what Darcy told herself as she headed north.

A steady, soaking rain was falling and Darcy frowned as she realised the wind was strong as well. She'd been very lucky throughout December with the weather, but it looked as if her luck had just run out. When she arrived at Nollick Balley she unlocked the gate and drove through it. Looking around, she felt tears forming in her eyes. The site looked abandoned and miserable.

Saying good-bye to everyone at the end of the day yesterday had been difficult, and now she felt almost overwhelmed by emotion. A strong gust of wind that blew huge clumps of soggy fake snow into the air snapped her out of her mood. Cleaning up the mess was going to be a much bigger job than she'd anticipated, given the weather.

She drove slowly towards Santa's Castle along rough ground that wasn't really suitable for her car. It took her several trips to unload her boot into the Castle. Inside, she plugged the mini vacuums into every outlet she could find and then grabbed a broom and a shovel. Opening the first box of rubbish bags, she stepped outside into the storm.

Two hours later she'd filled ten bags with the heavy and water-logged stuff, and when she looked around she couldn't tell where she'd been working. The wind was ferocious, blowing huge clumps of the fake snow in every direction. Just when she thought it couldn't get any worse, the rain began to fall even more heavily.

Darcy sighed as she headed in to get another rubbish bag from the castle. This was an impossible job, but at least the wet snow wasn't travelling all that far as it was being blown around. The clumps were too heavy to do much more than shift around and recover the area she'd just cleared. She just had to hope she and her crew could get it all cleared up before it spread to the rest of the farm.

In the loo, she glanced in the mirror and almost screamed. She was covered from head to toe in a heavy layer of snowflakes. Her hair was thick with the stuff and her shoes were caked in it. She'd been so busy shovelling and stuffing bags that she hadn't really noticed. A stray tear ran down her cheek, but she brushed it away impatiently. She could cry later; she had work to do now.

Back outside the rain was still coming down in sheets. She began filling bag number eleven. The wind howled loudly as it gusted again. Darcy's ears were half full of snow and she'd turned up the collar on her coat as well. She didn't hear the tractor as it approached. It was only when Kerron put a hand on her shoulder that she realised he was there.

"What are you doing?" he shouted at her.

"Trying to clear up the snow," she shouted back.

"Why?"

"Because it's the wrong snow, remember?" Darcy yelled.

Kerron shouted something back, but Darcy couldn't hear him.

"I can't hear you," she called.

Whatever Kerron was going to say was lost in yet another huge wind gust. Darcy shut her eyes tightly as the snow blew all around her. She felt Kerron take a step towards her and then he pulled her close, wrapping his heavy coat around her to protect her from the wind and rain. After a few moments, the wind died down slightly and Kerron pulled her towards the tractor. He helped her climb inside and then dashed around to the driver's side. Once he was seated, he started the engine. Darcy opened her mouth to protest, but it was too noisy inside the cab for conversation.

Back at the house, he climbed out and helped her down and then dragged her inside.

"You left the gate and the castle unlocked," Darcy gasped. "Anyone could get in."

"Give me your keys," he told her. "I'll send Don up to secure things."

"But...." she began.

Kerron held up a hand. "I've behaved very badly and I feel terrible. Please, let me send Don over to lock everything up while you have a shower and try to get warmed up."

Darcy realised that she was shivering and felt cold all the way through. A long hot shower sounded incredibly inviting. Much more so than going back out to lock doors and gates. She dug the keys out of her pocket and handed them to Kerron before heading for the stairs.

"I'll leave some clothes for you on the bed," he told her as she dripped her way up the steps.

Darcy stood in the middle of the loo, waiting for the shower to get hot before she undressed. She tried taking her ponytail down, but the fake snow made it impossible for her to get a comb through it. After half an hour in the shower, she started to feel a little bit better. Most of the snow had washed out of her hair and off of her face and neck.

She'd left her clothes in a pile on the floor, and now she decided that they weren't worth saving. Her shoes had been left at the front door and she wasn't sure if she wanted them back or not. She had a spare pair in her car, but that was up at Nollick Balley, probably covered in thick fake snow by now.

Kerron had left a pair of jogging bottoms and a T-shirt for her on the bed, and Darcy climbed into them, grateful that her undies had managed to stay relatively clean, if not exactly dry. She got dressed and then pulled her hair into a fresh ponytail. There was still some fake snow in it, but Darcy was optimistic that it would brush out once her hair was dry. She could only hope for better weather the next day, when she'd have to tackle the stuff again.

She pulled on the thick black socks that Kerron had provided and sighed deeply. Her toes had only just started to warm up in the shower and now they wiggled happily in the toasty socks. The bed looked incredibly inviting. Darcy hurt all over from all of the shovelling and heavy lifting she'd done, but she knew she had to go down and deal with Kerron eventually.

"I'd better get it over with," she muttered to herself before she left the guest room.

As she walked down the stairs, she could hear Kerron whistling in the kitchen. She stopped in the doorway to watch him for a moment. He had the kettle on and was hard at work preparing something on the long countertop. The cosy space looked exactly the way it had in Darcy's many dreams of late, and she sighed as she felt tears filling her eyes.

The noise had Kerron looking up from his work. "Ah, there you are," he said. "Are you feeling better?"

"Much, thank you," Darcy replied.

"I owe you an apology," he told her. "I had the report back on the snow a few days ago, but with my dad in hospital I didn't actually look at it until yesterday. The stuff Alastair supplied, while nowhere near as harmless as what I wanted, should be absolutely fine. It should eventually dissolve into the ground and won't harm the animals or the soil. It might put my efforts to go organic back a little bit, at least for that field, but I just bought a sizeable piece of land to the south of here that's already certified organic, so I can start there and expand slowly."

Darcy sat down at the table and let the words sink in slowly. "So we don't have to clear up the snow?" she checked.

"No. It's fine to leave it there."

Darcy wasn't sure whether she wanted to laugh or cry. Before she did either, Kerron handed her a cup of tea.

"You still look cold," he muttered as she took the cup.

Darcy took a sip and then smiled. "This is helping," she told him. "I'll probably warm up before February."

"I should have rung you about the snow," he said. "But I thought you were leaving for Lanzarote today."

Darcy shook her head. "I was never going to Lanzarote," she replied. "Alastair just couldn't imagine that anyone would ever say no to him."

"My father said you stopped to see him."

"I did. I was really worried about him."

"And I was behaving badly and not ringing you back," Kerron said, looking away.

"You blamed me for the snow."

"I didn't really," Kerron replied. "I knew that was all Alastair. No, I was angry about your relationship with the man. He was taking you on holiday, or so he said. I didn't know it wasn't true."

"You could have asked," Darcy told him.

"Yeah, but that makes sense," Kerron replied.

Darcy sipped her tea and looked out the window at the rain.

"Hello?" a voice called from the front of the house.

"We're in the kitchen," Kerron shouted.

"I'm too soaked to walk through the house," the voice, which Darcy recognised as Don's, called back.

Kerron chuckled. "I'll be right back," he told Darcy. When he came back in, he handed Darcy her keys.

"Don turned off the lights in the castle and locked it and the gate. He also brought your car down and left in out in front of the house to save me having to drive you back later."

"That was kind of him," Darcy replied.

"He had one of the other guys drive it down here, since he was so wet," he added.

"Very kind," Darcy amended herself.

Kerron went back behind the counter, and after a moment he opened the oven and put a pan inside it. "We usually have a feast on New Year's Day, but with dad in the hospital, it's just you and me, so I thought a little pork roast would do. I hope that's okay?"

Darcy counted to ten before she replied, letting her thoughts settle. "I don't want to be any bother," she began. "But it sounds wonderful if you're sure I'm welcome."

"As it was my fault you needed rescuing from the middle of a huge snowy gale, it's the least I can do," Kerron replied.

"Can I help?"

"If you want mashed potatoes, you can peel them," he told her. "I hate peeling potatoes."

"How many should I do?" Darcy asked as he handed her the bag of potatoes and the peeler.

"Three or four, I guess. Like I said, it's just us."

"I know your father is still in hospital, but what about Marion?"

"She's staying with her sister in Douglas so she can spend as much time as possible with dad. They're keeping him for another few days and then they'll both be back up here."

"What about the pretty blonde?" Darcy found herself asking.

"What pretty blonde?" Kerron asked, looking confused.

"When I drove by one morning you were helping a pretty blonde into her car," Darcy told him. "She was really stunning."

"I'll tell her you said so," Kerron said with a laugh. "She'll be pleased."

Darcy frowned and focussed on the potatoes. After a moment, Kerron laughed again.

"I guess I'm encouraged that you might be a bit jealous," he said. "But she's my cousin on my mother's side. Mum had a sister who moved across before I was born. She has one daughter, Jennifer. Anyway, Dad's always stayed in touch with her, at least sporadically, and they both came over and spent a few days with us at Christmas."

"Oh," Darcy said, feeling relieved and then foolish for having brought the subject up.

Kerron studied her for a moment and then moved over and sat down next to her at the table. "Were you jealous?" he asked quietly.

Darcy started to shake her head and then stopped. "I don't know," she said softly.

"We're not doing well here," Kerron said. "I was so jealous of your relationship with Alastair that I refused to speak with you. Then you saw me with Jennifer and jumped to the same sort of conclusion about me. I think we both need to work on our communication skills."

"Alastair and I were never a couple," Darcy said, staring into Kerron's eyes. "We went out a few times when I was in London or he was here, but things never got past the odd good-night kiss. He bought the trip to Lanzarote at that stupid charity auction he dragged me to, but I never agreed to go with him and I never would have. He, well, he isn't my type."

"And I wasted the entire month of December being angry at you for nothing," Kerron said sadly. "What sort of man is your type, then?"

Darcy took a deep breath and threw caution to the wind. "I like the rugged outdoor type," she said, voicing something she'd only recently discovered about herself. "Men who work hard but still have a soft side. Men who can cook, even if they don't like to peel potatoes."

Kerron laughed and then took Darcy's hands in his. "My father thinks you're too much like my mother," he told her. "He thinks you'll get tired of farming life and disappear like she did."

"How old was your mother when she married your dad?" Darcy asked.

"Nineteen," Kerron replied.

"I've nearly ten years of life experience on her," Darcy told him. "I've travelled just about everywhere, dated unsuitable men and enjoyed the wild side of life for many years. Working on Nollick Balley taught me how much I enjoy being in one place and working with a wonderful group of people. We became like a family up there and I'm really going to miss everyone. I had a thought..." Darcy trailed off.

"You had a thought?" Kerron asked.

"We did a day for children with special needs, and the parents were incredibly grateful," Darcy told him. She spoke slowly, her mind racing, not entirely certain that she was ready to share her idea with anyone else yet.

"My father told me about that. He said it was a really wonderful day."

"It was certainly that," Darcy agreed. "And the one thing I kept hearing was how the island could use more facilities for such children, really, for all children."

"Surely we can't keep Nollick Balley open all year around?"

"No, but what about starting a place with all of the best parts of Nollick Balley? Not Santa, of course, but maybe a petting zoo with farm animals. Maybe we could have fields where school groups could plant their own gardens and eventually enjoy the results. There could be a big indoor soft play area for children of all ages and abilities. Besides that, I gave part-time jobs to a lot of men and women who can't find regular full-time work because of their children or because of their own health issues. Some of my elves have trouble getting around, for example, but if they were put in charge of a gift shop that sold seeds and soil, they could sit down all day." Darcy stopped because Kerron was shaking his head.

"You think it's a bad idea," she said. "Never mind." She pulled her hands away and blinked back tears.

Kerron immediately took her hands again and then waited until she looked at him to speak. "I don't think it's a bad idea," he said softly. "I think it's an amazing idea. I'm just completely overwhelmed. You've clearly given it a lot of thought."

"I started thinking about it on Christmas Eve," Darcy told him. "When I realised Nollick Balley was winding down and I wasn't going to get to see George or the elves, or everyone again, I started to feel really sad. I had such a great team of people up there and they worked so hard."

"And there's a real need in the community for something like this," Kerron added.

"I think there is," Darcy replied. "I think it would have to be closer to Douglas, though. People were happy to drive out this far for something special like Nollick Balley, but I think a year-round place would need to be more centrally located."

"You've certainly put a lot of thought into this," Kerron said, sounding bemused.

Darcy blushed. "It's just an idea," she said. "Maybe a terrible one."

"Maybe a wonderful one," Kerron replied. "My father was very impressed with everything you did at Nollick Balley. I think your idea could be very successful and I know my father would love to be involved, as would I."

"Really?" Darcy asked.

Kerron squeezed her hands. "I want to be involved in whatever you do next," he said quietly.

Darcy's eyes met his and she felt herself getting lost for a moment. She took a deep breath just before his lips met hers. The buzzing noise that interrupted them was the cruellest sound Darcy thought she'd ever heard.

"What is that?" she asked breathlessly.

"The oven timer," Kerron told her. "The pork roast is ready."

"I never put a light under the potatoes," Darcy groaned.

Kerron found a microwave container and Darcy dumped the potatoes into it. While Kerron served the roast meat and vegetables, Darcy managed to get the potatoes cooked enough to mash. They were both laughing as she spooned the slightly lumpy results onto their plates.

"Shall I open a bottle of wine?" Kerron asked.

"I have to drive later," Darcy reminded him.

"You're welcome to stay," he told her. "It is pretty miserable out there."

Darcy looked out the window. The rain hadn't stopped and neither had the wind. She was very tempted to stay, but she wasn't sure that was a good idea. She and Kerron had a lot of things to work out and she didn't want to ruin everything by getting too serious too quickly.

Kerron was watching her face. Now he got up and pulled some cans of fizzy drink from his refrigerator. "I'd rather you'd stay," he told her. "But I don't want you to feel rushed into anything. I know I behaved badly last month."

"We both did stupid things," Darcy said. "At the very least, I should have made sure Alastair knew I wasn't interested in him from the very beginning."

"You're being kind," Kerron told her. "I was an idiot and I don't deserve you."

Darcy laughed. "Let's just agree that you were an idiot," she suggested. "Then we can move on."

Kerron grinned. "Somehow you make that sound reasonable."

After dinner, Darcy helped him with the washing up and then she insisted that she needed to get home. "Happy New Year," she said at the door.

The kiss that followed nearly had her changing her mind about leaving. "I have to go," she whispered against Kerron's neck as he held her close.

"You can't leave yet," he said. "I didn't give you your Christmas present yet."

"Christmas present?" Darcy echoed.

"Stay there," he told her before he dashed from the room. He was back a moment later with a small, flat box, wrapped in brightly coloured paper.

"I got you this before our, um, disagreement," he told her.

Darcy took the box and shook it gently. She heard nothing, so she slowly unwrapped it. Handing Kerron the discarded paper, she opened the lid of the box and gasped.

"The necklace from Christmas at the Castle? But how?"

"I had my father ring in and bid on my behalf," he told her. "I figured Finlo and Alastair wouldn't care if a stranger won. They just wouldn't want me to win."

Darcy sighed and held up the necklace. It was even more gorgeous than she'd remembered. "I can't accept this," she said sadly. "It was too expensive. You can't afford this."

Kerron sighed. "I think I know better than you do about what I can afford," he said a bit testily.

"But I remember how worried you were about repaying Alastair if you cancelled Nollick Balley," she said. "You need the money for the farm."

Kerron shrugged and gave her a sheepish grin. "I might have exaggerated slightly when talking about the precarious state of the farm's finances," he told her.

"Why?"

"It started out as a way to torture Alastair," he admitted. "When he sent that little blonde woman over I gave her a sob story about how I would lose the farm if Alastair sued me, but how I really didn't want the event held here. She ended up leaving in tears. When you turned up, it was easier to go with the same story than make up something new."

"But if you could afford to pay Alastair off, why didn't you?"

"I was planning on it," Kerron said, sheepishly. "Dad and I had a disagreement about something and he went behind my back and signed the deal with Alastair to get back at me. Then he took off to the Algarve and left me to clear up the mess. He thought I'd just pay Alastair back and it would all be over, and he could come back from the Algarve, so I dragged things out to make dad suffer a bit. Then I got in over my head."

"Financially?"

Kerron laughed. "Emotionally. You came in and took over and I found myself making excuses to see you again. Within a few days I realised I was going to have let you use the site just so I could spend time with you."

Darcy smiled. "So you aren't broke?"

"Not even close. We had a really good year this year. I've just extended the farm to the south and the east, and some of my other investments have done really well this year, too. In fact, I just bought some land on the outskirts of Douglas. They won't let it be developed for housing, so the price was rock bottom. It might be just about perfect for your plans."

Darcy's smile got even bigger. "We have a lot to talk about," she said slowly.

"We do, and we shouldn't rush anything," Kerron told her. "Anyway, Merry Christmas." He nodded towards the necklace.

"I can't accept it,' she said after a moment.

"Now why not?" Kerron asked with a wry grin.

"Even if you can afford it, it was too expensive. We haven't even been on a proper date yet. You keep it and you can give it back to me after we've been a couple for a while. Maybe for my birthday or something."

Kerron looked like he was going to argue, but he just shook his head. "I don't understand women," he told Darcy.

"And you never will," she replied with a laugh.

❧ 17 ❧

It was a beautiful June day, six months later, when Darcy cut through the ribbon and declared Ballakewley Children's Farm officially open. It was still a work in progress, but many of Darcy's ideas had already come to life.

Every primary school on the island had its own garden, and there was just enough time left in the school year for them all to get something planted before the summer holidays. Darcy's staff, most of whom had worked with her at Nollick Balley, were committed to keeping the plants thriving until the autumn when the schoolchildren could come back and harvest everything.

There were pens full of farm animals, a huge fenced-in field where children could safely simply run around until they were tired out, and in the centre of the site, an enormous barn was stuffed full of mats and soft play equipment that would be safe and fun for children of all ages and abilities.

Darcy stood back and watched as the first group of children, the sons and daughters of her friends, family and staff members, dashed into the site. Kerron slipped an arm around her waist.

"You've done a wonderful job," he whispered.

"You did a lot of it," she reminded him.

She smiled as Lisa waddled past, holding tight to her husband's hand. The baby was due in less than two months, and Lisa looked enormous but incredibly happy.

"Is it everything you'd hoped for?" William asked as he joined Darcy and Kerron at the entrance.

"I think it is," she replied. "Our afternoons for special needs groups are completely booked through the end of the year with school groups and other organisations. All of the schools are booked to bring their classes to do their planting, and our weekends are pretty much sold out until October with families who want to check it all out for themselves."

"And you haven't even built it all yet," William added.

Darcy laughed. As things had started coming together, Darcy's vision had kept expanding. There were now plans to add an open-air theatre where local music, dance and theatre groups could perform. A huge outdoor but covered playground specifically for special needs children was also in the works.

There were still a lot of people hanging around the entrance. "In you all go," Darcy told them. "Go and explore and then tell me what you think."

Lisa smiled at her from the small crowd of her dearest friends. Beside her, Kerron cleared his throat. Darcy turned and gave him her most dazzling smile.

"I think you know that the last six months have been the happiest time of my life," he told Darcy. "So now is the perfect time to give you this."

He handed Darcy a long flat box that she instantly recognised. She felt tears in her eyes and she took it from him.

"The necklace," she murmured. When he'd tried to give it to her six months earlier, she'd insisted it was too soon. Now, after six long months of working hand in hand to make her dream a reality, she knew she was madly in love with the man. He'd helped her realise her dream; the necklace was just a trinket.

She slowly opened the box and then gasped. The necklace wasn't inside. Instead, in the centre of the box was a gorgeous diamond ring. As Darcy began to cry, Kerron dropped to one knee.

"Will you marry me?" he asked.

Darcy was shaking so hard that she couldn't speak. For a long moment she could only stare at the man, unable to make a sound. Finally she managed to choke out a strangled "yes" that made the crowd cheer. Kerron slid the ring onto her finger and then pulled her into an embrace.

Dear Reader,

Poor Darcy was in such a hurry to get away from Alastair that she didn't even realise the significance of the woman she saw in the throne room at Castle Rushen. You spotted it, though, didn't you?

(If not, check the author's note at the front of the book.)

GLOSSARY OF TERMS

MANX WORDS

- **balley** — town
- **Nollick Ghennal** — Merry Christmas
- **Traa-dy-liooar** — time enough

ENGLISH/MANX TO AMERICAN TERMS

- **advocate** — lawyer (solicitor in the UK)
- **bin** — garbage can
- **biscuits** — cookies
- **booking** — reservation
- **boot** — trunk (of a car)
- **car park** — parking lot
- **chippy** — a fish and chips take-out restaurant
- **chips** — french fries
- **comeover** — a person who moved to the island from elsewhere

- **crisps** — potato chips
- **cuppa** — cup of tea (informal)
- **CV** — resume
- **estate car** — station wagon
- **fizzy drink** — soda (pop)
- **flannel** — washcloth
- **flat** — apartment
- **fortnight** — two weeks
- **full stop** — period (punctuation mark)
- **holiday** — vacation
- **jelly** — gelatin dessert (Jell-O, usually)
- **lift** — elevator
- **loo** — restroom
- **midday** — noon
- **pavement** — sidewalk
- **petrol** — gasoline
- **pudding** — dessert
- **queue** — line
- **rubbish** — trash (garbage)
- **starters** — appetizers
- **takeaway** — takeout (at a restaurant)
- **telly** — television
- **tannoy** — public address system
- **trainers** — sneakers
- **Wellies (informal for Wellington boots)** — rain boots

OTHER NOTES

A wardrobe is a large piece of furniture with rails for hanging clothes in it. Most bedrooms in the UK and the Isle of Man do not have closets as they would in the US, so a wardrobe is needed.

Boxing Day is the day after Christmas (December 26th) and was traditionally a day for giving gifts to servants and tradesmen.

When talking about time, the English say, for example, "half seven" to mean "seven-thirty."

When island residents talk about someone being from "across," or moving "across," they mean somewhere in the United Kingdom (across the water).

Noble's is Noble's Hospital, the island's main hospital facility, located in Douglas.

Ready meals are meals that are prepared and chilled (but not frozen) and sold in the grocery store, that can then be reheated at home.

An airing cupboard is a small closet space where the hot water tank is stored. Because it is generally quite warm, clothes or other items are often place there to dry (or air) out.

The Isle of Man requires work permits for anyone seeking employment on the island, except for "Isle of Man Workers" who need to meet certain birth or residency requirements in order to fall into that category.

ALSO BY DIANA XARISSA

The Isle of Man Cozy Mystery Series

Aunt Bessie Assumes

Aunt Bessie Believes

Aunt Bessie Considers

Aunt Bessie Decides

Aunt Bessie Enjoys

Aunt Bessie Finds

Aunt Bessie Goes

Aunt Bessie's Holiday

Aunt Bessie Invites

Aunt Bessie Joins

Aunt Bessie Knows

Aunt Bessie Likes

Aunt Bessie Meets

Aunt Bessie Needs

The Isle of Man Ghostly Cozy Mysteries

Arrivals and Arrests

Boats and Bad Guys

Cars and Cold Cases

Dogs and Danger

The Markham Sisters Cozy Mystery Novellas

The Appleton Case

The Bennett Case

The Chalmers Case

The Donaldson Case

The Ellsworth Case

The Fenton Case

The Green Case

The Hampton Case

The Irwin Case

The Isle of Man Romance Series

Island Escape

Island Inheritance

Island Heritage

Island Christmas

ABOUT THE AUTHOR

Diana Xarissa lived on the Isle of Man for more than ten years before returning to the United States with her family. Now living near Buffalo, New York, she enjoys having the opportunity to write about the island that she loves so much. It truly is a special place.

Diana also writes mystery/thrillers set in the not-too-distant future under the pen name "Diana X. Dunn" and fantasy/adventure books for middle grade readers under the pen name "D.X. Dunn."

She would be delighted to know what you think of her work and can be contacted through snail mail at:

Diana Xarissa Dunn
PO Box 72
Clarence, NY 14031.

Find Diana at:

www.dianaxarissa.com
diana@dianaxarissa.com

Made in the USA
Coppell, TX
15 November 2019